I0544614

WYCAAN MASTER: BOOK ONE

AT THE WALLS OF GALBRIETH

A Novel

ALON SHALEV

Tourmaline Books
Berkeley, California

At The Walls Of Galbrieth
Wycaan Master, Book 1
Copyright © 2012 Alon Shalev

Tourmaline Books, Berkeley, California
http://www.tourmalinebooks.com

LCCN: 2012950787

First Edition: November, 2012

This book contains an excerpt from the forthcoming book *Wycaan Master - The First Decree* by Alon Shalev. This excerpt has been set for this edition and may not reflect the final content of the forthcoming edition.

Published in the United States of America

DEDICATION

Deep in an ancient redwood forest, an 11 year-old boy on his family vacation, craved time with his father. Mighty trees bore witness to the creation of a new world and time, and the summoning of the Wycaan Masters.

To my son, Pele. I wrote this with you and for you. I hope you never need walk the path of Seanchai, but whether you do or not, you will not walk it alone.

ACKNOWLEDGEMENTS

- To Monica Buntin, my editor, for making sense of an awful lot of words.

- To William Kenney, my book cover artist, for your amazing ability to transform my jumbled ideas into a beautiful piece of art.

- To the Berkeley Writers Group, for your patience, honesty, and your reluctant acceptance of elves.

Ancient stories can change the destiny of the world. They give birth to myths, legends, and prophecies. In dire times, such stories fire the imagination, shape a culture, and alter history. But above all, such stories can provide hope, which is in itself a very powerful force.

One is told of a bygone age in which man, elf and dwarf lived together in harmony with other races. While each had their own villages, tribes, or towns, they shared the roads, marketplaces, and occasionally governance.

This story speaks of an alliance that lasted a thousand years before collapsing in a terrible battle. Blood flowed down the hillsides turning the streams red. After such chilling violence and death, peace was shattered. Greed and fear thrived, fueled by an unquenchable thirst of some for power.

The dwarves retreated deep into their caverns and mines, surfacing only to trade their fine wares of precious metals, iron, and stone, never allowing other races to enter their underground domains.

Men built cities of stone, with high walls and towers. They consolidated power, first subjugating weaker races and then fighting among themselves. They craved wealth, built great arsenals, and raised large armies. Man's seed spread through the land in great numbers.

The elves, the oldest and proudest of races, were decimated. Legend holds that even as the battle commenced, they tried to broker peace among the races and, in doing so, spread themselves perilously thin. They were massacred and the survivors left leaderless. Some disappeared into the mountains, others into the woods, while those who remained became little more than dispirited serfs.

Of the other races, no one knows. Only obscure scrolls, art, and pottery testify to the existence of aqua-skinned people, trolls, ferocious one-horned pictorians, and small gnomes who smoked pipes almost as big as themselves.

Thus, the alliance, forged in trust and hope, passed into legend. And, though recalled in universal lore, each race held to a different narrative.

But storytellers of each race also spoke of a time when a new alliance would be formed. They were laughed at, scorned, and became few and far between. Whispers, however, continued of a golden age that might once again emerge. Stories–good stories–never age.

ONE

The screams pierced his dreams and his eyes sprung open. His body went rigid with fear. Through the window above his bed he saw the first hues of dawn. They had assured him it would never happen, but the shrieks and cries proved them wrong. It was happening right now.

His father shook him roughly and dragged him out of bed. The young elf pulled on his breeches and boots while his mother quietly stuffed a few more provisions into a backpack that had been ready for weeks. As he took the bag from his mother, he glanced into her eyes. No tears, just immense sadness.

He slung the backpack over one shoulder, balancing it with a bedroll that hung over his other. His father grasped him with thick, muscular hands. No farewells. No last sentiments. No time.

"Run, son," he commanded. "Run and don't look back."

The young elf squeezed his tall, thin frame out the back door. He had practiced this many times in the last five of his fifteen years, always in the hours before dawn. And now he faded quickly into the shadows.

He felt heat on his back, heard the crackle of burning wood as villagers paid for their defiance. The once-proud race of elves would not passively give up their children to be conscripted as fodder for the Emperor's boundless ambition. Huts would burn, crops and livestock be confiscated, and those with children–including the young elf's parents–might suffer injury, arrest, or even death.

He disappeared into the forest, moving with practiced stealth among the trees and brush. The forest surrounding his village was thick, but he knew it well. He had played here all his life, mimicking the hunters and gatherers.

Only after several hours separated him from his village did he dare walk on the path that would lead him to the village in the Ardian Mountains where his father's brother lived. Though they had never met he had been assured his uncle would provide shelter and protection. He tried to imagine what his uncle would be like. His father was slight of build and mild of manner.

As dusk fell, the youngster stopped to rest awhile, though he was too afraid to sleep and dream of the consequences his parents may face for letting him leave. The gathering darkness made it impossible to recall from memory the woods where his mother had taught him to recognize herbs and roots in the hopes he would become a village healer like her. He instead needed to recognize the landmarks on the map his father had drawn. When the first rays of light found their way through the treetops, he was relieved to rise and continue his journey.

By the end of the second day the trees had become larger, thicker, and farther apart. The dark-leaved flora and moss were gradually replaced with flowering plants that basked in dim sunlight. He followed a stream that widened as he neared the forest's edge, pausing as he stepped out of the trees to adjust to the sunlight. He removed his backpack and knelt to drink some water and replenish his canteen.

With his thirst quenched, the teenager stretched and blinked a few times. He felt an abrupt coolness cast by a shadow behind him. He gasped and whirled around.

"Never stop to drink or leave the cover of trees without first carefully checking the terrain."

The deep voice was harsh. The young elf squinted into the light, but couldn't see anything more than the man's silhouette. He lifted one hand to protect his eyes while slowly reaching for his dagger with his other.

"Don't try it," the man warned, his face hidden in the cowl of his hood. "Our archers will cut you down before your blade is out of its sheath. Anyway, we aren't your enemy. The army uses that path there to move men and supplies." The man jerked his head in the direction of the road, "By stopping you here, I saved your life. Now, I suggest you follow me—and fast."

The man jogged back into the woods and hid behind a tree; the elfling followed. Almost instantly, a patrol of troops—in groups of half a dozen commonly known as sixers—marched by, oblivious to their presence.

The young elf observed the army's crimson clothes and black armor. The banners they flew were likewise crimson, bearing a tower's dark silhouette with a golden sun peering out from behind. Four sixers marched in this patrol, one composed entirely of huge, horned, bipedal, bear-like creatures, with enormous axes strapped across their backs.

The young elf gasped at the sight of these huge creatures. When only dust was left in the army's wake, he looked across to his rescuer.

"Thank you," he said. "What were those?"

The man had also been watching the patrols. "They are pictorians, brought down from the north. They are much stronger than us, and can grow as tall as eight feet. You don't mess with them more than once."

The man turned and whistled. A dozen hooded figures dropped from branches or appeared from behind tree trunks or bushes. One had been perched in the very tree where the elfling had hid.

"My name is—"

"Don't bother, *calhei*. We know who you are. Your uncle requested that we keep an eye out for a lost pup." The elfling was surprised to hear the word for youngster in his race's language. The man and his hooded friends laughed at this last remark. Feeling nothing malicious in it, the elf decided not to take offense. The man continued. "We're one of a number of resistance groups prepared to help you on your way."

As he finished speaking, the man removed his hood to reveal pointed ears.

"You're elves?" the youngster asked, relief obvious.

"Some of us," the man replied as the rest of the group removed their hoods, revealing more elves as well as several humans. "Others were born less fortunate."

The group laughed again at the evident ongoing joke.

"Elves and men together?" the young elf was shocked. "I've never heard of that."

One of the men stepped forward and put a big hand on his shoulder. "The world, laddie, splits into two groups: free and enslaved. We don't have the luxury of hating each other if we wish to remain free."

He then turned to the leader. "Yochai. The Emperor doesn't bring pictorians this far south. Aren't they usually posted on the battlefields and borders?"

"Yes," Yochai responded. "Something's afoot; something stirred the muck." He gazed at the young elf for a moment. "We'll head to our camp at the foot of the Ardians. In the morning, we will take you to your uncle."

"I am Seanchai, son of Seantai," the young elf said between mouthfuls of fish. "My village was raided for conscripts."

The others, eating with him around a fire, nodded sympathetically.

"They were burning everything," Seanchai said, his voice wavering. "I don't know what happened after I fled."

"Best not dwell on it," the big man next to him said and mussed Seanchai's hair. "You did the right thing. Serving in the army would only have meant your death, or by your hand the death of other innocents.

"Rhoddan," Yochai addressed a young elf, maybe a year younger than Seanchai. "Watch him, okay" The leader turned back to Seanchai. "Even if you want to relieve yourself in the night, you don't walk alone. Is that clear?"

Seanchai frowned and was met with a glare. "This is my camp," the leader hissed. "I'll do what I need to protect my people. I don't want a green-ear wandering off and giving us away, or for our sentry to put an arrow through him. While you're with us, you follow my orders. Understand?"

"I understand," the young elf replied as he tried to stifle a yawn. "Sorry," he grimaced. "I haven't really slept since leaving my village."

Yochai smiled. "Turn in. You'll never know how long you'll be able to sleep." He turned to a dark-skinned elfe, her cheekbones thin and arched. "Sellia, organize the guard but don't include the boy. I'll take the last shift."

Seanchai, who had never seen a dark-skinned elfe, watched her nod and then scowl at him. He turned to the leader. "I can take my share. Let me guard."

"Not tonight. You have a long walk to your uncle's village. If you join us again, you will share the burden. Go to bed."

"Come on," said Rhoddan. "Put your bedroll over here. Have

your bag packed and closed in case we need to flee. Wake me if you need anything."

As they stretched out, Seanchai glanced at the leader who stood near the fire, still barking out orders. "He doesn't like me."

"Yochai doesn't trust anyone who hasn't fought next to him," Rhoddan responded. "It's that simple out here. Don't take it personally."

"Have you fought?" Seanchai asked.

Though younger, Rhoddan was broader and more muscular from hard training. His demeanor suggested a *calhei* growing up fast. When he spoke, his voice was steady. "You don't live out here long without fighting. Now go to sleep."

TWO

Seanchai quickly fell into a shallow, dream-filled sleep, full of voices shouting, of fire, of hands shaking him.

Hands shaking him.

"Get up, quick." Seanchai sat up immediately when Rhoddan jabbed him in the ribs.

There were shouts and clashes of metal. Seanchai reached for his dagger, but the other elf grabbed his hand. "Not today, greenling. Yochai needs you delivered alive."

Seanchai hesitated, but Rhoddan's grip was as fierce as his glare. He thrust a finger in Seanchai's face. "Follow his orders, remember?"

Seanchai nodded and grabbed his bag to follow Rhoddan through the brush. A mounted soldier veered in front of them as they ran, propelled from his horse by an arrow through his throat. Seanchai gasped. Another soldier, another arrow found its mark, and Seanchai cried out when he heard the horse scream. But he and Rhoddan continued running, breaking clear of the forest and scrambling across flat, rocky terrain.

Seanchai felt the path gently ascend, and then abruptly it became steeper. As dawn grayed around them, Rhoddan pulled Seanchai inside a shallow cave to catch their breath. There were no longer any trees, only tall rock faces. They had entered the Ardian Mountains.

"Drink," Rhoddan said, as he raised his own canteen. "We must keep moving."

Seanchai looked at his guide in the light of the new day. Though Rhoddan was shorter he had muscles that were clearly the result of hard physical training. His hair was long and dark, held in place by a thin leather thong, as was the way of elves.

"Do you know where we're going?" Seanchai asked. "Do you know where my uncle's village is?"

Rhoddan finished drinking, closed his canteen and wiped his face on his sleeve. "Yochai gave me a place to head to. I doubt it's your uncle's village. I would give that information away if I were captured and tortured. No one ever knows everything, not unless they're willing to kill themselves or die before revealing it. We *calhei* are never given such an honor."

"Honor?"

Rhoddan glanced up. "When you strive to become a warrior, you must be prepared to sacrifice your life for freedom, for those who remain free, and for those who dream of one day being free. Don't you understand that?"

"It's new to me," Seanchai shrugged. "My life was quite simple until a few days ago. My father was a blacksmith and my mother a healer-storyteller. I assumed I would follow in her footsteps."

"Assume nothing," Rhoddan snapped. "Not even that you will live to see the day through. Come on, let's move."

"Don't you worry about your friends back there?"

"There is no time." Rhoddan was putting his backpack on.

"That's pretty heartless—"

Seanchai felt himself slammed against the rock face, a hand fisting his shirt, a rock jutting into his back. Rhoddan's eyes flashed. "Yochai is my father."

With that, he let go of Seanchai and left the cave. Either he never heard Seanchai's apology or didn't care.

Around midday, Rhoddan stopped abruptly and crouched by a feather protruding from under a rock. He looked around, moved a few paces and overturned another rock to reveal a small leather pouch.

"Drink," he ordered Seanchai as he opened the pouch. "And eat this." He held out something brown and brittle. "Chew carefully if you value your teeth."

"Thank you," said Seanchai, anxious to appease his guide. "What is it?"

"Smoked fish. It's tough; you'll need to work hard before you can swallow it." Seeing Seanchai vaguely hurt and confused by his abruptness, Rhoddan relented. "When you're in danger like this, it's wise to preserve your strength. Speak only when necessary. Move only on the chosen path. Eat and drink enough to satiate hunger and thirst. Otherwise focus all your energy on your surroundings and your goal."

"Where did you learn all this?"

"I train to be a warrior like my father. It's all that's important to me. Now, please, shut up and eat."

They chewed in silence until Seanchai noticed Rhoddan fiddling with the brown feather. When Rhoddan saw Seanchai watching him, he raised the feather. "Sellia," was all he said.

Seanchai looked around, expecting to see the beautiful, dark-skinned elfe. This made Rhoddan laugh, and Seanchai feel foolish.

"It's better that she and the others keep a watchful distance," Rhoddan said. "They can guard and provide us with food without compromising our presence. If we're caught, it'll be nice to know they're out there." Rhoddan rose, stuffed the remainder of the food back into his pack, and resumed walking.

Soon the path straightened out and began to descend. The elves saw a speck of blue ahead. "We can camp near that lake," Rhoddan said without stopping.

When they reached the lake several hours later, they found a mountain goat on the ground shot through its eye. Blood was still trickling down its face and onto the stony path.

"We're being well taken care of," Seanchai said as he helped Rhoddan pick up the goat. "Our feet may be sore, but we won't suffer from hunger."

Rhoddan grunted and gestured with his head toward a cavern where Seanchai noticed a small pile of firewood. Rhoddan took out his knife and said, "We will cook the meat, but then extinguish the fire. You rest."

Seanchai wanted to help, but he was exhausted and couldn't do more than slump against the rock wall. He watched as Rhoddan lit some dry moss under the wood and swiftly carved very thin slices of meat, laying them over the fire.

"Why are you cutting the meat so thin?"

"It needs to cook quickly. We don't want this fire going for long," Rhoddan replied.

The meat tasted raw to Seanchai but he didn't say anything. As they ate, Rhoddan cooked the rest of the goat. He wrapped the meat in small pieces of leather and put them to one side. Seanchai watched Rhoddan work, his guide's face as impassive as ever. After a while Seanchai spoke.

"I'm sorry about your father. I'm sorry about what I said. It must be—"

"You don't help me by speaking of this." Rhoddan's gaze

remained locked on his food, but Seanchai sensed he was working hard to maintain composure.

"I just wanted to …"

Rhoddan sighed. "I know. I appreciate it, but please don't."

They ate in silence and Seanchai stared out of the small cave. A thought occurred to him. "Why doesn't Sellia or the others join us? Surely it's safer in numbers?"

"Your safety is their only concern," Rhoddan replied, chewing and swallowing before he continued. "Whatever it takes, you must be delivered safely."

"Why?"

"You ask too many questions and I don't have the answers. All I know is that your escape has been carefully planned and many are ready to die for you. Stand guard and gradually put dirt on the fire. Not too quickly—we don't want to send up any smoke that might give our position away." With that, Rhoddan lay down and wrapped his cloak around himself.

"Thank you," whispered Seanchai from the mouth of the cave. He folded his hands against his chest and muttered, "… for whatever reason you're all doing this."

THREE

"Wake up." Rhoddan shook him. "It's dawn and we need to leave."

"What about breakfast?" Seanchai yawned.

"I cooked you some scrambled eggs and fried mushrooms," the young warrior replied, rolling his eyes. "Chew on some dried meat as we walk."

Seanchai stretched and moaned. "It's still dark out. Ouch! My back's so stiff. Do I have time to at least wash my face, and...relieve myself?"

Rhoddan nodded impatiently, and soon enough they were walking briskly around the lake. As he followed Rhoddan, Seanchai took in the soft hues of dawn on the rocks. What would become a harsh white was now a soft gold. He sighed as he adjusted his pack and wondered whether he would ever again live in a forest instead of rough mountains.

Seanchai's thoughts turned to how badly he wanted Rhoddan to like and respect him. He didn't want to be thought of as a soft village boy, though he conceded to himself that that's exactly what he was. Observing his guide's lean and muscular frame, Seanchai subconsciously flexed his biceps and felt a rather pathetic bulge.

They climbed the pass that led through the Ardian Mountains without event, save for Rhoddan, steady and confident in his purpose, occasionally turning to glare at Seanchai for inadvertently kicking pebbles into Rhoddan's heels. With the rising temperature, their water canteens were soon empty and Seanchai's mouth became dry. But Rhoddan kept the pace steady and he gritted his teeth. He was determined not to show any weakness and said nothing of his discomfort, though he was very much relieved when the path began to descend.

Rhoddan led Seanchai into a tight gorge between two rocks so narrow that they were forced to remove their packs from their backs in order to slip through. Seanchai smelled the moisture before he saw the water. It trickled down a crevice and into a puddle under a tall rock. Rhoddan knelt and filled his canteen and gestured for Seanchai to do the same. Both elves drank deeply.

They rested, enjoying shelter from the hot sun. Seanchai was dozing when he felt pebbles hit his head. He opened his eyes to see Rhoddan draw his long knife in a flash and gesture for Seanchai to hide under the rocks. Seanchai shook his head and drew his own knife, though his hand shook. Both crouched for what seemed ages to Seanchai, and then a soft bleating accompanied hoofbeats of animals dropping to the path from the rock further along.

"Guess we're not the only ones using this water source," Seanchai said as he stood up and sighed. He realized that he had been holding his breath.

Rhoddan nodded. He rose suddenly and slammed Seanchai against the rock as he had earlier. His nostrils flared and he held his blade up.

"When I tell you to do something, you do it without question," he growled. "I signaled for you to hide and you disobeyed me. Don't play hero until you've learned how."

"I wasn't going to leave you to—"

Rhoddan tightened his grip. "Listen to me. There're a lot of people risking their lives for you. This isn't a child's game in your village. You're no good to anyone dead and you dishonor those who have already died for you. Maybe my father is one of them. You must make it alive to your uncle."

A confused Seanchai stood frozen for several seconds before Rhoddan loosened his grip with chagrin. He patted Seanchai on his chest. "Come," his said in a softer tone. "We must reach our base before dark."

The mountain path descended now surrounded by rocks turned a soft red by the sinking sun. Seanchai marveled at the different colors the same rocks took throughout the day, stopping abruptly as they rounded a sharp curve that opened into flat grassland.

"The Kuro Plains." Rhoddan waved his hand. "My role ends when I get you to the other side."

Seanchai saw what he hoped was a forest on the far side of the flat land and started to cross. He stopped when he saw Rhoddan hesitating. A slight breeze ruffled his guide's long dark hair and Seanchai saw uncertainty on his young face as Rhoddan glanced back at the peaks behind them.

"What is it?" Seanchai asked, his hand moving toward his dagger.

"We should already be across. I'm not sure if we should stop for the night or keep going and try to pass. The road is patrolled and I don't know their routine. We wouldn't be able to see the dust they kick up like we would in the daylight. There are also others waiting for us at the edge of those woods, and I'm worried they might misidentify us in the dark." He looked at Seanchai carefully and said, "Close your eyes and listen to your inner voice. Try and see if there's anyone out there."

Seanchai stared at him. "Me! Why?"

"Because I trust your instinct," Rhoddan sighed.

"You do?"

"No, but my father does. I was told to if…" There was a slight panic in his voice as he explained. "Please, try."

Seanchai leaned against a rock and closed his eyes. He breathed deeply as a village healer would, relaxing his mind and sending it out over the plains. It was a strange feeling but somehow felt natural. Suddenly something cold and foreboding stopped him, like a black wall. Scared, he withdrew his mind and opened his eyes.

"Let's camp here in the mountains," Seanchai said. "We'll cross the plain in the morning light."

Rhoddan nodded his assent and doubled back on the path. They settled nearby in a small clearing with rocks shielding their perimeter, chewing on dried goat meat. Rhoddan's eyes darted in the direction of every sound he heard, whether a whistle in the wind or the rattle of falling pebbles. Occasionally he glanced over at Seanchai.

"Why do you keep rubbing your head?" Rhoddan asked.

Seanchai frowned, only now noticing a dull throb. "I don't know," he replied, "It's just a headache."

"Sleep," Rhoddan suggested. "I'll wake you when I tire."

Seanchai lay down and wrapped his blanket around himself. But despite his fatigue he was unable to sleep. Why were others risking their lives for him? Why had Rhoddan's father trusted his instinct? And what was this dull ache in his head?

His eyes flew open to the sound of cries and the clash of steel on steel from the plains below. Rhoddan put a hand on his shoulder and a finger to his lips. They crawled over to the clearing's edge to see what was happening. The moon revealed fleeting silhouettes of riders on horses. Two groups were fighting.

It was over in minutes. There had been an ambush. Once back

in the clearing, Rhoddan and Seanchai sat and looked at each other.

"We'd have walked straight into an ambush," said Seanchai, his breath quick. "It was lucky we didn't try and cross tonight."

"No," his companion replied with awe in his voice. "Luck had nothing to do with it."

FOUR

Seanchai woke just before dawn, cold and shivering. He wanted to begin walking immediately and tried to warm himself by breathing into his cupped palms and then rubbing his body vigorously. When that didn't work, he jumped up and down on the spot until he saw Rhoddan glaring at him.

"We should cross as early as possible," Rhoddan said. "It'll be easy to see us on flat land, even from a distance."

"What will we do if a patrol spots us?" Seanchai asked anxiously as he scanned the terrain. His hand rose to his forehead to shield his eyes from the rising sun.

"You will run like the wind. Drop everything and fly," Rhoddan's voice became harsh, "and this time … don't hesitate. And don't look back."

Seanchai opened his mouth to protest, but then thought better of it. Hopefully, this was all theoretical. They walked briskly for several hours, stopping only to drink water. Midway between the mountains and what Seanchai was now thrilled to see was indeed a forest, they found a narrow brook. It would be easy to jump over, just a little more than a big step. But Rhoddan scanned all around and then signaled Seanchai to crouch with him.

"Keep vigilant," he said and bent over to fill his canteen. When he was finished, he motioned for Seanchai to do the same.

The water was cold and refreshing, and Seanchai drank copiously. After he had quenched his thirst and replenished his canteen, he rose, saying he was ready.

Rhoddan grabbed his arm and pulled him back down roughly. His nails dug into Seanchai's forearm. "Fool. A bowman can fell you even if he's a hundred yards away."

"Well, one of us has to rise," Seanchai said in a high-pitched voice revealing how upset he was at his own stupidity.

Rhoddan glared at him before standing cautiously. After surveying their surroundings, he muttered, "Let's go."

With each hour the forest loomed bigger before them and Seanchai became angry at the arrogant younger elf. If they had been in the village, Seanchai would have had the upper hand, being older and already apprenticing with his mother.

But they weren't in the village. Rhoddan was in command because he was battle tested. His anger faded to shame as he realized that Rhoddan was willing to die to ensure Seanchai's safety. He wondered if he would ever be brave enough to risk his life for another, much less a stranger.

His thoughts returned to the forest that was fast rising up before them. He was comforted at the prospect of being back among trees, which felt more like his village surroundings and offered a sense of security. But he wasn't secure yet–both boys stopped in their tracks as they heard a high-pitched screech.

"What bird –" Seanchai froze in mid sentence when he saw his guide's face.

"No bird. A signal. Run," Rhoddan hissed, and there was no mistaking the fear in his voice. He unsheathed both knives and whirled behind Seanchai. "Run fast!"

Seanchai hesitated for just a moment but fled for the trees when he heard the hooves and shouts.

Arrows crossed in the air over his head, and he realized they were flying from different directions. Suddenly a dozen men on horses were charging toward him. He cringed, covering his head and screwing up his eyes. But the horsemen galloped past him with swords and long knives drawn. One stopped and held out an arm. Seanchai grabbed it. If this man were an enemy, he would hardly be offering Seanchai a ride.

The horseman whirled, drove his horse back into the forest, and dumped Seanchai next to a row of archers before he turned back to join the fray. An elfe grabbed his arm and steered him toward a horse without a rider.

"Come, we must move you away." She grabbed the horse's reins.

Seanchai started to climb onto the horse, then stopped and looked back at the fight. "We must help Rhoddan."

"Who? Your guide? The others will help him if they can. But they were told to hold off only long enough to get you out."

"But Rhoddan—" Seanchai began.

"—has served his purpose," she snapped. "If he dies, he will die well."

"No!" Seanchai ran toward the sound of clashing swords. He struggled to draw his long knife from its sheath.

The elfe leaped onto the horse and cut off Seanchai's path. "You must come with me. They will help him if they can."

"He's willing to risk his life for me," Seanchai yelled. "I can't leave him!"

"Many others have risked their lives for you," she screamed back. "Don't let it be in vain." There was an edge of panic in her voice and, though Seanchai couldn't see her face beneath her helmet, he thought for a moment that she might also be young. "You must come with me."

"I don't leave my friends."

Seanchai dodged around her horse and ran out from the cover of trees. The fighters protecting him were retreating. He ran past them to find a half dozen heavily mailed soldiers in black and crimson armor. Lying on a horse behind them was Rhoddan. He wasn't moving, and Seanchai could see he had been beaten.

Something inside of Seanchai snapped. Red mist erupted into his vision and a primeval scream escaped his lips. He would not know the words he cried for several months afterward, but he instinctually dropped his knife and ran forward awkwardly, his palms out.

The soldiers screamed and dropped lifeless to the ground as Seanchai ran through them. He jumped onto the horse holding the limp body of Rhoddan and grabbed the reins. The horse set off at a wild, hysterical gallop, shaking its head from side-to-side and bellowing in panic. Seanchai jerked back the reins and half jumped, half fell off. The horse cantered nervously in place and then calmed.

Seanchai turned back. He instinctively knew that no soldier was alive where he had dropped his knife. His breath caught as the realization of what had just transpired became clear to him. What had he done? Where had that power come from? He stared at his warm, tingling hands and felt a wave of fear.

He decided to return to find his knife, a final gift from his father. He also needed to see what he had done to the soldiers. He checked Rhoddan's neck and, feeling a strong pulse, grabbed the reins and steered the horse back the way they had come.

He found smoldering, charred men and huge creatures that he thought might be pictorians. They were horned and bear-like, but walked on two feet. He could see from their thick muscles why they were such ferocious soldiers. He crouched and saw their melted metal armor, horror carved into their faces. A large elf—clearly not a soldier—watched Seanchai approach. His expression was a mix of awe and fear.

"I believe you dropped this," he said, returning Seanchai's long knife. "We should go."

FIVE

The slap cracked across Seanchai's face and snapped his head to the side. His skin burned and his eyes filled with tears. He focused all his strength to hold them back.

As he accompanied his rescuers deep into the woods, Seanchai had bathed in their awe. He assumed it was because of his bravery and prowess, though he chose not to dwell on the fact that he had killed people. He tried to put such thoughts out of his mind by looking at the trees. They were bigger and older than those in Morthian Wood, where he had grown up. These had knurled trunks and branches. This was the Kurostan Forest, and had been around since the age of faerie.

But now, in the rebel camp, Seanchai was no longer basking in awe, but instead stood before a huge elf with a very bad temper.

"As long as you are with my people, you will never disobey one of my orders again, ever," the elf roared. "Whether it comes straight from me or through someone else, you will obey it as law. I don't care who you are. You put good elves and men at risk. What you did was stupid and impulsive."

Seanchai took a deep breath. "Look, I'm sorry I put others in danger, but Rhoddan is my friend and…" His voice trailed off as he saw the veins in the huge elf's neck begins to throb. "How should I address you?"

"Call me Uncle."

"You're my uncle?" Seanchai arched an eyebrow, seeing no resemblance between this elf and his mild-mannered, loving father.

This question was met with laughter.

"Sure, if that works for you," replied a smirking Uncle. "But Uncle is my title. It goes unnoticed in the ears of our enemies."

Seanchai stood as tall as he could and willed himself not to look away. "Well, if we have finished, Uncle, I would like to go see how my friend is doing."

After a long pause, Uncle cleared his throat.

"Your guide?" he corrected venomously. "Sure, you may go to him. We will speak again after dinner. Ilana, please escort him to the healer."

An elfe approximately Seanchai's age approached. She was shorter than him, with dark and shiny hair held away from her face by a plain leather-braided thong. She averted her eyes and signaled him to follow her.

"Thank you," said Seanchai. "I appreciate you taking—"

"Uncle told me to," she interjected.

"Yes, um—" Seanchai stopped talking and surveyed the thick perimeter of trees around the camp. It made him think of the forest that surrounded his village. Thoughts of his parents slipped in. What had happened to them? He shuddered. He might never find out and perhaps that would be for the best.

"You shivered," Ilana said, her voice now softer. "Do you require a cloak?"

"I was thinking of my parents." Seanchai lowered his head, regretting the admission.

"I'm sorry. Many of us have lost parents, siblings, and friends. My mother…" her voice shook and she took a deep breath. "It never gets any easier. The healer's area is there beyond those fronds." Her voice was warm now and Seanchai regretted that they were about to part.

"Why so far away from everyone else?"

"If we need to hide, the wounded cannot give us away."

"That's kind of callous." Seanchai impulsively remarked, immediately cringing at the slip.

"Survival is callous," she snapped. "We do what we can for them. We collect herbs and provide them with whatever the healer requests. But we can't help them if we are dead and they can't run away. And the healer, by the way, is an elfe."

Seanchai stopped, sighed and rubbed his forehead with his hand. "I'm sorry. I seem to be saying all the wrong things. Everything is happening so quickly and it's all just...just confusing. A few days ago, I was just an innocent *calhei* playing and studying in my village. I was about to begin my apprenticeship as a healer.

"Now look at me, at what I did. I don't understand what's happening, what I'm doing, or even who I am. I don't know what I should be saying and, well," his voice quivered and became a whisper, "I understand why you have no patience for me."

Ilana turned to face him. She started to reach out but changed her mind and withdrew her hand. Instead, she smiled and looked him in the eyes for the first time. "It's not about patience," she said softly. "You scare me. You scare us."

She turned and left Seanchai by the entrance to the healer's area. He watched her go before he entered the hut.

Rhoddan lay on a bed of straw off to the side. His face was covered with thick green leaves Seanchai identified as comfrey—an herb that helps reduce inflammation and bruises. Seanchai leaned over his friend, who was awake but struggling to open swollen eyes. He put a hand on Rhoddan's shoulder.

"How are you, my friend? You look rather dashing."

Rhoddan's attempted smile became a wince. His voice was weak and hoarse. "They say you came back for me, that you took down a half dozen soldiers."

Seanchai shook his head. "They exaggerate."

"But you came back for me?"

"Yes, I did."

"Then you're a fool. I should have died protecting you."

"Your gratitude is overwhelming." Seanchai half-smiled, but Rhoddan shook his head, causing himself more pain.

"No, no." His voice was slightly louder now than a rasping whisper. "You're the important one. It was wrong. They should have stopped you."

"They tried, but I can be very persuasive."

"Stubborn, you mean. You were wrong to come back for me. Why did you do it?"

Seanchai felt his frustration rising. "Because you would have done the same for me. Because maybe your father and others paid for my safety with their lives. That's what we do for our friends."

"No," Rhoddan panted. "I'm not your friend. I'm your guide. That's what I was assigned to be."

Seanchai snapped back. "They can choose my guide and protectors, but they can't choose my friends. I want you as my friend, Rhoddan, and I'd like to be yours." He took a deep breath to calm himself and put his hand back on Rhoddan's shoulder. "Now get some rest. I'm sure I can find someone else to tell me off. In fact, I'm supposed to meet with this Uncle after we eat." Seanchai rubbed his still-sensitive cheek. "I'm hoping he'll use words to express himself this time."

Rhoddan allowed a small smile. "Ask him to slap you once as a favor to your new friend."

Seanchai grinned and stood up. "I'll look in after I meet with him."

As he turned to leave, Rhoddan said, "They say you felled the soldiers with a word and a brilliant red light. What was this power?"

Seanchai turned back. His face creased and he felt his chest tighten. "I don't know, Rhoddan. It was both awesome and frightening. I need to find out what it was and who I am."

SIX

Seanchai took a bowl and filled it with dark stew from the cooking pit. He saw some of the elves who had helped him earlier sitting on some logs. They were chatting and laughing as he approached but went silent when he sat down.

Seanchai was determined not to show that their silence hurt. "Thank you, all of you. I know you risked your lives back there to save me. I appreciate it."

The elves stared at him and then at one of their own, a big elf with unusual red hair.

"Glad we could help," the elf said in a deep voice.

Seanchai cleared his throat, unsure of how to continue. He decided to focus on his food. He hadn't eaten a good meal in days and went back for more when he finished his first bowl, despite the dirty looks. As he tried to decide if the others' scorn was worth a third helping, Ilana tapped his shoulder.

"Uncle is ready for you now," she said, her voice stiff.

"Has he eaten?" Seanchai asked.

"Yes. Why do you ask?"

"I'm hoping a full stomach might put him in a better mood than he was before."

Ilana laughed out loud, an unbridled and throaty sound that took Seanchai off-guard. "I think you'll find yourself engaged in a sound discussion," she said. "And then he'll thrash you to within an inch of your life."

"Really?" Thoughts of making the elfe laugh again disappeared, replaced by a tight knot in his stomach.

She smiled now. "Maybe you are alright. Come on." She took his arm and gently pulled him along.

Unfortunately for Seanchai, who was enjoying Ilana's attention, she only guided him a short way, leaving him outside of an entrance between two thick tree trunks that he had mistaken for a clump of fronds and branches.

When he stepped inside, Seanchai was met by Uncle and three elder elfes. The elders had deeply wrinkled skin and thin, gray hair. One hobbled over to him, taking his face in her leathery hands. Seanchai flinched as she pressed the bruise from Uncle, but she held him firm. She stared into his eyes and he felt powerless to look away. When she returned to her chair, she nodded to the others.

Uncle offered Seanchai a log to sit on. It was situated lower than the others and he was sure that this was intentional, perhaps a way of showing respect for the elders.

"How is your guide?" Uncle asked.

"My *friend* seems well," Seanchai replied with as much defiance as he could muster, "though he took quite a beating."

"He's in good hands," Uncle said, ignoring the challenge and switching topics. "We have heard what the elves with you in the clearing witnessed. And your guide told me about your scrying."

"My what?"

"Remember when you were able to reach out with your mind and sense that you shouldn't cross the plain at night? That is called scrying. The elders and I have spoken about these things."

One of the old women leaned forward. "You don't understand your powers, do you, my *calhei*? You must learn who you are and what you are capable of. If you are what we suspect, you must go find a master who can teach you. Shehlid knows of one about two weeks' journey from here."

"Where?" Seanchai asked, trying to imagine such a long journey and regretting that he would need to leave Rhoddan and Ilana.

Uncle spoke. "You'll travel with two guides, both purposely young. They will know the way. You'll be able to tell captors that you were on your way to a school in Marsfield and got hopelessly lost. You'll wait three days and then leave."

"Why wait?" Seanchai was not sure why he blurted that out. He felt unhappy having his life mapped out by strangers, even when they obviously knew better than him.

"We'll see how quickly your *friend* Rhoddan recovers from his wounds." Uncle said, and a small smile crossed his face.

"Thank you," Seanchai said and smiled back.

Seanchai and his companions didn't leave for four days, partly to allow Rhoddan enough time to recover, but also for Seanchai to receive instruction and training from Uncle.

If Uncle knew who or what Seanchai was, he didn't let on. He focused solely on teaching Seanchai how to use the equipment he would give him.

They trained with the knife sets common to elves, the long and short. But Seanchai told Uncle that he would like to improve with the bow.

"There's no time to teach you more. You need to become proficient with one weapon. Focus on depth rather than breadth. Practice your bow work when we're not training or grab one of my archers if you can."

With the long knife, Seanchai learned to spar with elves and humans, and with the short knife to stab and slit throats, practicing on dummies that also served as archery targets.

"You'll never have such an effective weapon for close and quiet combat," Uncle remarked, unaware of how wrong he was.

Seanchai had used a bow before when he hunted and thought himself a pretty accurate bowman. He confidently shot three quick arrows into a target that was twenty yards away. He looked up proudly at Uncle who stood expressionless with his arms folded.

"Do you see the rock over there?"

"Yes," Seanchai replied.

"Good. I want you to run as fast as you can around that rock and back here. Then fire three arrows as you just did a moment ago. Make sure you run as fast as you can."

Seanchai was surprised but did as he was instructed. All three of the arrows he shot missed the target.

"Now," said Uncle, ignoring the missed shots and Seanchai's labored breathing, "I want you to run around the rock again. This time, when you return to this spot, roll, and shoot the arrows while you're kneeling."

Seanchai did and, to his credit, one of the arrows hit the edge of the target.

"Shooting a stationary target with both feet planted firmly on the ground and your breathing stilled is one thing," Uncle explained. "But the enemy rarely stands there like a deer grazing. Neither will your heart or breath be stilled when you are in danger. Even if you have not been running, in battle, you will be stressed."

"He trains hard," Ilana said to Uncle a while later. "Does he have what it takes?"

Uncle was hiding behind a bush and watching Seanchai practicing the exercises by himself. He looked down fondly at Ilana and put his arm around her shoulder.

"You're quite taken with him, aren't you, my daughter? I have seen you watching him."

"He's so vulnerable and innocent." Ilana flicked some strands of hair that had slipped over her face behind a pointed ear. "Yet, when he refused to leave the battlefield—when he told me that his guide was his friend—well, there was power and strength there, something very special."

Uncle sighed and his voice became heavy. "I understand, Ilana. But he has a long and dangerous path ahead of him. I would hate for you to fall in love and lose…"

His voice trailed off. Ilana impulsively hugged him tight, knowing he was thinking of the elfe he had loved—that they both still loved—and had lost.

"Perhaps it's the destiny of our family," she said.

Uncle looked down at her, shook his head and sighed. He could see how Ilana was watching Seanchai. He knew the expression on her face. "Does he know you're my daughter?"

"Not from me."

"Good." He pursed his lips. "Keep it that way."

SEVEN

Seanchai woke early to the pungent smell of moss, thankfully banishing dreams of a burning village. He took his hot tea over to a log around the smoldering embers of the fire. His exhalations rose into the crisp morning air.

Ilana approached. "Did you sleep well?" she asked.

"No, Not really."

"I have been instructed to help you collect supplies for your trip. Come along."

She offered her hand and pulled a groaning Seanchai up from the log. His body ached from sleeping on the hard ground. But he forgot this as soon as their hands touched, though his exhilaration was short-lived. Once he was on his feet, she let go and started walking with a smug grin she hid from him. He sighed and followed.

They came to a small cave that had been turned into a storeroom. Ilana nodded to two men just leaving with some clothes. They smiled but Seanchai could sense their unease with him. Ilana inspected Seanchai from head to toe and then turned to rummage through the barrels and piles on the ground. "How are your boots?"

"They're fine," he replied. "Not a year old."

"Good," she said, and threw him a pair of pants. "Try these on."

"Here?"

Ilana laughed. "I'll wait outside."

Seanchai hoped she hadn't noticed that his ears were almost certainly burning red. He tried on the pants. By the time they left the supply cave, he held two pairs of trousers, two shirts and some thick woolen socks.

Ilana had also foraged a cloak. "You only get these when Uncle gives permission," she said. The cloak was dyed in a range of dull grays, browns and greens designed for camouflage and travel.

"It's so light," Seanchai said, feeling the mesh on the inside of the cloak.

"It retains your body heat and keeps you warm even in the highest passes," Ilana explained as she modeled one.

"You look good in it," blurted Seanchai, who instantly blushed. He turned away wincing and again missed the smile on her face.

Ilana folded and picked up two cloaks in addition to the one Seanchai carried and led him out of the cave.

"Where now?" he asked.

"The blacksmith," she replied. "We haven't finished our shopping."

A bit later, they passed through a slit between two walls of rocks and found a muscular, bare-chested man standing by a makeshift forge. He was sharpening weapons on a spinning stone wheel that he pumped with his foot.

"What do you want?" His voice was deep and gruff, but not half as attention-grabbing as his bloodshot eyes.

"We need our knives, please." Ilana said. She had warned Seanchai that the blacksmith was a tough character. He was a craftsman, deprived of the environment he needed to create quality weapons and tools.

"Your blade is of good quality," said the big man, handing Seanchai the long knife Seanchai's father had given him. "But you treat it badly. An elf knife must be respected and cared for."

Seanchai looked up at the blacksmith and frowned. "Will you show me how, please?" he requested.

The blacksmith stared at him and, seeing that Seanchai meant it, oiled Seanchai's blades and explained at length how to sharpen and store them. He warned him not to abuse the blades by using them for cutting vegetables, or knocking them frivolously against stone.

Seanchai listened intently, asked questions, and even volunteered to sharpen a knife under the blacksmith's supervision. He was rewarded with a compact sharpening and oiling kit, as well as a short boot-knife with a carved handle.

"Back in the day I could have fashioned you a serious blade," he growled. "Once I had a mighty forge, built by my grandfather and passed down to my father."

"What happ—"

Seanchai stopped when Ilana squeezed his arm.

"Thank you, but we must go," she said to the blacksmith as she pulled Seanchai back through the slit.

"Thank you," Seanchai called over his shoulder.

Away from the enclosure, Ilana let go of Seanchai. He stopped abruptly.

"Why did you interrupt me? Where I come from—"

Ilana touched his arm again, but this time it was gentle, and his irritation subsided.

"I know you meant well, Seanchai, but you might need to forget some of the civilities you learned in your village. Gorthan lost his entire family to the Emperor's army. His forge was destroyed, along with tools that had been handed down through generations. Craftsmen like him measure their worth by their tools. It is just as well that he has no offspring. He would be so ashamed not to have any tools of worth to pass on."

"I still don't understand why I couldn't ask him what happened."

"Gorthan is our only blacksmith. Did you see his eyes? We need him to keep fixing and making weapons. We need him sober, and that's more difficult when he's dwelling on his past.

"The Emperor has destroyed our race and many others. This is why we need you, Seanchai." She paused and smiled when she saw panic on his face. "Come, I shouldn't burden you with more than a few supplies."

Seanchai followed her for a few moments, thinking of Gorthan. Then he noticed what she was carrying.

"Who are those other knife sets for?" he asked.

"Your guide and your friend," she replied with a smile.

"Rhoddan is coming with me?" He had doubted that Rhoddan would recover in time. "My friend?"

"Yes," she replied. "And the other set is for your guide."

"When will I meet him?" Seanchai asked.

"You already have," she replied and laughed. "And it's not a he."

They left before dawn, twelve in all—more than the three Seanchai was expecting—clad in identical gray hooded cloaks and carrying gray satchels carefully packed for balance and to keep food fresh for as long as possible. Their monotone matched the cloudy sky and the fog that hugged the ground.

They each led a mountain pony capable of taking its rider great distances without rest, and extremely adept at negotiating difficult mountain passes. Seanchai was perturbed. The only time he had ridden a horse was when he rescued Rhoddan and that was really just grimly clinging to the horse for a few moments, and he wasn't convinced he could repeat even that. He dreaded the other elves discovering this, as they had apparently just assumed he could ride. For now, at least, his pony clopped along with no resistance. So far, so good. Even so, he felt his stomach muscles tighten.

Seanchai looked down the line at the identically dressed figures and he was sure it was intentional. With cowls covering their heads, only the most observant tracker would be able to distinguish them by size or weight. Was this to make Seanchai more difficult to identify? He couldn't help feeling like a target.

"How are you doing?" Seanchai asked Rhoddan when they stopped to rest at a fork in the path. "Perhaps you shouldn't have come. Maybe it's too soon." Seanchai had watched Rhoddan wince when he removed his pack and struggle to lift his water skin to drink.

"Actually, I doubt we could have stopped him," said Ilana, drawing back her hood. "I hear he demanded to be included in the party, and there aren't many who tell Uncle what to do."

"So why did Uncle agree?" Seanchai asked.

"He has a talent for identifying strengths," Ilana replied. "He probably saw something in Rhoddan that he thinks will help you along your way. I'm sure it had nothing to do with Rhoddan threatening to track you on his own if he wasn't allowed to come along." This last part she said with a grin.

"Extreme stubbornness is a good tool to have on a journey," Seanchai laughed, "even if he is a wounded soul."

"I'm fine," Rhoddan said, sidestepping Ilana's jab. "I just need to focus my energy on healing as well as walking."

He sipped from a small hip flask and shuddered at the taste.

"What's that?" Seanchai asked.

"It's an herbal tonic—a strengthener," Rhoddan explained. "The healer who prepared it purposely made it very concentrated so that it would last. Yuck. It's so bitter. Now stop looking at me like that, or I'll make you drink some."

All three laughed at this, causing others close to them to turn and frown. Seanchai didn't care. Being with Ilana and Rhoddan made him feel that he might be able to do whatever everyone seemed to expect of him because he wouldn't have to do it alone.

Seanchai leaned closer to keep his voice down. "Can I help you at all?"

Rhoddan shook his head, but Ilana thought differently.

"Why not?" she asked. "Let him try."

"Try what?" Seanchai asked as Rhoddan continued shaking his head.

"Maybe one night after we've set up camp," Rhoddan conceded. "It'll tire him and that might be dangerous while we travel."

"Try *what?*" Seanchai asked again, impatience clear in his voice. "I *am* standing here, you know."

"Not now," Rhoddan almost pleaded. "Not while we're on the road. Let me be, please. I am a warrior, let me bear my pain."

He turned away and Ilana nodded to Seanchai to comply. She picked up her pack and tightened some cords that had loosened. When Seanchai put his pack on, she stepped forward and tightened his cords, adjusting the whole way his pack sat on his back and it felt considerably more comfortable.

"Thank you," he said and thought her smile shone through the grayness around them.

As the line moved off, three figures took the other fork in the path.

"Where are they going?" Seanchai asked.

"Decoys," Ilana replied. "They will walk through the mountains for a few days. Once they're certain they aren't being followed, they'll return to camp."

"And if they *are* being followed?"

"They will keep heading westward to draw any spies away from us. We will soon swing north to the Snowdons."

"How do we know spies will follow them and not us?" Seanchai asked.

Ilana shrugged. "We don't. But they have to choose between four groups. Let's hope they choose wrong."

Over the next two days, as Ilana had mentioned, others broke off in groups of two or three. Finally, it was only the three of them left. Seanchai watched the last three leave them and then addressed Ilana.

"So … you're my guide?"

"Yes," she replied and Seanchai heard pride in her voice. "I have been trained for just such a mission."

"And you're my bodyguard?" Seanchai turned to Rhoddan.

Rhoddan shrugged. "I happen to have a few days with nothing to do."

Seanchai put a hand on each of them. "I'm glad," he said, and meant it.

When they stopped for the evening, Ilana showed Seanchai how to help Rhoddan heal using his hands. Seanchai had seen his mother doing this, but wasn't sure what it was. Ilana explained.

"We can all channel energy into and through our bodies. Sometimes we can direct the excess to another person. Our healers believe that this energy comes from within. Others think we take it from our surroundings–like trees and plants, or animals. Parents lay hands on their children to soothe them. I reckon you have a greater ability than others to store and pass it on.

"Just follow my lead," she continued. "But if you feel an instinct to do something different, then follow it. Learn to trust your intuition."

With Rhoddan lying between them, Ilana and Seanchai settled on their knees, tucking their feet under. They put their palms on their own chests. Ilana began breathing more deeply.

"Imagine your breath coming in with energy from the trees and the forest and filling your stomach. Then exhale out through your chest into the palms of your hands."

Seanchai imitated Ilana until he felt warmth gathering beneath his hands. He faced his palms to each other and allowed the heat to grow. Then he leaned over and put his hands on Rhoddan's chest and stomach. The wounded elf was dozing and sighed deeply. Seanchai imagined his energy flowing into Rhoddan.

After they finished, Ilana and Seanchai rose together and quietly moved away so as to not wake up Rhoddan.

"I'll guard first and then wake you," she whispered. "If he does get up and feels better then he can switch with you. But it would be better if he sleeps all night."

"Ilana, what is this energy?" Seanchai could still feel his hands tingling.

"It's called ryku. It can heal, vitalize, and invigorate. It stimulates and strengthens the body's own rejuvenating powers."

"I really felt it, Ilana."

"It is amazing," she replied, and her eyes sparkled in delight. "I can't wait for you to master it. We'll be able to do great things together."

EIGHT

Rhoddan's condition visibly improved as the days passed. Seanchai was not sure whether to attribute it to the ryku energy work, the herbal drink, or simply Rhoddan's stubborn desire to be useful. Rhoddan took charge of security, dividing the guard rotation into four shifts instead of three and guarding the two middle shifts himself so as to allow the others several uninterrupted hours of sleep.

"A warrior is trained to sleep for short periods of time," he argued when Ilana expressed concern. "I know my limits and I'll tell you if it becomes a problem. I won't endanger the mission."

"But you've been wounded," she protested, her hands on her hips, a sign Seanchai was quickly recognizing as time to back down.

"I know my limits," Rhoddan replied, "and I won't do anything stupid. I promise."

Seanchai felt bad for Rhoddan but did not object too vigorously. The reality was that he, Seanchai, was having the hardest time physically. The longest hike Seanchai had taken before this was when he had fled his village, and fear, he realized, had proven a powerful energizer.

But without so much adrenaline now, his feet were sore and his back ached from climbing narrow mountain paths strewn with protruding stones. It was not safe to ride a horse, which could easily turn a leg. Not that he would have felt safe on a horse even on a flat grassy field. He also struggled to adjust to the high altitude's thinning air, feeling perpetually short of breath.

The terrain was rocky and steep. All around him, Seanchai saw nothing but boulders, crags and mountaintops. He had the feeling that there was always a higher peak ahead of them, though the peaks were shrouded in fog, which made this impossible to discern.

Ilana's knowledge of the terrain as a guide and tracker impressed Seanchai, though he had to admit that everything about her impressed him. She confidently led them as they changed paths and backtracked to obscure their tracks. Seanchai had learned not to question her after the first time.

"Hey Ilana," he said. "We're going backwards."

"I know," she replied.

"This track parallels the one we just took."

"I know."

"Well, that means we're essentially going back the way we just came. We—"

"*I know,*" she hissed, wheeling around to face him with clenched fists digging into her hips. She glared at him and then abruptly turned back to the path.

"Err ... Seanchai," warned Rhoddan, "I think you should leave the directions to Ilana. She really is very good."

"Oh I think she's extremely competent. It's just that—"

Ilana whirled around again, her hair whipping behind her. "Competent? Competent? I am...*competent?*"

"Well, what I mean is... Rhoddan, what do I mean?"

Rhoddan was having a hard time hiding his grin, but he made an effort. "I think you were just about to compliment Ilana on her brilliant backtracking tactics."

"Err, that's exactly what I wanted—"

Ilana stomped toward Seanchai with reddening cheeks and hands back on her hips. "Did it ever occur to you that we might be being followed and that retracing our steps could throw them off track?"

"No," Seanchai replied, chagrined. He sighed. Ilana softened and punched him playfully on the arm.

"We're going to get you to your teacher, Seanchai, but you're going to have to learn to trust us."

"Oh I do, I do," he replied rather too quickly. Then, involuntarily, he glanced over his shoulder.

Ilana led them to a remote monastery of elves, dwarves, and humans who rigidly practiced meditation, physical exercises, deep breathing, and a very austere lifestyle. The monks were of the Kundzu Order.

When he saw the Kundzu Monastery an hour up the mountainside, Seanchai almost cheered. There would be a fire and warm food, a mat to sleep on, a roof, and other people guarding while they slept uninterrupted by guard duty.

As they neared the monastery gate, Ilana stopped and signaled to hide behind some nearby rocks. "There should be smoke coming from the chimneys and a flag on the post above the gate."

"Maybe they're meditating or something," Seanchai offered. He was desperate for the comforts that had propelled him forward the last day.

"Then maybe you would like to join them?" A deep voice snarled behind him.

Seanchai swung round to find a thick broadsword inches from his face. A dozen burly soldiers materialized out of the shadows and surrounded the elves. Rhoddan reached for his long knife.

"Don't," said the soldier facing him. "Even if a mite like you could take me, there are archers itching to shoot you down. You wouldn't even reach me."

"Rhoddan, stand down," said Ilana, her voice surprisingly calm.

"Keep your weapons sheathed and put your hands behind your heads. Good. Now, let's go inside, shall we? Nice and quiet."

The soldier barked to another to bring their horses and then turned towards the monastery. The surrounding walls were built of dark stones stacked about double Seanchai's height, and covered with lichen. They entered through an archway that opened into a courtyard with huts on each side and a stable at the far end. They ended up in a large hall and, once inside, were instructed to remove their weapons and boots.

"My boots?" Seanchai objected and then saw Ilana roll her eyes. "What?"

"You'll miss your boots more than your weapons?"

"We're not too happy about it either," a nearby guard snarled. "Judging from the stench, you haven't washed in days."

Seanchai glanced around and realized that all the soldiers were human. Elves traditionally shunned humans because they were known to be violent and unpredictable. Seanchai knew that once, elves, dwarves, and humans had lived together in harmony, but that was a long time ago. He had been brought up to fear humans, and right now he was petrified. The soldiers seemed so big and broad. They all had beards and long knotted hair.

Seanchai sat down on the floor of the main hall and looked around. There were long tables along one side of the room. On the other side, sacks of vegetables and grains were piled next to a big stone fireplace, where a heavy pot was hanging above a fire. In front of the fire was another long table with plates, spoons, and bread. At the end were cups and a barrel.

A huge man with a ruddy complexion and a potbelly that spilled over his trousers, stood behind the table serving a stew. He kept a careful eye on who took drinks. When all the soldiers had eaten, he called to the three elves.

"Come over here, you three. The Emperor probably doesn't want us to starve you. This here is prime mountain goat. Its meat is dry and lean and tastes like rotting strands of rope. But the monks had dried vegetables and I've a few tricks up my sleeve." Seanchai saw that he rubbed his ample belly, which quivered under his touch. "Come on. You might only be elves, but you're kids, and kids are always hungry."

Seanchai approached him and took a bowl. "Thank you," he said as the big man raised a full ladle. "You're very kind."

The cook grinned and signaled to the other two. The three took their stew and retreated to their corner where they sat on the floor. Seanchai had only taken a few spoonfuls when a boot kicked his bowl across the room.

"Get up," the man barked. "I am the sergeant here and you'll obey everything I tell you. Tomorrow we march down this wretched mountain to the garrison at Galbrieth. What General Tarlach does with you, I don't know and I don't care.

"Don't think of trying to escape. We have eighteen battle-hardened soldiers here. Three sixers. All of us hate elves and this mission. If you try anything," he stared at Seanchai while pointing at Ilana, "your she-elf goes first. Understand?"

Seanchai nodded. This was the second time he had been addressed directly. They seemed to know that he was the one they wanted. Then he recalled what the cook had said; the Emperor apparently wanted him alive.

"You sleep in here and don't leave the room. There will be guards at each door and along the walls outside. We know how to take care of ourselves."

Seanchai nodded again. He didn't doubt the officer. So he was surprised when he awoke in the morning to find all eighteen dead, a single black-feathered arrow protruding from each of their still bodies.

NINE

They crept through the monastery in disbelief. Rhoddan kept count of dead soldiers by retrieving the arrows from their bodies. When all but four of them were accounted for, Rhoddan suggested they return to the hall and retrieve their bags and weapons.

"Whoever did this might want to refill their quivers," Rhoddan remarked with awe and fear.

Seanchai took an arrow from Rhoddan and examined it. It felt heavier than elf arrows, but perfectly balanced, and had tightly bound, black feathers.

"What about the other soldiers?" Ilana asked.

"They're probably at the gate or wherever else they stand guard," Rhoddan replied, keeping his voice low. "Maybe they're chasing the people who did this."

"Shouldn't *we* try and find who did this?" Seanchai asked. "We need to thank them."

Rhoddan grimaced. "Whoever pulled this off will decide when and where to introduce themselves."

They retrieved their cloaks, weapons and packs from the main hall. Seanchai knelt over the dead cook who had had fed them He was staring lifelessly at the ceiling, a look of horror across his face. The young elf felt a wave of sympathy. The fat human had shown them kindness and Seanchai regretted his death. When he looked up, he saw Ilana watching him.

"There're too many innocent victims," Ilana said, joining him. "Had he not been conscripted he may well have been a jolly father at the head of a long table of happy, well-fed children."

"He chose to serve in the army," Rhoddan said without a hint of sympathy.

"He was conscripted," Ilana snapped.

"So would I have been, and Seanchai too. We chose not to serve."

Ilana glared at him. But before she could respond, Seanchai sighed loudly, bent over and gently closed the cook's eyes. His voice was so despondent.

"Please don't argue. He was kind when he didn't have to be. We know nothing of what came before, of his struggles and sufferings. All we know is that he showed us gentleness when no one else did. I think that makes him different, and for that, I mourn his death."

Rhoddan and Ilana both gaped at him. His distraught tone disarmed their anger and they silently nodded a truce to each other. Rhoddan packed some extra food into the packs as Ilana placed a hand on Seanchai's shoulder.

"You're right," she said. "It becomes too easy to hate and then we're no better than the worst of our enemies. You do well to remind us."

She bent down and covered the cook's face with an apron. "May the spirits of your ancestors receive you in love," she said and then rose to help Rhoddan pack some extra food.

They slipped out of the monastery and retrieved their horses—which seemed to have been well taken care of—from the stables. The sergeant had clearly planned to travel in the morning. Rhoddan retrieved the arrows that had killed two more soldiers there. They found the last two bodies as they passed through the archway of the front gates.

"I guess we are free to go," Rhoddan said.

They had barely left the monastery when Seanchai stopped and pointed at a figure on the rocks above them. They had to shield their eyes from the sun's glare. The silhouette stood up and held his bow in the air.

"I think he's trying to signal something," Seanchai said.

"Rhoddan," Ilana whispered, though the bowman couldn't possibly hear her. "Put the arrows down there for him."

Rhoddan made a show of piling the arrows onto a nearby rock and the figure waved them on. They continued at a brisk pace, feeling compelled to distance themselves from the soldiers, even though they would not be following. Ironically, they had slept well since they had no need for guard duty, and they had eaten a hot meal. Seanchai again thought of the cook. Would he ever get used to the killing? Did he want to?

The path through the mountains remained stony and uneven, with large walls of sullen brown rocks rising on either side of them. They contrasted with the east-facing mountainside, which was a bright warm red and sharply defined by the rising sun.

They rested in a cavern that protected them from the chilling wind after two hours of steep climbing. For a few minutes they sat in silence, adjusting their packs, retying boots, or in Seanchai's case, just staring out at the mountain range in exhaustion.

"We should have taken some more supplies." Ilana spoke first. "We don't have enough to get us through our journey. There are no elf villages on our way, but we will need to buy supplies."

"How will we pay?" Seanchai asked.

"Uncle has taken care of that," Ilana replied, patting a leather bag she wore.

Seanchai stared pensively outside the cavern. "Is he out there, do you think?"

"Yeah," replied Rhoddan. "Frankly, I'd be happy if he's on the ledge above, watching out for us."

"I don't envy him out there in this wind," Seanchai replied. "He'd be smarter coming inside."

"Can I take that as an invitation?" The voice was so close it made them all jump. "Thanks for returning my arrows; the black ones are my favorites. A shame to waste them on such scum."

Ilana was the first to recover, though Seanchai could feel her apprehension. "Please ... come in. Thank you for saving us."

The figure came inside and perched on a rock. He was wrapped in a black cloak and hood. He swept the hood back, revealing that he was a human, not much older than them. His long, spiky, jet-black hair was held back with a leather band in similar fashion to the elves. But it was his eyes that caught their attention. They were very dark, almost black—intense, and cold.

"A human?" Seanchai exclaimed. "Why did you save us?"

"Not all humans hate elves." The stranger took a swig of water from a leather flask. "Some of us like and respect your race. I grew up hearing stories about men, elves—and dwarves, even, if you can believe it—once living together in harmony. It sounds like a better time, if it ever existed."

"It did," Seanchai said fervently, and then blushed at his own intensity. "I–I mean, it had to, if you get my meaning."

The others nodded, though he wasn't sure if they were just humoring him. He also wasn't sure why he was becoming increasingly certain a better time had existed, and why it had begun to take on such immense importance to him. Humans had treated elves as an underclass ever since the great battles when the Emperor's ancestors had seized control of Odessiya.

"Still," Ilana continued. "That doesn't really explain why you risked your life for us, taking down a dozen soldiers, or how you happened to be there."

The stranger snorted. "Maybe I just hate them more. Anyway, there were eighteen, the officer, and that fat cook."

Seanchai stiffened. Ilana probably noticed as she quickly continued the conversation. "But why?" she asked again.

He sighed and rubbed his spiky hair. "The why is for another time. But the how … I saw that you were about my age and it piqued my interest. I've been tracking you for a few days, and knew by the way you kept backtracking that you were either on an important mission or really, really lost."

The stranger grinned and Seanchai laughed before withering under Ilana's glare.

The human continued. "You can pick up supplies in Tripath. It's two days' walk from here, though most of that is descending from the mountain range."

"Is that a human town?" Ilana asked.

"Yes. It used to be a small trading post but has grown very quickly over the last few years."

"I'm not sure a group of elves should just walk in." Ilana was fiddling absentmindedly with her hair, which Seanchai now interpreted as a nervous trait. "We need to stay as anonymous as possible."

"I can help you with that," the stranger said. "Where are you heading from there?"

His question was met by silence. The story they had rehearsed seemed disrespectful, given what this stranger had just done for them, but they still feared revealing the truth. Seanchai, actually, realized that he didn't know where, and that if anything were to happen to his companions, he would have no idea how to continue. He decided to ask Ilana when they were next alone.

"You don't have to tell me," the young human said. "I understand. But I need to know how many days you will need supplies for."

"We're traveling in search of a teacher," said Seanchai, breaking the silence. "We are to study with him to become healers."

"Really?" the stranger turned his dark eyes on Seanchai.

"No," Seanchai met his gaze and responded without hesitation. "But it's the best I can do for now."

"Very well. I understand."

"What's your name?" Ilana asked.

"Shayth," he replied. "It means 'the darkest shade of black'."

"Really? Shayth is your name?"

"Yes. As far as I remember, at least."

"Your family?" Ilana continued.

Shayth shook his head. "That's the best I can do for now." He smiled and the elves breathed a collective sigh.

"Well, Shayth," Seanchai said and offered his hand. "Thank you for saving us at the monastery. Whatever your motivation, it is gratefully received."

Shayth now walked with them. He rarely spoke, but continually scanned their surroundings to determine if they were being followed. Seanchai realized that this was a well-practiced behavior.

"You're on the run, aren't you?" Seanchai blurted as the thought occurred to him.

Shayth nodded.

"For how long?"

"This is not the time," said Shayth. "Drop it."

But Rhoddan blocked Shayth's path. "It is the time. You might be endangering our mission." His voice was firm.

"Mission?" Shayth smiled.

"I mean journey."

Shayth rolled his eyes, making sure Rhoddan knew he didn't appreciate the questions. "Half the kingdom is chasing you, right?"

Seanchai saw his friends nod.

"Well, half the kingdom is probably after me too. Let's just hope it's the same half. Look. He pointed to thin pillars of smoke.

"Tripath?" Ilana asked.

"Dinner," Shayth replied.

TEN

Rhoddan was nervous and skeptical about accompanying Shayth into town, but necessity dictated that they buy food, so they had no choice. Tripath sat, as its name suggested, at the junction of three main roads. It had flourished as a trading town far away from the Emperor's gaze, it had also earned a reputation as a center for shady business. Traders sold their wares in the vibrant marketplace and were promptly tempted to part with their money in the surrounding drinking or gambling establishments.

Shayth and Rhoddan wore their hoods closely over their heads. Shayth had told Rhoddan that elves were tolerated in this town because of their economic contribution, but would not be welcomed in the bars or back alleys. Rhoddan noticed how other elves on the road walked with their heads bowed, trying to avoid drawing attention. He mimicked their gaits.

They were prepared for the rough and ready populace and to keep a low profile, but by the way Shayth jerked upright at the sight, he was clearly not expecting military checkpoints.

"This is new," Shayth whispered to Rhoddan. "I'm not sure whether they're searching for someone or just levying a toll for the Emperor." He looked around at the people waiting to pass through the checkpoint. "I have an idea. Follow me and don't say a word."

They joined the traders waiting in line to pass, taking position just behind a farmer whose mule pulled a wagon stacked precariously with small cages, all carrying squawking hens.

Just as the farmer approached the sentry, Shayth stepped forward and, with a small knife concealed in his sleeve, sliced through a piece of rope that was barely holding the stacked cages, sending them scattering. Immediately, he began scrambling to collect the squawking birds, yelling apologies to his 'father'–the farmer–and hailing insults down on Rhoddan.

"You clumsy elf," he yelled. "Father told you several times to make sure these were tied well. Don't just stand there, you idiot–help me. Sorry father, we've got them. You'll pay for your incompetence, you dumb elf. Mark my words. I'll ring those ugly, pointed ears of yours, so help me."

The farmer, an old, bent man, looked on, too stunned to speak. The soldiers began yelling at him for holding up the line, forcing him to find his voice and begin stuttering apologies. With the cart precariously restacked, and Rhoddan and Shayth holding the cages, Shayth slapped the mule and it lumbered through the checkpoint. The exasperated soldiers let them go, as both the farmer and Shayth apologized profusely.

Once through the checkpoint and safely inside the town walls, Shayth passed the still-unsecured rope to the bewildered farmer.

"You really should double-check these knots every few miles." He patted the old man on the shoulder, grabbed Rhoddan's arm, and disappeared into the crowd in search of the supplies they needed.

Back at camp, Rhoddan told the others how well Shayth must have bartered and haggled, for their money seemed to stretch an impressively long way. He harbored a few doubts, but kept them to himself. They ate heartily and prepared for bed.

Before they went to sleep, Shayth addressed the elves. "You'll need to decide your direction in the morning, if you haven't already. You don't have to tell me anything, but you should know I might deduce things as we walk. I know the land very well. You should decide whether or not you want me to accompany you."

"Let's talk more in the morning," Ilana said, nodding at Seanchai, who was already half-asleep, and soon everyone was out except Shayth, who stood guard, staring out into the darkness, deep in thought.

When they woke just after dawn, Shayth allow them some space so they could discuss whether he should join them the rest of the way.

"He's extremely useful," Rhoddan admitted. "He can fight. He knows the country and how to deal with other humans. He's also a valuable source for food. But he's on the run himself. He might be a murderer, thief, or traitor. I worried about letting him guard while we slept."

"He's very bitter and closed," added Ilana. "I think we'll find him unpredictable. We're all very committed to each other, and he doesn't share that commitment. Poor human. He's been on his own for way too long."

Then Ilana looked at Seanchai. "What does your instinct tell you?"

"I don't know," he said without thinking.

"Seanchai," Rhoddan said. "Remember when we couldn't decide whether to cross the plain the night before we met up with Uncle?"

Seanchai immediately shook his head in protest. "I don't know what I did. Uncle called it scrying."

"Maybe you don't understand it, but it worked," Rhoddan argued, "and we trust you, even if you don't trust yourself yet."

Seanchai nodded and tried to clear his mind as he looked at Shayth, recalling what he had done when Rhoddan had pushed him to decide about crossing the plain. He thought he could feel the bitter young man, his anger and hostility. He felt himself reaching out...

Shayth whirled round and raged, "Stop that! You don't have my consent!"

Ilana, looking from one to the other, shook Seanchai. "Seanchai! Seanchai! What's happening?"

Seanchai gasped and blinked rapidly, shaking his head. Tears welled in his eyes. "Wh-what was I doing?" he stammered.

"I'm not sure," she replied. "I think you entered his mind, or at least attempted to."

"What? I didn't..."

"Seanchai," Ilana put her hand on his shoulder and squeezed gently. "You just need to decide. Trust your judgment."

Seanchai rose and started toward Shayth, rubbing his forehead. He felt the dull scrying headache growing. Shayth was already standing up, his fists clenched and his eyes black as his name. Seanchai held up his hands, palms out, in the universal sign of surrender.

"You had no right to try that," Shayth yelled. "What do you take me for? After what I've done for you, why..." He trailed off. "You had no right," he repeated, now more sullen than angry.

"I don't know what I did," said Seanchai earnestly. "Ilana told me to use my instinct and this just started to happen. I don't control it or even understand it. That's why we're going where we're going, so that I might learn from one who understands and can teach me how to use and channel this power I possess. And it's why I am being chased.

"I don't know what my role is in this messed up world. But there seem to be a lot of people who fear me, and far too many who are willing to lay down their lives to ensure I survive. I have apparently even caught the Emperor's attention. I appear to be very important, and this terrifies me. A few weeks ago, I was a simple villager hunting, fishing, playing pranks, and chatting up young elfes."

Seanchai's voice cracked. "A few weeks ago I had a community and a family. Now I doubt they're even alive, condemned to die maybe for the crime of sheltering me. I'm afraid, Shayth. I'm in way over my head. I need friends I can trust, and I need to find this teacher. I want you to come with us but you need to know what you're getting into."

Shayth had been watching Seanchai closely as he spoke. Now he rubbed his spiky hair back and forth a few times. Finally, he cleared his throat. When he spoke, Shayth's voice was soft for the first time since they had met.

"I will help you find your teacher, Seanchai, if that is your request. I offer you my allegiance and my loyalty until then." Shayth's voice abruptly became harsh. "But don't ask me to stop hating, and don't ever stop me from killing. This is how I live. And don't ever scry my mind without my permission, or I will kill you." He paused and looked away for a moment. Then he turned back and grinned. "Other than that, I'm happy to help."

He and Seanchai grasped each other's forearms firmly in the custom of Odessiya. Their eyes were still locked.

"Thank you," said Seanchai, shakily. "Thank you. I don't have many friends."

Shayth withdrew his hand. "I never said anything about being your friend."

Seanchai blinked, but then saw Shayth was smiling. Seanchai smiled back, for the first time in quite a while.

ELEVEN

When they were ready to leave, Shayth suggested the elves ride since they would be following well-traveled roads rather than mountain paths.

"What about you?" Seanchai asked. "We only have three horses."

"I'll follow off the path," Shayth said. "It'll be easier for me to see and help if you get into trouble."

"But you have no horse. We should walk, all of us, together." Even Seanchai heard the panic in his voice.

Shayth came over to Seanchai's horse and adjusted some of its straps. Actually, Seanchai noticed he adjusted all of the horse's straps.

"Had this horse long?" Shayth asked, casually patting the horse's mane.

"No," mumbled Seanchai. "They gave him to me." He nodded toward Ilana.

"Ah-ha," Shayth said. "You're a forest elf? From Morthian Wood, you said?"

"Uh-huh," Seanchai replied, feeling panic rise.

"The elves of Morthian Wood are excellent woodsmen—err, woodelves. Fine hunters and foragers, I hear. Not much need to ride horses in the thick brush."

The hand in front of Ilana's mouth hid her grin but not her red cheeks. Rhoddan had turned his back to them and was walking away. Seanchai noticed his shoulders shaking with laughter.

"Okay," said Seanchai accepting his fate. "I don't have much experience with horses." They all turned together and stared at him. "In fact," he sighed, "I have *no* experience with horses."

"Why didn't you tell us?" Ilana asked after she got her giggles under control.

Seanchai shrugged.

Ilana glided over playfully and wrapped her hands around his neck. "I think it's cute." Abruptly, she sharpened and pulled away from him. "But what if we were attacked and needed to flee on horseback? Rhoddan and I could be miles away before we realized you had fallen off or been thrown.

"Rhoddan, please bring your horse over here and show our ward at least how to mount and dismount. The rest he'll manage, for now, by hanging on. Shayth, let's scout ahead a bit and choose our path."

Seanchai turned to Rhoddan, who was approaching with his own horse. His friend was still grinning, and Seanchai was quite convinced that the horse was smirking, as well.

For most of the day they rode. Seanchai, to his credit, never fell off, but quickly lost all feeling in his thighs and backside. They passed fields and meadows surrounded by clusters of farmhouses and barns. Cows, pigs and sheep grazed in groups. Still, Seanchai noticed that they never actually saw anyone working in the fields or tending the livestock. He asked the others about this.

"I think it might be fear," Shayth answered. "The army passes this way and might decide to conscript a strapping young farmhand."

"I doubt the women would wander far from the buildings either," Ilana added.

Shayth appeared and disappeared at various intervals, always joining them when they rested. At one such break in the late afternoon, he watched Seanchai staring at his horse. "Ilana," he asked. "What is the name of Seanchai's horse?"

"Snowmane."

The horse was chestnut with a long white mane. Shayth patted him and signaled for Seanchai to join him.

"Stroke him," he instructed. "Feel the contours on his neck, chest, and flanks. Let him know you care about him, that you're a partnership. Make him your best friend, and he'll be as loyal as Ilana and Rhoddan." He glanced over and saw they were watching him. "He's a lot cuter, too."

As Shayth turned, Seanchai said, "You know a lot about horses. Why don't you have one?"

Shayth turned, and Seanchai saw that his eyes had darkened. "I did—a powerful and intelligent stallion named Windstar. I could call him from anywhere with a whistle and he would gallop to me and nuzzle. I spent hours grooming and caring for him."

"What happened?" Ilana asked, a sick feeling in her stomach.

"Same as everyone I've been close to," Shayth replied, his back to them and his voice cold. "He's dead."

Seanchai touched Shayth's shoulder, but the human threw off his hand and spun to glare at Seanchai. Shayth's face was contorted with rage, and he bared his teeth.

"It's the hate that fuels me," Shayth hissed. "Don't ever try to temper it."

Seanchai thought about Shayth as they rode through the afternoon. They were so close in age, yet Shayth was already burdened with such terrible experiences. Seanchai wished there was something he could do.

They continued to ride as the sun began its descent. They were approaching a sharp bend in the road when Shayth, who had not been with them for some time, hissed from the side. "Checkpoint!"

They froze. Rhoddan and Ilana immediately backtracked their horses, but Seanchai didn't know how to. Shayth dropped silently beside him and grabbed Snowmane's reins just under the muzzle. He murmured into the horse's perked ears and turned it around.

"We have another half a day before we enter the Seven Peaks," Ilana said when they were a safe distance away and off the road. "I'm not sure what to do. There's only one way into those mountains."

"Maybe not," Shayth replied. "I know another way, a pass, but it's dangerous. There's a particularly nasty gang of bandits who camp up there."

"We could try and bluff our way through the checkpoint," Seanchai suggested, and was met with some astonished looks. "Then it's settled. We take our chances with the bandits."

Shayth ruffled his unruly hair again, a sign they now recognized as anxiety, but he didn't say anything further.

They doubled back to a small path that led north. Seanchai admitted to himself that he probably wouldn't have even noticed it if he hadn't been following his guides. The path began to ascend and they led their horses up it, single file. Shayth jogged ahead to scout. Ilana followed and Seanchai saw her glancing around.

"What's the name of your horse, Ilana?" Seanchai asked from behind her.

"Night," she replied with pride. Her horse was a stately black stallion with a sliver of white on her nose.

"It's a fitting name," Seanchai said and then called over his shoulder. "What about yours, Rhoddan?"

Rhoddan was bringing up the rear and mumbled under his breath.

"I can't hear you," Seanchai called back. Ilana laughed.

"His horse is named Riverwader," she said. "He's always loved galloping through water–river, lake or even a puddle after the rain– and kicking up dirt on everyone around him."

"I should have a battle horse," Rhoddan grumbled from the back. "I am a warrior."

Ilana stopped and turned to look at them. "I have seen River-wader in a fight, Rhoddan. He's disciplined and brave. You shouldn't judge him so."

Riverwader neighed loudly and Ilana and Seanchai burst out laughing. Rhoddan shook his head, trying unsuccessfully to maintain a scowl. Then he patted his horse affectionately. "I guess we'll make it work, huh, buddy?"

It was getting dark as they reached the rock face.

"I'm torn about whether to start through so late in the day," Shayth said. He stood thinking for a while and then turned darkly to the others. "You camp here. I'll go in, find the bandit camp, and try to talk to them. Perhaps we'll have better luck negotiating than fighting."

Ilana began to protest, but Shayth cut her off.

"I don't think we would have much chance in these gorges against hardened men and elves who make a living out of surprising and robbing people. Besides, their leader is a man called Calreith, and we go back a time."

"He's your friend?" asked Seanchai feeling upbeat.

"We've had some fun together," Shayth replied, "though I believe his parting words when last we met were, *I'll slit your throat if I ever get my hands on you,*' or something like that. I can't be sure since I was riding away from him in quite a hurry."

"Riding away from him?"

"Yes, on his horse." Shayth grimaced, then turned and disap-peared into the dark.

TWELVE

Seanchai woke with a start to Ilana's cry cutting through the silent dawn. He sprung from his blankets and scrambled for his knives. But when he looked at her, he saw she had not dropped into battle position, but was looking at an approaching figure.

Shayth was barely recognizable as he stumbled toward them. Seanchai saw that the young human's face was swollen and one eye was puffed shut. Rhoddan flew to his side to steady Shayth and lower him to the ground.

Shayth slumped back against a rock. "Water," he rasped.

Rhoddan scrambled over to his pack and retrieved his canteen. When Shayth stopped drinking, Rhoddan loosened his neck scarf, poured some water onto it, and pressed it to Shayth's face. The others knelt next to him, staring at his beaten face.

Rhoddan glanced sharply around. "Shayth. Were you possibly followed?"

"For sure," Shayth replied. "But they won't approach."

"Why not?" Rhoddan asked.

Shayth just shook his head.

"I'm sorry they did this to you," said Ilana sadly. "Seanchai and I can perform healing on you and then we'll go back the way we came."

"Go back? Why?" Shayth tried to sit up, gasped in pain and gave up.

"We can't face those animals," she said. "We should never have let you go alone."

"No," Shayth replied. "I was successful. He'll let us pass, but first he wants to meet the special student."

"You call this success?" Ilana shook her head. "What kind of success is this?"

"The kind of success that gets Seanchai to his teacher." Shayth winced briefly before continuing. "Anyway, Calreith actually seemed quite pleased to see me."

"Pleased?"

"Sure. If he still held a grudge, I'd be dead. Now let me rest a while. Perhaps we should eat before we head in."

After breakfast, Seanchai offered to lay hands on Shayth to help speed his healing. "I won't be touching your mind; I think I can control it now that I know what can happen," Shayth couldn't deny that it would help him on their day's journey and begrudgingly accepted the help. He lay back and let Seanchai work on him, thanking him warmly when he finished.

While Seanchai was healing Shayth, Rhoddan signaled for Ilana to join him a distance away.

"Ilana," he whispered. "I need you to trust me and do as I tell you."

She nodded and Rhoddan wet her hair and face, rubbed dirt and ash on both, and twisted her hair into loose knots. When he had finished, she looked eerily gray.

"From now on, wear your hood tightly drawn so that no one can see your face. When we approach the camp stay in the rear and pretend to be tired and weak. Don't overplay it in case we need to keep the act up. Just sow some seeds in their thoughts."

"You have a plan?" she asked. When he nodded, she added, "A good one?"

He smiled weakly. "All that is important is that Seanchai gets through the mountains. Remember that."

He called the others over to explain his plan.

Calreith stood scowling in the middle of his camp, his crossed arms bulging with muscles. He was a towering man with bright red hair and a wild beard. A huge battle hammer was slung across his back.

"So," he sneered when Seanchai, Ilana and Rhoddan stopped their horses in front of him. "This is the miserable band of followers who have attached themselves to my dear friend Shayth. We would rob you, but if he is the best guide you can afford, I doubt you have any money or jewels."

His gang laughed crudely. Rhoddan guided his horse forward. When he spoke, his voice was quiet but steady. "Calreith, we are on an urgent mission. We respectfully request safe passage through your territory. We have very little time."

"Are you the special one?" Calreith asked.

"Aye," Rhoddan replied with the same calm tone.

"I doubt it," Calreith countered. "You're probably bluffing to protect..." he looked at the others, though their hoods gave little away, "him." He pointed at Seanchai, who felt a shiver of fear as he thought of the beating Shayth had received.

But Rhoddan laughed. "He can barely ride a horse, as you have seen. And he bears arms like a child. His mind is a child's, too. He's harmless, pathetically so."

Everyone laughed and Seanchai hung his head. Rhoddan was playing a dangerous game. Seanchai did not like the idea of Rhoddan putting himself in danger by pretending to be him.

"Then what about..." Calreith stopped and glared at Ilana. Though her hood masked her face, he could see the feminine curves of her chest. "A woman?"

"An elfe," Rhoddan corrected him. "She is sick and we must deliver her to a healer at the monastery of Trewent before I can continue on my mission. Her father provided us with safe passage through his land in return for this. We must be careful. People seem to die if she touches or breathes on them. That's why I have the simpleton to attend her."

A murmur went through the bandits. Only Calreith seemed doubtful. He stared deeply at Ilana and then at Shayth before speaking to Rhoddan again.

"How, then, have you managed to buy the services of Shayth? You must have money to give him?"

"No," replied Shayth, moving next to Rhoddan. "Her father has my horse."

There was a dangerous silence and then Calreith started laughing. His huge shoulders shook and he held his stomach. "You have nerve, Shayth. Did they use your own tricks on you?"

"Yes," Shayth replied, "and I would appreciate if you would hold off killing me until I have had my revenge."

Calreith laughed again. Then he addressed Rhoddan, abruptly serious again. "Swear to me that you hate the Emperor. Swear that you will never reveal us, and swear that you will never take the Emperor's service."

Rhoddan dismounted Riverwader and approached Calreith. The big man towered over him but the elf looked unflinchingly into his eyes. "The Emperor's army has destroyed my village, tortured my people, and killed my family and many of my friends. If you are a fellow enemy of the Emperor, then you have my oath. *Ashbar.*"

Calreith and Rhoddan stared at each other for a while, recognizing mirrored suffering in each other. Then Calreith glanced over to two elves in his band, both carrying long bows like Shayth, and one of them nodded back. Seanchai realized he was holding his breath.

Then Calreith spoke. "You swore in the ancient elven language. This binds you forever. You and Shayth are welcome at our fire. Eat with us, sleep here tonight and then in the morning, we will see you through the mountain pass. The girl will stay over there," he nodded to an area by a large rock, "and the simpleton will bring her food. She will not come near any of my men, or they have my permission to strike her down. Am I clear?"

"So be it," said Rhoddan. "Thank you. One day I hope to repay the debt."

"If I have need," Calreith replied, "I'll make sure you do."

THIRTEEN

Seanchai played his part, walking with his head down and staying close to Ilana. Rhoddan, on the other hand, strutted around the camp and loudly gave orders to both of them. After a generous dinner, Calreith's men settled around the campfire and became more raucous as ale and mead flowed. Rhoddan was invited to join them, though he became increasingly intimidated as they drank.

Shayth stayed in the shadows, out of the way of Calreith and his men. He knew the band's leader was not alone in harboring a grudge against him. An anonymous blade in the dark could be blamed on any one of a number of men.

After several hours, when the men began to either fall asleep or give in to drunken stupors, Shayth pulled Rhoddan aside.

"Come, we should return to the others."

"Where are you going, elf?" someone shouted. "You walk far too straight. I think you haven't been keeping up with the ale. Can't elves take their drinks like men? Perhaps that is why your race is no longer strong."

There were cheers and laughter. Shayth felt his companion stiffen.

"Steady," he whispered.

Rhoddan turned slowly. By the time he was facing the fire, he had a placid smile on his face. "I need to check that the oaf has fed our horses with the oats and water that you gave us. I am worried that he confused it with beer and it'll be no fun in the morning riding a horse with a hangover."

The bandits laughed, allowing Rhoddan to turn and walk away.

"Very nice," said Shayth. "I think being arrogant suits you," and he patted him on the shoulder.

Despite the heavy drinking the night before, Calreith and two of his men were ready at first light. The steam that wafted from the cups they were holding was clear in the crisp morning air. They already had their horses saddled, along with a third for Shayth, and had packed some additional bundles of food. Calreith pointed at Seanchai.

"Elf. Take these supplies to your horses. Mind you tie them well." As Seanchai scurried to comply, Calreith turned to Rhoddan. "These men volunteered to escort you through the mountains. They are not under my command, so treat them well if you want their service. This is Mainch and Rovert."

Thank you," Rhoddan said, turning his horse around.

"And Shayth," Calreith pointed a long finger, "don't ever come back here again unless you plan to repay past debts."

"It was good seeing you too, big man, and thanks for the horse. Now I owe you two."

Thankfully, it was Calreith's deep belly laugh that escorted them away from the bandit camp.

Calreith's men guided them steadily along the path. They snickered at Seanchai's horsemanship, but otherwise kept to themselves. The path rose, as did huge, pale granite rocks on either side. Once through the pass, they began crossing a small plateau. Seanchai enjoyed the openness—the blue sky and the mountains behind them—but realized he was indeed a wood elf. He craved the smell of moss and the security of trees and daydreamed about the herbs that his mother had taught him, trying to recall their names and properties. It all seemed so long ago.

In the late afternoon, they reached a stream and let the horses drink. Mainch approached Rhoddan and pointed at the elf's horse. Riverwader was splashing through the current and whinnying.

"He's brave in battle and strong on the long road," Rhoddan muttered.

Mainch smirked. "We'll camp here tonight. The ground ahead is stony and the horses need to see where they are going. We will stay with you and guard for you, but we will leave in the morning. You need—"

He stopped as Ilana approached.

"Are you discussing directions?" she asked.

Mainch drew his sword and glared at her.

"Keep your distance, she-elf," he growled.

Ilana froze, and then, remembering she was supposed to be sick and infectious, retreated quickly to Seanchai. Mainch stared after them. "What if she infects the boy?"

"Then I'll kill him," Rhoddan answered without hesitation. "But meanwhile, he has his uses."

Shayth nodded approvingly at Rhoddan behind Mainch's back. He was enjoying Rhoddan's act. The elf had seemed so rigid and square up until now. This had been most revealing.

The next morning, as they watched Mainch and Rovert's disappearing forms, Seanchai turned to Rhoddan. "Impressive. When did you decide to take on the role?"

"Over breakfast, when Shayth had rejoined us," replied Rhoddan before blushing under their admiring gazes. "Actually ..." he hesitated, then continued. "I once saw a play in Castleton and always thought of becoming an actor."

"Well, I think you make a great actor," said Seanchai. "Am I right, Ilana?"

Ilana glared at them. "Sick! Infectious! You might be a good actor, but I'm not impressed with your casting ability."

They all laughed, except Rhoddan. "You know why I did that?" he protested.

"Yes," she replied and her tone was warm. "It was good thinking. I appreciate it."

They saddled their horses and began to follow the stream. Seanchai leveled his horse with Ilana's, bumping it in the process, much to both horses' apparent disgust. They neighed their objections and Ilana tried to hide her smile.

"How long are we going now?" he asked.

"Not far, I think. We follow this to the foothills of Cadhria. Then we climb into the mountains and follow the path to a hidden lake where we are to wait. If your teacher is around, he will find us when he comes to the lake."

Seanchai glanced across at her face. He enjoyed her cheekbones, her full lips and cute nose. But this time he felt something else. "You seem worried," he said.

"Those men were scared to bring us out of the mountains and in a hurry to leave us. I'm worried about what lies ahead. Remember, Seanchai: whatever else happens, you must go on and find the lake. Forget about Rhoddan, Shayth and myself. You must find your way to the lake."

"Lighten up," Seanchai replied. "It's a beautiful day. What can possibly happen?"

As if summoned by her cautionary words, an arrow whistled past them fired from behind and Mainch reappeared, galloping toward them at full speed and lying flat on his horse.

"Ride!" he yelled.

FOURTEEN

Seanchai's horse broke into a gallop almost without any prompt and the tranquility he had just been enjoying vanished in the dust the horses kicked up. Still uneasy riding, he had to focus desperately just to stay in the saddle.

They were chased over the plain. Mainch cut sharply across the stream and headed for the foothills of the Cadhria mountain range's tall, sharp peaks. The occasional arrow flew near, but it was clear their pursuers seemed content to just keep up for now.

The path steepened into a narrow gorge as rocks rose on either side. At a growth of flat rock ahead of them, Shayth leapt off his horse and onto the rocks, climbing higher as his balance allowed, to cut off the ambush.

"No," shouted Seanchai, but it was all he could do just to keep himself on Snowmane.

They rounded a corner and brought their horses to a stop. Rhoddan was immediately on his feet, long knife drawn. Ilana called to Seanchai to take the horses and lead them away from the fray. Snowmane had advanced twenty yards ahead of the others before he had managed to halt him and dismount.

Seanchai was angry at being given the task of tending the animals, but had no time to argue. Already he could hear cries behind him—ones he hoped were from soldiers falling to Shayth's deadly bow. Then the clash of metal and he knew that his friends had joined the fray. He hurriedly tied the horses to a bush, freeing him to battle with the others. He drew his knives.

Seanchai crept along the path, careful to keep against the rocks. He was very close now and could hear shouting and swords parrying just around the bend. He stopped as the sounds came closer and felt his chest contract. Fear rooted him to the ground.

Then as he rounded the bend, he saw Ilana backing up, frantically fending off a huge soldier's sword with her long knife. She retreated past Seanchai and then tripped on a rock, stumbling back. The soldier snarled and leapt forward, his sword raised above his head.

But the soldier's blade never made contact. Seanchai had learned well during his few days with Uncle, and Rhoddan had diligently made him practice when they stopped every night. Seanchai sprang at the soldier from behind and pulled up his helmet with one hand, slitting his throat with his short knife in the technique Uncle had taught him.

He stumbled back in horror as blood spurted from the man. Though he had killed the soldiers on the plain when he rescued Rhoddan, he had been frenzied and unaware of his actions. This time, he had planned his attack, felt the man physically in his hands. It was so much more real.

Ilana, back on her feet, jumped at him and yelled. Another soldier had crept up behind him and Ilana's long knife was just able to deflect it from cleaving Seanchai's head. She kicked the soldier in the groin, sending him off-balance, howling in pain. Then she leapt forward and pushed the man over the ridge.

"Get out of here!" Ilana yelled. "You're not ready!"

Seanchai stood frozen with fright, then began to back away as Ilana commanded. But if had listened to that command the last time, Rhoddan may not be alive, or maybe Ilana just now. He stopped, took a deep breath and, teeth clenched, stepped back into the fray.

Another soldier had Ilana pinned against the rock face, his sword locked between her knives, but he was far stronger and using his body weight to bring the blades closer to her face. Again, Seanchai grabbed the soldier's helmet, yanked his head back and slit his throat. Ilana screamed as the man's warm blood spurted onto her face.

Seanchai suddenly felt a wave of calm descend. The controlled detachment of his power took over as he watched Mainch desperately fend off two soldiers who were pushing the big man toward the ridge. He knew immediately that the distance was too great for him to reach Mainch in time to help.

Without thinking, Seanchai sheathed his knives and held out his palms. A strange, alien word left his mouth and both soldiers were picked up like feathers in the wind and sent sprawling. Mainch quickly dispensed with them, then turned and stared at Seanchai, stunned, before going to help Rhoddan.

With so much damage done already, the fight was over in a matter of minutes. Ilana shouted as one soldier mounted a horse and fled.

"Get him," Mainch yelled, presumably at Shayth, but the soldier escaped unhindered. "Why didn't you shoot him down, you idiot? He'll bring more soldiers from the patrols below."

"I have no more arrows," snapped Shayth. He began retrieving those protruding from a dozen soldiers.

Ilana was tying a tourniquet around a wound on Rhoddan's arm, ignoring his protests that it was just a scratch. Seanchai knelt to help retrieve Shayth's arrows so he could avoid dwelling on the fact that he had killed more men. He had heard their screams and felt their warm blood leave their bodies.

The young elf sighed and told himself that it had killed these soldiers to save his friends. They would be dead otherwise. As he struggled to pull out the arrow from a lifeless body, Mainch approached him. "You are the special one, aren't you?" he said.

Before Seanchai could react, a drawn arrow was inches from the man's face. "And the elf saved your life. You owe him a debt." Shayth's cold tone made Seanchai flinch. "Never reveal who he is or what he did, or I will find and finish you."

"He saved my life," Mainch repeated, his voice steady. "I understand."

"We should not let him go back," Shayth continued, his tone still icy, his bowstring taut.

"No," said Seanchai quietly but with authority. He slowly pushed Shayth's bow away from Mainch's face. "He risked his life for us, too, so we are also in his debt. That is enough."

The man nodded at Seanchai. "Your secret is safe with me. But I'll ride with you for a while if you'll let me."

"What for?" Shayth spat, still suspicious.

"Well, first, there's half a garrison of soldiers coming from the direction in which I would be headed." Mainch stopped for a moment to consider his words. Then he looked up at Shayth and nodded towards Seanchai. "But also, I don't know—I want to help him."

Shayth lowered his bow and nodded. "Yeah," he said, rolling his eyes. "He has that maddening effect on people."

The tension broke with their shared laughter.

"And the girl?" Mainch asked.

"She's not sick," Seanchai replied. "But you still might want to keep your distance. She can be, well, somewhat unpredictable."

Ilana coughed a warning, but when Seanchai met her eyes, they were soft. "You shouldn't have..." she began but Rhoddan interrupted.

"Come. We must make haste. You two can argue later."

They mounted their horses and began to move— Shayth took one of the soldier's horses and released the rest. Seanchai saw how stiffly Rhoddan sat in his saddle as they trotted alongside each other. "Are you okay?" he asked.

"Just stay on your horse," Rhoddan snapped and clicked his horse forward.

They rode alongside and then away from the ridge into the mountains, each listening keenly for pounding hooves behind them. Seanchai looked over the ridge to the trees and bushes far below escorting the stream as it grew into a river.

He sighed and tried to force himself not to think of his village and the forest that he had grown up in and felt certain he would never see again. It made him think of his parents and friends, and he realized he could never return to the life he once had. Four men lay dead from his hands today. He sighed again. No, things would never be the same.

FIFTEEN

With Mainch urging them on, they rode as fast as they could across the plateau they were crossing. The short rests they took were to keep the horses as fresh as possible. Their hurry was because the flat land revealed their position, even from a distance. On the second day after the battle, they saw signs of their pursuers and quickened their pace as the Cadhria Mountains rose on the horizon.

"Those are the mountains that you have heard mentioned in stories," Mainch said to Seanchai as they cantered side-by-side. "What we were in before are just the foothills. These mountains are dangerous, steep, angry and unpredictable. And haunted! When I was a kid, we were told tales of the angry spirits who live there. Not many men dare enter, and even fewer return."

Seanchai said nothing. Right now he was more fearful of his horse than ghosts. His body was numb from riding and he doubted he would ever again be able to straighten his legs or sit down with ease. He was feeling more in control of his horse but not comfortable. No, definitely not comfortable.

As the sun began to set, they came across a shallow stream. Ilana stopped and jumped down from her saddle to fill her water skin.

"We must keep moving," Shayth called and they all turned their heads toward the cloud of dust in the distance where the Emperor's army rode toward them. There was no doubt they were catching up.

"They ride hard," Mainch said. "I think they will ride through the night."

"Why?" asked Seanchai, who had also dismounted.

"The ground is smooth and poses no danger to the horses turning their hooves."

"But their horses need to rest if they are to catch us, and be able to return to where they have come from," Seanchai said.

The silence that met Seanchai's comment spoke louder than words. "Oh," he said as he filled his water skin. The soldiers cared only to find and capture him. If they had to walk all the way back to their fortress then that was what they would do. The fear in his voice was unmistakable. "Will we stop?"

"We must," said Rhoddan. "We need to find somewhere off the path."

It was already dusk when they entered a canyon between two mountains and found what they were searching for.

"Let's set up camp in there," said Rhoddan, pointing, and then turned his horse back to the main path to join Shayth.

"Where are you going?" Seanchai asked.

"Clean your tracks. Then we will lead them on some," Shayth replied, "and give them something to think about."

As Rhoddan and Shayth rode off, Seanchai turned to Ilana. "What are they up to?"

She smiled. "I think I know."

Seanchai, Ilana and Mainch unsaddled and rubbed down their horses. Their camp was only a short way from the main path, so there was no chance of a fire and they whispered, rather than spoke.

Though concealed from view, an alert tracker might still hear or smell something.

Ilana took the first watch that evening. Seanchai fell asleep quickly and felt he had passed half the night by the time she woke him.

She signaled for him to remain silent by putting a finger to her lips. Seanchai heard the sound of horses' hooves back on the path. He crept over to their own horses to help Mainch coax them to stay quiet. Ilana crouched at the entrance with her back against the rock face, her knives drawn.

They heard muttering about ghosts and evil spirits, quickly silenced by an authoritative voice. The troop slowly passed, and Seanchai returned to his bed. Mainch relieved Ilana from guard duty and she brought her bedroll over beside Seanchai and spread it out right next to him.

"It's going to get really cold later," she whispered. "Do you mind?"

Seanchai solemnly nodded his consent, secretly thrilled.

"Also," she continued, "if I'm right, we aren't through tonight and I don't want you getting scared and giving us away."

"Very funny," Seanchai said, but then saw that she was not joking.

His pride wounded, the young elf turned onto his side away from her. Then he felt her move closer.

"I'm sorry," she whispered in his ear. "We're in a dangerous place and I'm just trying to look out for you. I care for you."

Seanchai was confused. He was attracted to Ilana, though this was hardly the time to explore a relationship. Then there was what she just said—*I care for you*—and the fact that she was lying close to him. Did she share the feelings that he had for her—whatever those feelings were? He yawned and thought how complicated this was, then promptly fell into a deep sleep.

It felt as if he had been asleep again for only a few minutes when a harsh, piercing cry woke him. A vivid image of the demons that Mainch had mentioned filled his mind. Ilana felt his fear and clasped her hand over his mouth. Then she turned him onto his back so that she could whisper in his ear. "It's okay. Don't make a sound."

Another screeching cry carried on the breeze. Seanchai could make out human voices and clearly heard their fear. He tried to sit up, the panic welling up inside of him, but Ilana tightened her hold.

"It's *not* spirits or demons," she whispered, pulling Seanchai toward her to comfort him. "Rhoddan and Shayth are putting on a show and trying to chase the soldiers away from us."

He breathed a sigh of relief and quickly raised his head. "I guessed," he shrugged, though he was sure she could see the tips of his pointed ears reddening, even in the darkness.

She smiled at him and then leaned forward and kissed him on the lips. "I know you did," she said and, turning her back on him to sleep, she pulled him so that he cradled her in his arms.

Seanchai was stunned. His ears was burning now for sure, but not from embarrassment. He barely heard the next demon scream.

Near dawn, Seanchai woke to more cries, horses neighing, and what sounded like a rock fall. He jumped up and moved to the rock walls. Ilana, her knives drawn, was immediately by his side, and Mainch had gone to their horses.

No one wanted to return to sleep and silently, they tied their bundles to the horses and returned to the main path. Around a sharp bend, they came across what appeared to be a rockslide. Men and horses were trapped underneath—some still twitching and groaning. Seanchai watched as Mainch ended their misery. Blood dripped from his blade and his face was grim.

"Now we ride fast," the man said.

"Where are Shayth and Rhoddan?" Seanchai asked.

"Not here," Mainch growled. "At best, they are chasing down other soldiers, assuming they weren't caught in this."

SIXTEEN

Seanchai was anxious to put distance between them and the carnage. The horses couldn't gallop, as there were still stones scattered along the path, but the smell of dead bodies, horse and man, was enough to motivate them forward.

They rode through a gorge and steadily ascended into the mountains. Though he saw no one, Seanchai felt as though they were always being watched, always being followed. The feeling of high alert kept them silent until they stopped for lunch in a crevice off the path that hid them from sight.

Seanchai ate standing up, stretching his muscles. He ached everywhere.

Ilana and Mainch crouched by the horses, whispering together. Seanchai thought the discussion was about their route, but when he saw them both glance at him, he knew he was wrong. As he approached, they stopped talking.

"I'd like to be a part of the conversation," he said, trying to muster a tone of authority. "Our party is down to three. I think I need to know everything."

They glanced at each other and nodded. Then they looked up at him expectantly. He shuffled. "But I don't think I can crouch. My body is so stiff from riding. Can you please stand up?"

They laughed and rose. With a certain satisfaction, Seanchai noticed they were also stiff.

"You're right. You need to know the route at this point, in case..." Ilana hesitated but quickly recovered. "We'll be on this path for several more hours before we reach another stretch of flat, open terrain. Tomorrow, we'll come to a fork in the path where three trees stand in a place where hardly any trees have survived. We must take the right path, which leads to a lake. Then we wait," she sighed, "and hope that your teacher is there."

Ilana made Seanchai repeat the directions back to her until she was sure he had them memorized.

"Seanchai," said Mainch. "If any of the soldiers got past Shayth and Rhoddan's ambush—and I'm sure some did—they'll be waiting on the open ground to capture you. We're considering crossing it at night, but if neither of us make it through you need to be able to find the correct path on the other side."

"I will," said Seanchai with a new feeling of confidence. Then he put a hand on each of their shoulders. "But let's hope it doesn't come to that."

He smiled at them. They did not smile back.

As they stopped by a stream later that afternoon, Ilana again had Seanchai repeat the directions back to her. Then she took his hand in hers and looked at him with sad eyes.

"Promise me that you won't turn back to help us if we are attacked—that you won't try to be a hero. Finding your teacher is all that is important, and we are so close. So many people hope that you and your gift are the bringers of freedom and dignity. Promise me that you won't put our...our friendship first."

Seanchai sighed. "I can't promise that. I'm not sure how I'll react; I never am and I'm too exhausted to lie to you."

"You must get through."

"I don't want to lose you, or Rhoddan, if he is still alive. Even Shayth has grown on me, though he still scares me some."

She laughed, but quickly became serious again. "Promise me you'll try."

"I'll try," he said and they both knew he hadn't promised.

They left at dusk and entered the plains when it was dark. Mainch led the way, periodically adjusting their direction as he looked up at the stars. Ilana brought up the rear and was constantly looking behind her. Seanchai drew up his hood as though it would protect him.

The moon moved across the sky and there was quiet all around. But just as Seanchai allowed himself to relax a little, they heard sounds of combat to the right. Mainch veered off to the left without hesitation. There were cries of pain and surprise, a brief clash of steel, and then silence.

Flaming arrows arced in the sky, illuminating two figures riding hard toward them. Mainch had his massive broadsword drawn to confront the horsemen, but Rhoddan's welcomed voice reached them first. "What are you waiting for?" he yelled. "Ride, fools!"

"Rhoddan!" Seanchai called. "You're alive!"

"Not for long if we don't move!"

They surrounded Seanchai, Ilana left, Rhoddan right, Mainch in front and Shayth behind. The heavy rhythm of hooves close behind spurred them on. Despite the danger, Seanchai was happy they were together again.

More fire arrows flew overhead. Seanchai gasped as he realized they were now under attack on three sides. Another wave of arrows, these unlit, dove into the ground around them. Mainch veered to the right, trying to move out of range of the archers on his left as they were closest.

Two riders closed in on Rhoddan's side. Shayth brought one down with his bow and stabbed the second while the soldier's blade was locked with Rhoddan's.

Then Night, Ilana's horse, swerved toward Seanchai, baying loudly. Ilana tried to balance herself as riders bore down on her. Seanchai tried to turn his horse to help her, but Shayth yelled at him to keep going before going to her aid himself. Mainch swerved back to join them, too.

Whatever happened, Seanchai couldn't see, but in very little time, Mainch, Shayth and Ilana returned to their original formation. He was aware that there was still cavalry on either side of them. He wondered why they were not attacking and why the arrows had hit no one. Then it occurred to him.

He yelled at Mainch. "It's an ambush! They're herding us into a trap."

SEVENTEEN

Mainch stared up at the stars again to gain his bearings and determine which direction might avoid the trap. He raised his hand in the air to get their attention and swerved to the left.

Mainch had his sword out in front of him. Rhoddan and Ilana sped up to move alongside him. Shayth closed up next to Seanchai. Seanchai admired their fluency in an attempt to occupy his mind with anything but what lay before them.

Mainch, Rhoddan and Ilana charged into the infantry. The soldiers were crushed under the momentum of the powerful mountain horses as the group flew through them.

The horsemen to their left attacked, and this time Mainch, Rhoddan, and Shayth met them with swords and long knives. Seanchai kept riding, fighting internally between the panicked impulse to flee and the desire to face the enemy together with his friends. Ilana read his thoughts.

"Keep riding," she yelled and moved her horse to position herself between him and the fight.

It was over quickly and again they were five.

"We are cutting through them like hot knives throu–" Mainch's maniacal cry was cut short by an arrow that pierced his back and protruded through his chest.

Mainch roared with pain and blood poured out of him. He turned his horse to charge their pursuers. "Ride on," he yelled as he rode into the fray and another arrow took him down. Ilana and Rhoddan closed their horses alongside Seanchai's and rode into deeper blackness. They had made it to the other side of the valley.

The enemy was close behind, emboldened by killing Mainch. Both cavalry troops had joined together and, as the elves and Shayth reached the path into the mountains, a horn blew and the line of horsemen charged with one long, disciplined cavalry gallop.

The elves turned to watch in horror. Only Shayth didn't hesitate. His bow took down three soldiers with incredible accuracy and speed.

Seanchai raised his arms to draw his power and stop the charge. He took a deep breath and waited. Nothing. His fear froze him into silence.

"Into the canyon," Rhoddan yelled and signaled first at Seanchai and then Ilana. "We have a plan."

"What—" Seanchai started to ask, but Rhoddan slapped Snowmane's rump and the horse flew forward with Seanchai barely managing to stay on its back.

Ilana was close behind Seanchai and propelled him on. He looked back and watched Rhoddan and Shayth take up positions facing the cavalry, blocking the narrow entrance of the gorge.

"Go," urged Ilana grimly.

They let the horses gallop as fast as they dared in the near-darkness. The first light of dawn was crowning the top of towering rock face and Seanchai could now see the path before him.

As the sun rose in the sky, they began to feel their fatigue and looked for a concealed place to rest. It was another hour or so until Ilana found something to her satisfaction.

"I need to hide our tracks," she said and walked briskly back to the path.

Seanchai collapsed to the ground, and when Ilana returned she went straight to the horses. She unsaddled them, then rubbed them and massaged their legs, fretting. They were pushing the horses far beyond their limits. Reluctantly, she returned the saddles and strapped the horses so they were ready to move at any moment.

She threw some dried bread to Seanchai. "Drink, as well," she said. Then she took some more bread and fed it to the horses. Seanchai reached into his pack for his canteen and found an apple, already soft. He rose, body aching from riding, and moved gingerly to Snowmane, offering the horse the apple.

"Thank you, my friend," Seanchai murmured as he hugged his horse. Then, turning to Ilana, who was now sitting and drinking: "What *plan*?"

Ilana blinked, surprised at his abruptness. She took another drink and then gazed back at him. "You know already," she said. Her voice was calm, but her body language told him she was bracing for an argument. "Our purpose was to get you across the plain. Nothing else. Rhoddan and Shayth made a stand at the entrance because it was the best place to defend and slow the cavalry down."

"Why? Why was that the best you came up with?" He knew he was not being fair or rational, but the image of Mainch, two arrows protruding from his chest, was forever burned onto his mind, and didn't want to think of his friends meeting the same end—or worse. He could feel tears welling up in his eyes. "Why is it only you left?" he pushed, when she didn't answer.

Ilana let her hair loose and closed her eyes. "I think you know why I didn't stay to battle with them."

"Because you're my guide?" he oozed sarcasm.

"No."

"Then why?" he persisted.

"What do you want to hear, Seanchai?" she hissed and then took a deep breath. "Isn't it enough that three stayed behind? Are you sorry that I'm not dead like Rhoddan and Shayth may be?" Her eyes begged him to stop, but he just couldn't seem to back down.

"I need to know," he rasped. "How do people choose who lives and who dies?"

She stared at him, eyes blazing as she spit the words out. "Because there was more chance you would obey our plan if I stayed with you." Her anger vanished and tears welled in her eyes. "We didn't think you could bear to leave me behind."

Seanchai turned away from her. It had been cruel to make her say what he already knew. He shook his head, bewildered. Then he allowed himself to cry.

EIGHTEEN

"It makes no sense," Seanchai wailed as he collapsed against a rock, his head in his hands. "I'm no warrior. I was about to apprentice as a healer, and now I've been thrown into a world of such senseless violence."

"We can wait a few hours and rest," Ilana murmured. "Maybe they will join us if they are still..." She stopped and sat next to him opening her arms. She wasn't sure how he would receive the offer, but he leaned into her embrace without hesitation.

From inside her embrace, she heard a muffled whimper. "I just don't understand it."

"What?" she asked and tried to stifle a yawn.

"This way of living. How you all decide who stands and who runs. How you decide who shall live and who..."

His voice faded as he pulled away from her. He was too ashamed of his behavior to look her in the eye and instead lay on his back, staring at the sky, his hands behind his head. She laid her head on his stomach.

"It's what we have to do," she whispered. "It's the way we survive."

"It's cruel and unfair," Seanchai rasped.

"Yes it is," she replied. "It's sad for those who must die, but also hard on those who must live. Those who die fighting die with honor—with meaning. Those who live must forever try to prove themselves to those who are no more, because they were chosen. It's a heavy burden to bear, and you carry it for the rest of your life."

"It's barbaric. It's not…"

"Not the way of the elves? Not the code of life that we're taught by our elders? Our way is not relevant today in this violent world. It was meant for a better time. Maybe one day we will all live by the Elven Code again. Maybe your gift…" She stopped as she felt him bristle. "Maybe it will be like that again," she corrected weakly.

There was silence. When Seanchai spoke again, his voice was sleepy. "Tell me more about the Elven Code and how it once was."

"Not now. We must rest. Hopefully by tomorrow night you'll have a better teacher than me to explain things. Okay?"

His reply was a low snore and, despite all the pain from that day, Ilana couldn't help but smile to herself as she succumbed to exhaustion.

Ilana woke after only a few hours. The echoing clop of hooves had her wide-awake. She nudged Seanchai and shushed him before he spoke. Both were standing with knives drawn within seconds. Ilana signaled for Seanchai to stay with the horses and keep them quiet.

She crawled up onto a rock and watched twelve soldiers ride past. They rode slowly, clearly exhausted. Then she realized only eleven of them were soldiers. In the middle, tied across his horse, was Rhoddan. His body was limp and she could not see if he was even conscious. She wondered if he might continue being Seanchai again as he had with the bandits. If he did, she thought, it might be his final acting role.

There was no sign of Shayth and she tried to wipe the image of him lying dead from her mind. Then she quietly lowered herself back down. As she turned to face Seanchai, she knew another showdown was inevitable.

"You can't be serious!" Seanchai yelled moments later when Ilana described what she had seen. "He saved both of our lives. He's our friend. We must follow and try to rescue him."

"Keep your voice down," Ilana snapped. "There might be more soldiers. Do you have any doubt this is what Rhoddan would want? You *must* reach your teacher. You must learn to harness this power."

They continued arguing, and as he got angrier, Seanchai got louder. Ilana briefly contemplated slapping him—she knew this needed to stop immediately. The crunch of rocks behind them confirmed this.

They froze and turned slowly. Two soldiers stood before them, swords already drawn.

"Well, well, Hendrick, what do we have here?" one sneered. "Two babes out camping? Lovers squabbling?"

Hendrick laughed, revealing yellow teeth. As his body shook, he winced and clutched a bloodstained sleeve.

"And they're elves, too," the first man continued. "I hear their blood is green, Hendrick. Shall we find out?"

"Cut the boy, but don't kill him. He might be the one with the reward on his head," Hendrick suggested. "And the girl looks quite pretty."

"What! She's an elf," his friend said. "That's disgusting; they have all kinds of diseases."

"Yes, but a pretty face—even a pretty elf face—can collect a higher price in the slave market."

"Good point, my friend. You're truly a businessman."

He limped toward them, revealing that his left thigh had been cut. The newly congealed blood was barely staunched by a clumsily tied tourniquet. Still, he whirled his sword as he approached.

Ilana took a step in front of Seanchai. "This pretty face can fight," she snarled.

The men laughed, which gave Seanchai the chance to move and face Hendrick. The first, mid-chuckle, suddenly kicked dust and pebbles into Ilana's face. He drew his sword on the choking and temporarily blinded elfe. But the blow he intended never landed. Seanchai leapt forward and kicked the man's wounded thigh, sending him down, screaming from pain.

Seanchai whirled on Hendrick. His long knife was blocked by Hendrick's sword, but his short knife made contact with Hendrick's wounded arm and he staggered back, swearing.

Ilana had recovered by this time and was in no mood to be gentle. Her target was slow and tired. He went down, blood gushing from his throat. Seanchai gasped, both at her speed and ruthlessness.

Hendrick lunged, roaring, for Seanchai. Seanchai's eyes glazed and he crouched under the soldier's onrushing body, clashing with his upper legs. He rose and sent Hendrick flying into the rocks. Propelled by his own momentum, he smashed into the black slate. A black-feathered arrow from behind them finished the job.

They turned and saw Shayth, bow in hand.

"Nice move, Seanchai," he said, his voice hoarse. "Let me guess: you have no idea how you did that?"

Seanchai shook his head in shock, then said, "Glad you're a—"

Shayth finished the sentence. "Alive? Yes, I can be quite resilient. Nice move making so much noise, too. Not only would these oafs have missed you, but so would I. The company moved on ahead. They left these behind, as they're wounded."

"They have Rhoddan," said Ilana.

"He's alive?" Shayth's face lit up.

"I don't know. He was strapped over a horse, but I couldn't see if he was even conscious. Still, wouldn't they have left him if he was dead?"

"Possibly not," Shayth replied. "They may need to prove they killed him." He turned away, scratching his chin and thinking, and then spun back around. "Is that what you were arguing about? Going after Rhoddan?"

Seanchai and Ilana looked at each other, now embarrassed.

"Seanchai," Shayth continued. "I know you want to go after him. He's your friend and, believe me, I have noticed how highly you hold friendship and loyalty."

"We can't leave him in their hands," Seanchai protested.

"We won't. Listen to me, please. There are at least thirty soldiers still searching these mountains. We need to get you to the lake.

"Once you're safely there, I'll leave you and go after Rhoddan. It won't be hard to track them, and Ilana can come with me if she wants. We'll return to the lake after we free him." The young human put his hand on Seanchai's shoulder. "You have my word that I'll do everything I can. I swear. But first, we must get you to the lake."

Seanchai looked at him. "Why are you doing this?" his voice was cracking.

Shayth ruffled his hair. "I don't know. I think it's this friendship thing of yours again. It's frigging annoying."

NINETEEN

There was no sophisticated plan, no riding formation. They rode in an exhausted daze, tense and silent. Ilana had drilled Seanchai with final instructions for this part of the journey and he found himself recognizing landmarks that she had mentioned.

The mountain path continued to ascend toward a deep blue sky without a cloud to be seen. It was beautiful, but Seanchai was fed up with rocks, even these smooth beige ones. He missed the forest, the trees, and the smell of mulch and moss—everything he had taken for granted growing up.

He was also painfully aware of the danger they were in and kept thinking of Rhoddan incarcerated. Seanchai had no doubt that elves were treated far worse than men were by the human guards, and probably even more so by pictorians. He was also worried that Rhoddan might impersonate him and therefore suffer all the more once they broke him.

"Get ready," Shayth hissed. Suddenly an arrow whizzed past. Shayth swore behind him and Ilana leaned down close to her horse's neck. Seanchai copied her.

"Go Night, go," she yelled and her horse instantly sprung forward.

Snowmane took off after them, jerking Seanchai backwards with the sudden acceleration. The trail curved around a bend where two riders waited for them, blocking the path. Night whinnied, lowered her head and charged between them, opening the way for Snowmane to follow.

The thunder of the warhorses' hooves behind them echoed off the rocks, and the winding trail narrowed, sheer, smooth rock formations rising on either side. The ground was littered with small rocks, preventing a full gallop from the horses, though the experienced cavalry was slowly closing the distance between them.

They came to the fork in the trail by the three trees, and Ilana dove to the right. Seanchai followed her, but Shayth continuing straight to force the soldiers to split up or hesitate while they decided which of them to follow.

Ilana and Seanchai rounded another bend, and the path rose. They crested the hill and looked down onto the lake. It was sparkling and beautiful, but now would have to serve as a battleground.

They reached the water's edge with the soldiers close behind and Ilana frantic. "I never planned we would arrive being chased. I don't know where to go and with the ground leveling out, the cavalry horses will be faster than ours."

She looked around and pointed. She led Seanchai toward a narrow trail leading away from the lake. They snaked along the tight path for a minute before coming to a halt at an eighty-foot tall rock wall. They had ridden into a dead end.

"Seanchai," Ilana's voice shook. "Start climbing. I'll hold them off as long as I can."

"Don't bother," he said as he drew his knives. For once she didn't try to argue. Seanchai felt the intensity in his own expression and a surge of confidence and energy welled up inside him. Then he turned and saw a tear rolling down Ilana's face.

"What is it?" he asked.

"Seanchai," she whispered, "I don't want you to escape and leave me. No matter how important this mission, I don't want us to..." She gulped. "I have failed–failed our people, failed the land of Odessiya, and I have failed as your guide."

She took a deep breath, turned toward the path, and drew her knives. "Seanchai?"

"Yes?"

"You afraid?"

"Yes, but less than I expected." He was actually surprised at how calm he felt.

"Seanchai?"

"Yes?"

She couldn't get out the words she wanted to say.

"I know," he said. "Me, too. I've felt it for while now. And never think you failed me. No one else, not even Rhoddan, has given me what you have."

She looked over at him and arched an eyebrow. His gaze, however, was firm and looking ahead to where the soldiers would momentarily come into view.

"Your faith and belief in me has made me believe, too," he continued. "Even if this is the end, I will die believing in my own self-worth. And we will go down together. That also helps."

Into the canyon rode eight armor-clad soldiers on massive horses. The steeds also wore armor and panted clouds of steam. The soldiers assembled in line blocking the trail opening where Seanchai and Ilana would need to exit.

One soldier edged his horse forward. "I think we can agree that we have you trapped," he called to them. "Come peacefully and I guarantee you'll be treated well until we reach the garrison."

"And then what happens?" Ilana edged Night slightly forward.

"And then I hand you over to my superiors. I can't vouch for what they'll do to you."

"That's very honest of you," said Seanchai pleasantly, trotting forward next to Ilana.

The soldier eyed him, his face muscles tense. "We just want to avoid any trouble."

"Well, we don't want any trouble, either," replied Seanchai smiling as though they were discussing the weather or crop rotation. "So how about we allow you to turn around and trot along back to your garrison."

"There are eight of us, elf, in case you haven't noticed. Eight experienced warriors. And you are only two elves—young ones, at that."

Seanchai didn't flinch. "I *had* noticed. I have also noticed that there were considerably more of you before you began this mission. And I doubt you can work for a tyrant and call yourselves warriors. Soldiers, maybe. Mercenaries and conscripts, most likely. But please, not warriors. A warrior serves a noble cause, not a despotic ruler."

Seanchai's confident detachment obviously unsettled the officer. But he checked himself and decided that he still just saw two young elves against his trained cavalry line.

He lifted his sword and waited, challenging Seanchai. The elf, however, sheathed his knife and faced his palms out, summoning his power with words he didn't even know he was speaking. The officer's sword began its downward stroke and froze midway. His eyes bulged and he gasped for breath, his sword clattering to the ground with him. At the same time, two of his men jerked forward and fell, white-feathered arrows protruding from their backs.

A figure stood behind them, crouched, ready to spring. He wore a sandy cloak with a hood that covered his face. His long staff struck quickly at two soldiers who charged, sending them tumbling from their horses and the horses galloping out of the canyon.

Ilana and Seanchai charged forward while the troops were distracted, stabbing at the soldiers' chain mail, looking for a place to pierce.

Meanwhile, the hooded figure sent two more soldiers flying from their horses, crumpled all four dismounted men with his staff. Seanchai thought he glimpsed steel being thrown as another soldier crumpled from his horse. Their rescuer then turned on and dispatched the soldiers fighting Seanchai and Ilana. He showed no mercy, and those who fell lay still.

Ilana dismounted from her horse, gasping with pain. She crouched on one knee and held her arm; a slash in her sleeve was beginning to redden.

"Show me." He tore a strip of cloth to tie off the wound.

A scrape behind them revealed a soldier who had survived and crawled onto a horse.

"He's getting away!" cried Seanchai.

Their new battle companion spun round and extended his palm in a way Seanchai now recognized. The soldier and his horse smashed into the rock wall with a sickening crunch. When they hit the ground, the soldier was still but the horse kicked in pain. Approaching the stallion with caution, the man tried to touch it, but the horse was hysterical from pain. The figure again offered his palm and the horse stilled.

"We must leave. Can you walk, elfling?"

Ilana nodded and the warrior turned to Seanchai.

"Check that they all stay dead this time. Then collect my bow and arrows from that rock. After that, please bring both your horses and follow me. I will help your friend. We shouldn't tarry. We've had enough exercise for today."

TWENTY

The hooded stranger erased the tracks behind them once they had returned to the main path. A thin palm protruded from the cloak and a swift wrist movement moved sand and gravel over their footprints. This was repeated this every fifty yards or so.

"I value my privacy," he declared.

"Why did you come to help us?" Seanchai asked.

"I know who you are."

"Are you my teacher?"

"Maybe. In nobler times the student petitioned to study with the teacher, not demanded it."

Seanchai lowered his head. "How should I address you?"

"My name is Mhari. But introductions can wait. Let's get out of here."

Seanchai wished he could see Mhari's face, that he would pull back his sandy cowl and reveal himself, but he didn't. They walked for a while in silence, leading the horses. When Ilana began to feel weak, she mounted Night and held on doggedly to the reins.

Suddenly, Mhari stopped and looked slowly around.

"I suggest you come out. If I must come after you, you will die. I have killed enough for one day. And please, loosen your bowstring. I assure you, I am quicker than your arrow."

A shadow rose on the rock face to their left.

"Is he with you?" Mhari asked, looking at Shayth.

"Yes!" replied Seanchai, thrilled to see his friend. "I can vouch for him."

"Vouch for him!" A sharp bark of laughter came from the hood. "Can you even vouch for yourself?" The figure turned back to Shayth. "Come down here."

Shayth hopped down from the rocks, scowling no doubt because he had been discovered despite his skill at stealth. But when he saw Ilana on her horse, he forgot his pride and immediately went to her. "Are you okay?"

Ilana nodded but didn't speak.

"She looks pale," Shayth said to Mhari.

"She's an elf. They're generally pale. But she's lost blood and needs rest. Bring up the rear, please. Mask our way if you know how."

They're all pale? Seanchai always assumed that his teacher would be an elf, not a human.

"Rest here and keep an eye on the elfe," Mhari said a bit later. "I want to check we aren't being shadowed."

Seanchai went to Ilana and leaned against her leg. He could feel the heavy breathing of her horse. "I'm sorry about shouting at you before. I was just upset about Rhoddan being caught."

Ilana's only response was a slight nod. She rested her head on Night's mane and closed her eyes.

"We're alone, as far as I can see," Mhari said when he returned. "Come, we're close to my castle." A laugh came from the cowl, but cut off when Ilana began to fall from her saddle. Mhari moved with lightning speed to catch her, causing the hood to fall and reveal an old woman's face.

So. Not only was Mhari human, but also a female. Yet she looked like no human Seanchai had ever seen. Her shiny, straight white hair was tightly tied behind and this accentuated her slanted eyes; high cheekbones; and a tanned, leathery face. Seanchai was so absorbed in his teacher's appearance that he failed to notice she was now looking at him.

"When you've finished gaping, could you please help me with your friend?"

Seanchai shot forward and together they disentangled Ilana from her saddle. Night whinnied. The woman took Ilana in her arms and spoke to the mare. "She'll be fine, my friend. Don't worry."

Shayth offered to carry Ilana, but Mhari shook her head. "The horse knows you. Better you lead it. We are here."

They moved through a tight gap between tall rocks that would be easy to miss. The horses were not too enthused with being herded down the narrow path. Shayth told Seanchai that mountain elf horses were very brave and Seanchai got the distinct feeling that Shayth was really speaking for the benefit of the horses.

The path opened into a circle surrounded by sheer cliffs with caverns interspersed. Large rocks jutted out of the sandy floor. Mhari lay Ilana down on a large bed of straw near a cavern. Ilana grimaced as Mhari washed and dressed her wound.

"You are a tough one," Mhari smiled at her before addressing Shayth. "Lead the horses over there to graze on the reeds after you unsaddle and groom them."

Shayth left to complete his task while Mhari lit a fire under a rock.

"Won't the smoke reveal our camp?" Seanchai asked. He had learned well from their long journey.

"There is a natural chimney that threads through the rock," she replied without looking up. "The smoke will be released above the rock faces, not anywhere near here. Now, please go help your friend with the horses. He is also tired."

Seanchai tended to Snowmane, taking note of a trickling

waterfall nearby. A water-carved channel guided the water toward where the horses stood.

At length, Mhari called them over to eat around the fire. She ladled a thick soup into bowls that Seanchai had retrieved from their packs.

"You will have to excuse me for not having any utensils save for my own; I so rarely entertain." She cackled at her own joke.

Mhari took a third bowl over to Ilana, tenderly waking her and encouraging her to sit up and drink the soup. Seanchai noted the woman's tenderness, as Ilana both laughed and winced.

When she returned, Mhari busied herself gathering ingredients for and making an herbal tea. She kept going into the cave next to the cooking area, bringing out herbs, roots. or a sliver of bark. She constantly fussed over the pot and Seanchai realized that she had not eaten. Seanchai ladled out a bowl of soup and offered it to his teacher.

"Thank you, but I'll eat after this is ready. It mustn't boil, and it takes time to brew when there is bark and roots."

"I can do that," Seanchai persisted.

"Do you understand herbs?"

"A bit. Actually, I started to apprentice in my village. Let me stir it. You can watch while you eat."

Mhari passed the spoon and smiled. "I am hungry. Thank you."

Seanchai tended to the tea while Mhari sat close by, sipping her soup and observing him.

"Are we going to talk?" Seanchai asked.

"No, not tonight. We're both very tired. Take it off the fire and bring some tea to Ilana."

Ilana had fallen asleep again. She smiled as he woke her and helped her sit up.

"My special recipe," he quipped when she grimaced at the taste.

"I got you here," she boasted between sips. "I got you to your teacher."

"You did. Thank you." They gazed at each other and Seanchai smudged away the single tear trailing down her cheek. She took his hand and held it to her chest, wordlessly conveying her love and gratitude in a universal gesture he understood at once. Seanchai enjoying the feeling of her heart beating and the flood of his own emotions.

"Your teacher is a woman," Ilana said. "Surprised?"

"At first," Seanchai admitted, "but so is my guide and she has proven to be both brave and... competent."

Ilana laughed and winced simultaneously. She drank half of her herbal tea and then lay down again, still clutching Seanchai's hand. He waited until her breathing told him that she was asleep before he withdrew it and went to talk to Mhari.

But the old woman had no desire to talk, content instead to puff languidly on the pipe she had lit. The pipe's stem was long and bent, with carvings around the bowl. It was a dwarf's pipe, Seanchai thought.

Shayth sat next to her, struggling in vain to stay awake. She signaled to Seanchai with her head.

"Go to sleep, Shayth," Seanchai said. "You've had a long day."

"You should both sleep near the elfe in case she needs help," Mhari said. "I sleep in there, but wake me if she needs anything."

Shayth nodded and rose, his muscles stiff. He checked on the horses before taking his pack and spreading it near to Ilana. Mhari's eyes followed him and when she spoke to Seanchai, she kept her voice very low.

"How well do you know this boy, Shayth?"

Seanchai shook his head and recounted what little he had gleaned. His teacher listened carefully and nodded. "He carries a heavy load, too great a weight for such a young man."

TWENTY-ONE

When Seanchai woke the next morning, cold and cramped, he was surprised to find Ilana out of her bedding. He sat up, yawned, and found her crouched near the fire, hugging a steaming cup of tea and in deep discussion with Mhari. Shayth was still asleep, so Seanchai lay back down, content to doze.

It took the smell of food frying to get him up. He went to the waterfall and stuck his head under the spray. It was freezing and he let out a startled cry. The others laughed.

"Lesson number one, my student," Mhari called out. "Know what you're sticking your head into before you commit."

"Oh, I'm learning that one," Seanchai retorted.

Ilana handed Seanchai a bowl of hot, sweet broth when he joined them by the fire pit. He cupped his hands around the bowl and listened to Ilana explain developments in the wider world information that Uncle might have wanted passed on, he thought.

Seanchai took the opportunity to observe his teacher and her uncommon appearance. The woman's long, straight, white-gray hair now hung freely down around her shoulders. Mhari's skin was tanned and crinkled; the sun had not been kind. But it was her slanted eyes that had surprised Seanchai when he had first seen the woman's face. He could still see the woman's pupils and whites, but her eye structure was narrower than any human or elf that Seanchai had ever met.

He surmised that Mhari must have been born in a land far away and wondered how old she was. She caught him staring.

"I know you're the one who has come to learn," she said. "I saw what you did to the officer yesterday, and I can sense your power. But I do not know your name."

"Seanchai."

Mhari nodded. "Really? That is an apt name. It means 'storyteller' in the elf language and is an ancient name. Storytellers were important members of their villages, held in high esteem."

"You speak our ancient language?" Seanchai was surprised. Most elves today had not learned the language—certainly no humans. In his experience, it was considered an unkind reminder of a noble past and those who tried to revive it were often frowned upon. His own mother had learned the language when she had studied to become a healer and had taught him many words.

"Here and there," Mhari replied. "I am privileged to have studied with the Markwin."

"The Elves of the West!" Ilana exclaimed. "They exist?"

"I thought they were just a myth," Seanchai added.

Mhari nodded. "All things as they are, it is probably better that way. But no, they exist outside of Odessiya, far away from all this."

"Then why don't they come to our aid?" Ilana snapped. The edge in her voice reminded Seanchai of how tough life must had been in Uncle's band.

"They live a very different life than you; a very different existence. It's best you focus on your own reality for now."

Ilana furrowed her brow and rose to talk with Shayth, who lay on his bedding, staring up at the sky, with his hands behind his head. Seanchai noticed that she walked rather gingerly.

"Don't worry," Mhari said. "I can see there's much between you. Her wound is not as deep as I first thought. Her exhaustion just amplified the effects. She'll be fit to leave the morning after tomorrow."

"Leave?"

"Yes, they both will—to rescue your other friend and then return here if they're successful."

"I should go with them," Seanchai grumbled. "I need to help them."

Mhari laughed. "That's admirable, but rather short-sighted, given that all their efforts so far have been to bring you here. It's good that they leave. You will better focus on your lessons."

Tense silence followed as Seanchai scuffed the dust with his feet. The old woman leaned forward and spoke sincerely.

"Work hard with me, Seanchai, and I will not keep you here long. It seems that we do not possess the luxury of time."

Seanchai nodded and then looked up. "Let's begin."

Mhari smiled. "We will begin when they leave. For now, you can wash the dishes. Then, over the next two days, we'll collect food and wood so that we don't need to break for such tasks when we are alone."

Seanchai cocked his head, sensing she was leaving something out.

"The soldiers are not that smart, but their officers are." Mhari relented. "They'll be back, and we may find it difficult to wander around at times. We may even have to move on. This has begun to feel like a home for me—always a mistake for our kind."

"Our kind?"

Mhari sighed. "Please, Seanchai, take a bowl of oats to the young man, and then clear up breakfast."

Seanchai picked up a bowl and spoon. Then he looked across at the old woman.

"What does your name mean?"

"Your people gave me my name. In the elf tongue, Mhari means *one who must sacrifice.*"

Though they hadn't truly started lessons yet, Seanchai was already learning. Mhari taught him the different herbs they found, to read tracks, and to move quietly in the rocky terrain. They foraged for mushrooms, roots, nuts and fruit, and collected more wood.

Shayth and Ilana spent most of the next two days resting and planning their route. Mhari drew a map in the sand, explaining different routes the soldiers might have taken. She also had a constant brew of the herbal drink on hand for Ilana.

"You must do everything you can to catch up and rescue him before they reach the garrison at Galbrieth," Mhari said over supper the following night. "You've lost some time by recovering here, but you could make up the distance."

"Why?" Seanchai's voice became tense whenever they discussed Ilana and Shayth going to rescue Rhoddan. "What makes you think they can catch up?"

"Life in the garrison is very structured and rigid. Once they reach the valley, here," she pointed to her map with a stick, "they'll encounter inns, ale, and women. They're confident that they aren't being followed, so why rush? Also, their horses are tired. It'll be an excuse to let them rest and recover.

"However, once they reach Galbrieth, I'm not sure what they'll do with your friend. After they have extracted all the information they can from him, they could him enslave or execute him."

"There is something else to consider," Shayth spoke, though his mouth was full and they had to wait until he swallowed his food before he continued. "Rhoddan might let them think that he's Seanchai—he's done it before. It would draw their attention away from Seanchai and might keep Rhoddan alive longer."

"That would be admirable and brave," Mhari replied, "but it won't buy him too much time and they'll make him suffer for his deceit if they find out he's not who he says. On the other hand, there's a good chance they won't execute him if he can be used to lure Seanchai to Galbrieth."

They absorbed this in silence, each focusing on his or her own plate. Then when she had finished her food, Ilana looked at Shayth.

"Are you packed?"

"Yes. Have you decided on the route?"

Ilana pointed to the straightest line on the ground map. "The fastest. We can double back if need be. I don't fancy our chances once they have Rhoddan inside the garrison."

Shayth nodded.

"I should come with you," Seanchai pleaded.

"I'm turning in," Ilana said, straining to get up. "We leave at first light."

Seanchai's voice broke as he said her name.

Ilana turned to him with steely determination. "Study hard and don't argue. Be ready when the three of us return. That is when it will really begin."

Seanchai blinked. He couldn't think that far ahead—couldn't imagine being here without his friends. But more than that, he feared for Ilana, knowing that she was leaving him and heading into great danger and he could never see her again or know how they were faring. He stared intensely into the fire. He would not say or do anything stupid.

TWENTY-TWO

When Seanchai woke the following morning, Shayth and Ilana were already checking their horses' bridles. Seanchai shook himself alert and quickly dressed.

He walked over to Shayth. "I appreciate you doing this," he said, and then felt foolish. He opened his mouth to continue but nothing came out until he glanced at Ilana talking with Mhari by the maps.

"Um," Seanchai cleared his throat. "Look after her." He ducked his head.

Shayth grinned broadly and put his hand on Seanchai's forearm. "Try not to think of her, or Rhoddan. The best way to help will be for you to be ready when we return, and to be the best you can."

Seanchai waited for Ilana next to Night, stroking her mane absentmindedly. Ilana finished her conversation with Mhari and put a scroll into a pocket of her saddle. Then she moved closer to Seanchai.

"Don't look so worried," she said. "We'll find Rhoddan, I promise."

"It's—"

"I know what he means to you. We won't rest until we free him."

Seanchai swallowed hard and nodded. "Yes," he said looking at his feet. "And you...you be careful too. You..."

Ilana raised an eyebrow, waiting for him to continue.

"You know," he said, shuffling the dust beneath his feet.

"Know what?" she arched the other eyebrow.

"Well, you won't be able to rescue him if you get caught or hurt."

"Right."

"And..."

"And?" Ilana had put her hands on her hips, a bad sign, Seanchai knew.

"And I've kind of grown fond of...of Shayth."

"Right, Shayth." She moved closer to him and softly touched his cheek. "Anything else?"

He looked into her eyes. "You know," he could feel the tips of his pointed ears burning.

"Yes, I do." And suddenly she pulled him tight to her. "You know, too, right?" she whispered in his ear.

"Yes, I do," he replied and they hugged each other until Mhari loudly cleared her throat and reluctantly they parted.

After Shayth and Ilana had left, Mhari put a hand on Seanchai's shoulder and said, "Come, we have a lot to cover. It's best that we plunge straight in. I don't expect you to forget them. That would be disingenuous. But you will need to focus entirely on what I'm going to teach you."

They filled water canteens, gathered their weapons and set out on foot up a steep, narrow path. When they reached the peak, Seanchai slumped heavily on the ground next to his teacher, panting. Mhari sat waiting on a smooth rock, one leg held close to her chest. Her white, shiny hair was tied back, but a few strands had come loose and danced in the wind.

When he had his breath under control, Seanchai pulled out his water skin and drank enthusiastically. Apparently, in the silence that surrounded them, his gulps were noisy and he realized that Mhari was glaring at him.

"Sorry," Seanchai said, feeling even more miserable.

"Look around you. You can see for many miles. Perhaps more lands than you will ever visit, if you are lucky."

"Lucky?"

"Yes. Your talents will be in great demand. You will be called to visit many lands."

"What am I, Mhari?"

"You are an elf, my student. Don't forget that. Whatever else you may be, whatever else you may become, you are first and foremost an elf. Now, tell me what you have done; how your uniqueness has expressed itself."

Seanchai told her about scrying for patrols with Rhoddan, about rescuing Rhoddan when they were ambushed on the plains, and about the fight on the cliff. He recounted how he had used energy to push the men who were attacking Mainch over the edge, and also the time that he tried to wield the power and nothing happened. He was going to continue, but stopped himself.

"What is it?" the old woman asked.

"It's nothing, kind of silly."

Mhari looked him in the eye. "I have trained others before you. They went through long apprenticeships, questions and answers, tests and quests. I prided myself on prodding them to find answers from within or through the learning experience.

"But you and I don't have time for that now. I'll teach you all I can as quickly as I can. I'll give you exercises and you will discover your own results through your daily practice long after we have gone our separate ways.

"You have no time to hold things back from me, Seanchai. Now tell me what is on your mind."

Seanchai stared out over the land, absorbing the view. "I'm changing, Mhari. I'm not the elf I was when I fled my village. I feel something happening inside. One minute I can speak with authority and clarity, and the next I'm back to being the self-conscious calhei, in way over his head—the teenager that I really am. And it makes me feel alone and adrift."

Mhari nodded and tapped her forehead. "What do you feel up here on the mountaintop? Close your eyes and tell me whatever comes into your head. Don't stop to analyze it."

Seanchai breathed deeply to focus. "The wind. I feel the wind and the air. It's very quiet up here and yet very…powerful. Being so high up gives perspective, but also shows how small we really are. And yet, everything fits. Does that make any sense?"

"Yes," his master replied. "It makes sense because it's what you feel. There's no right or wrong answer. But let me ask one thing: Do you feel the silence?" When Seanchai nodded, she continued. "Seek out the silence, even in the darkest times. There is strength in it and it will nurture you.

"Now, listen carefully, for on this everything I teach you will be based. The world is made up of five sources of energy, of power: air, water, earth, fire, and wood. You will learn each of them individually, but what binds them is a universal energy. It flows through the world, its elements, and through us. Does this make any sense?"

Seanchai nodded. "Ilana taught me ryku."

Mhari was pleased. "And did you feel healing energy coming from your hands?"

"Yes I did."

"That's what I'm talking about. You must learn to harness this energy—to store it inside your body—and wield it for healing or violence."

"When you smashed the soldier and horse into the rock,"

Seanchai asked, "were you using this energy then?"

"Yes, I was."

Mhari watched her new apprentice digest what she was telling him. When he didn't speak, she quizzed him.

"You are shaking your head as you think. I find that interesting. Tell me what's bouncing around in there?"

"I can't get used to the killing," Seanchai said at last. "I hate taking someone's life. It feels so…" he struggled to find the right words, "so wrong."

"That's good," Mhari replied. "You should never be comfortable with violence. It is a last resort, for times when good can be served in no other way. It's also often a failing of sorts. The art is to change someone's harmful actions without harming them, or even better, to help them make that change themselves."

"But I will have to kill again won't I?"

"Yes, Seanchai. I believe you will, and many times, I'm afraid."

Seanchai stood up and stretched. "You said there were five elements?"

"Yes."

"I think you're wrong. I think there are six."

"What is the sixth?" Mhari asked.

"Love. Love for your friends, love for the land, and love for one special person."

Seanchai was aware that Mhari was watching him, but he let the tears flow anyway.

TWENTY-THREE

A shimmering haze of cool mist hovered over the water as Mhari and Seanchai walked to the lake. An early morning breeze whipped through their clothes and Seanchai pulled his cloak tighter around him. Despite the cold, he enjoyed the view.

Seanchai carried a small pack that held what he hoped were the necessary items to brew some hot tea. As they continued along the water's edge, Mhari pointed out tracks of different animals and explained how to discern how long ago they had been made.

Abruptly, she rapped Seanchai sharply on the back of the head.

"Ouch! What was that for?" the young elf said, rubbing his head.

"We aren't out on a stroll. Everything we do is a lesson. You just passed the tracks of two horses and didn't even stop to check them."

They walked back until Seanchai found the tracks, which he couldn't deny were very clear.

"Are they your friend's mountain horses?"

"No," said Seanchai, bending down. "The horses who left these are bigger and heavier. These are cavalry horses, but the tracks are old. There are layers of dust and sand covering them."

"Good," his master said. "But if there was a sentry checkpoint twenty paces ahead of you, you might have walked straight into them. You must put your friends out of your mind and focus on being in the present. There's no time to dwell on that which you cannot influence."

They passed by an old tree, about fifty feet high, but almost entirely bare of leaves and covered in peeling bark.

"It's dying," Seanchai said sadly.

"No," Mhari replied. "Do not assume too much just from appearance. The tree struggles to survive out here. This is not the lush forest you grew up in. We're still a few months from the rainy season. The tree is almost sleeping, living off water tapped from deep below. It's in hibernation with the great mountain bears. In the spring when the rain comes and the river swells, the tree will show off its leaves and berries."

"Impressive."

"And you can learn from it. The tree focuses on its survival. It stores resources, conserves energy. Come stand by the tree. I want to teach you the fundamental exercises that you will need to master. They are very simple and yet very complex. Try and do exactly as I do."

The old woman stood in the shade of the tree, her legs shoulder-width apart and her hands at her sides. Her breathing was deep and slow and her eyes were closed. Seanchai copied her, though he kept adjusting his stance to find comfort. Every few moments he opened one eye to peek and see if his teacher was doing anything different. She wasn't. The human was as still as the tree. After a while Seanchai got frustrated. He cleared his throat, prompting Mhari to open her eyes.

"Yes?"

"What are we doing?"

"Standing."

"Standing?"

"Standing," she replied, "like the tree."

"Okay," said Seanchai, determined not to let the old woman get under his skin. "Let's stand still."

"Stand still, and achieve everything."

"What? What are we achieving?"

"What is the tree achieving?"

"Survival? Existence?"

"Yes, and that is no easy feat out here. It is gathering and storing energy. You must do the same."

"By just standing."

"No! Not by *just* standing. By standing in a way that opens up your energy channels. *Just standing!* Why must my final student have to be *just* you?"

Seanchai wasn't sure Mhari was joking so he appreciated having his eyes shut.

The old woman walked over to him. "Come, plant your legs shoulder width apart. Good. Balance your weight on the soles of both feet, and keep them flat on the ground. Rock backward and forward a bit. Good. Now, bend your knees, but do not focus on the knees. Focus on sinking into the ground. Let your roots dig down, like the tree. Very good.

"Now, straighten the bottom of your spine. Curl your tailbone in like this." She put one hand at the base of Seanchai's spine, pushing gently, while her other hand constrained his stomach. "Good. Now, shoulders relaxed and down.

"Imagine small, round rocks under your armpits. Your arms should slightly arc at the shoulder, but drop freely by your sides. Barely curl your fingers to relax the muscles. Yes, good," she said as she adjusted Seanchai's stance. "Pull your chin in and extend the top of your spine. Imagine there's a piece of string attached to the crown of your head and it is gently pulling your head up straight."

She pulled up some hair at the top of his head and he felt his neck straighten.

"Ouch."

"Not bad. Now, breathe in through your nose and fill your stomach. When your stomach is full, contract those muscles and expel the air back out your nose."

Seanchai stood there with his eyes closed. He began to feel stable and that there was something very familiar about this position, though he had never tried these exercises.

"Now," Mhari said. "The last thing for this lesson is to imagine that when you breathe in, you are inhaling the air up through your feet, from the ground, like the tree is bringing up water from deep in the earth. It is the energy of the earth. Let it nourish you."

When Seanchai felt he was getting too tired, he opened his eyes. He was astonished to see that his hands were out in front of him, as though he was hugging a big ball. There was a warm vibration flowing through his body and when he looked at his master, also in stance, he saw a shimmering film surrounding her. Then he noticed the tree—and yes, he himself—were also encased in this light, this energy.

He took a deep breath and stretched his cramped muscles.

"Please, make us tea," Mhari said. Though standing next to him, her voice sounded far away.

Seanchai took the small pot down to the edge of the lake and filled it. On his way back, he watched Mhari standing by the tree. He could see her vibrant posture and that the deep creases on her face had disappeared. Mhari's arms moved from her sides to in front of her, as though she were hugging the tree, and then rose as though they were holding a ball above her head. A few minutes later, she returned them to her sides with palms facing down before extending them in front of her as if holding a ball from underneath.

Seanchai arranged the fire between three stones. He rested the pot of water on top of the stones and sat down. His teacher's hands had now moved in front of her as though she was holding a ball from underneath, the ball resting against her stomach.

"Come here, Seanchai," she called softly.

Seanchai rose and obeyed.

"Put your hands between mine."

Mhari's eyes were closed, her expression serene. Seanchai put his right hand between hers.

"Aagh," he yelled and yanked it back, cradling it under his left armpit and hopping about. His hand felt burned and there was a sharp tingling vibration coursing through his arm.

"What the… What *was* that?" he cried out.

Mhari opened her eyes and smiled. "That is what you have come here to learn," she said. "That is what might just save the kingdom of Odessiya."

TWENTY-FOUR

Ilana and Shayth rode slowly down through the mountain range. She was still feeling weak and needed to rest frequently. Mhari had provided her with an herbal tonic to help speed her healing.

They rode mostly in silence and she found herself glancing at Shayth and wondering what was going through his mind. She could see little beyond his cloak and hood, even when it wasn't wrapped tightly around him.

When they stopped to eat, he insisted she rest. He collected wood, brewed her tea and tended to both horses. When he finally sat down to eat she had already finished her food. She sipped her tea, staring at him over the rim of her steaming cup.

"How about you look somewhere else?" he said, his own eyes focusing on the smoldering, charred wood.

"I'm sorry," she said. "I started this…this *journey* with all my focus on Seanchai. Rhoddan and he share a special friendship and he fitted easily into the picture. But you…"

Her voice trailed off as she sank into her own thoughts. Shayth didn't move or respond. She felt compelled to finish the sentence and struggled to find the appropriate words.

"You're different. It's not just that you're human. There are men in Uncle's band, but you aren't like them. They're so much louder than elves and more freely express their emotions verbally and in their behavior. But I have no idea what you are thinking or feeling. It's…it's disconcerting."

Shayth shifted, nudging a piece of blackened wood with his boot. Ilana continued. "It was easier when we were four, but now that it's just the two of us, I find it very intense."

Shayth looked up. "Do you doubt my intentions? I will help you rescue Rhoddan. I would have done it without you if your wound had been worse. I'm not a human who looks down on elves. I've met some good and bad men—mostly bad. And I've met good and bad elves. I choose to try and free Rhoddan because he is good, regardless of whether he's man or elf. Race is irrelevant."

"But we're all strangers to you. How can we matter enough to you to do all this?"

Shayth thought for a while. "I don't know. We've talked about Seanchai. I'm drawn to him, as you all are. Rhoddan is honorable and brave. He's quick in his mind as well as on his feet. I like him. And I know what they'll do to him in Galbrieth. He's too good for that."

They fell silent as Ilana finished her drink. Then she said: "You still haven't told me anything about yourself. You trust me to fight alongside you and watch your back. But I know nothing about you."

He did not reply.

"It's just us, Shayth. There's no one else to hear."

She looked at him, but he was staring behind her. "Yes, there is. We had better get going."

Shayth hesitated as they left the mountains about an hour before dusk. He surveyed the flat land ahead of them and then looked back at Ilana.

"We might want to go back and camp for the night. It'll be easier to defend ourselves there. We're still a few hours from the forest."

"I can keep riding," she said, her voice flat.

"No, you can't. If we need to fight or run, then you can't be drained of energy."

Shayth had not seen or heard anyone even though he had doubled back a few times to check. But he remained convinced they were being followed.

They turned their horses and found a cave a short way back the way they had come. It was not big enough for them and the horses, so Shayth took off the bags and saddles and laid out Ilana's blankets for her. He left and moved the animals further along until they were out of sight and sound from Ilana. If anyone startled them, they might not give away the sleeping elfe.

When Shayth returned, he was relieved to see that she had fallen asleep. No more questions for tonight. Taking his bow, he decided to check again if they were being followed. He climbed a rock and sat, motionless, scanning the area. Nothing.

He was perturbed he could not see who was there. It was not a clumsy soldier for sure, but someone well-practiced in stealth.

Shayth had a dilemma. Ilana needed to sleep as much as possible, but he didn't think it was wise for him to guard all night and then ride all day. As he said to Ilana earlier, they couldn't risk exhausting themselves.

He settled down in between two rocks and wrapped his hood and cloak around his body. His bow lay across his knees, an arrow already nocked. If he stayed here, perhaps he would see them approaching down below. If he couldn't take them down, then he could at least lead them away from Ilana.

Shayth yawned and thought about the elfe. He had not known any human woman as tough as she was and as willing to live such a life. He was impressed at how she stoically coped with her wound, by her fighting abilities, and with her dedication to Seanchai. He yawned again and thought of her questions earlier in the day. She would not let up, he realized. But he could not tell her the truth, not if he wanted to stay with her, Rhoddan and Seanchai. And he did.

He shook his head as he felt his eyelids droop. The next yawn was long and deep.

TWENTY-FIVE

Seanchai yawned and forced his eyes open to a brightening sky. Hadn't he only just fallen asleep? He rose with some effort. His training regime, particularly the standing exercises, was leaving him discovering muscles that weren't happy being discovered.

He stumbled over to the waterfall and leaned forward to let the cold water wake him up. He dressed and went to tend Snowmane. The horse was agitated and restless without the other horses or regular exercise.

He nickered when Seanchai approached and pricked his ears as his rider spoke, complaining about the hour, his stiff limbs, not traveling with Ilana and Shayth, and more. Snowmane seemed very attentive until the elf sat down. The horse nudged the riding blanket and saddle that were next to it. When Seanchai shook his head, Snowmane neighed and turned away to graze.

Seanchai started a fire for tea and settled down, waiting for the water to boil. Mhari was awake and meditating. Her hands rested in her lap and he marveled again at how her many facial lines diminished when she meditated.

The young elf rose and assumed his own meditative stance. The five poses felt increasingly natural and had become easier to maintain. When he studied with Mhari, she would correct his stance or breathing, and instruct him in which pose to take and when to change. He liked it better when he stood alone, and allowed his body to guide him in slow, fluid movement.

However, no matter what stance he took, or whether Mhari was watching or not, as soon as Seanchai began the meditative breathing, he now felt the warm vibration of energy rise from his feet and fill his stomach. Under instruction, he began to learn how to direct the energy through his body and into his hands. The feeling became more intense in his fingers and he even found that he began to crave it.

As they ate breakfast, Seanchai turned to his teacher. "Snowmane is getting restless. He could do with a run and change of scenery."

"Good," Mhari smiled. "Let's take him for a ride."

A half hour later, Mhari was cheerfully perched upon a trotting Snowmane who was nickering while Seanchai jogged alongside them. Seanchai was not happy. Mhari and Snowmane had bonded and were enjoying having Seanchai run after them.

"You must build your stamina and be able to sustain yourself through a fight at any time of day," Mhari called from the saddle. "As you wield the energy, you will discover that it can be very draining. You cannot aim an arrow when you are breathing heavily, and you are more prone to make the wrong decision when exhausted."

Seanchai thought of Uncle's instruction. Would he ever see the big elf again, or had he paid for playing his part in delivering Seanchai to the master? How many others have died for him? Was Rhoddan being tortured while Seanchai jogged alongside a lake? He hoped Shayth and Ilana were faring well on their journey and would return with Rhoddan safely.

They reached a small wooded area that connected the lake and mountains. Mhari dismounted and whispered to Snowmane to rest. The grove of trees was humid compared to its arid surroundings.

"This is a magical place," said Mhari, admiring the trees and vines.

"Magical? Really?"

"No," Mhari smiled. "At least, not magic of man or elf. But, you know, maybe it is magic…earth magic. Come, I want to show you something."

Mhari moved a cluster of ferns aside to reveal a knee-high plant with narrow leaves. She unhooked a trowel from her belt and dug carefully around the plant. Soon she was sweating.

"Can I help?" Seanchai asked.

"No. Thank you," Mhari replied, stretching her back. "But watch carefully so you can do it next time."

It took at least forty minutes with Mhari working slowly and carefully. The plant's tuberous root had four offshoots that Mhari was careful not to break. When she finally released the plant from the ground, she sat back heavily, the root lying across her lap.

"It is truly beautiful, no, Seanchai?" She held it up. "I need to drink and rest. Please bring the water skin and use your fingers to gently rub the dirt from the root and shoots."

Seanchai cleaned the roots, thinking that, not long ago, he had helped his mother prepare herbal mixes the way she had learned from her mother. They had dried leaves and flowers in their house, and had even grown some plants for their roots, but this was different. This was far bigger and older than anything he had seen.

He felt a wave of concern and longing for his mother that he fought to push from his mind. He glanced up and saw Mhari watching, concern in her eyes.

"What is this root?" he asked, eager for distraction.

"Well, what does it look like?"

Holding the stems, Seanchai lifted the plant up. He laughed. "Why, it looks like an elf. Here are the legs, arms, and a body." He pointed to the tip where the root met the stems. "This could be the head, but I can't find the pointed ears."

Mhari laughed too. "He doesn't need pointed *or* round ears. He is not symbolic of only one race. This is *Danseng* in man's tongue. I believe the elves call it *Janenseng*, from the old tongue. I am sure the dwarves have a similar name, too, though I don't know it."

"What does it mean?"

"It means Breath of Youth," she replied, "or something there-abouts. It is a powerful herb that helps strengthen elders of all races as we try and stretch a couple more years out of life.

"I believe it's given to a male elf only when he is preparing to mate and create life. This is a rare plant, Seanchai. And the older the plant, the more potent it is. I think this one might be eight or ten years old."

"I'm not ready to mate," Seanchai said, blushing, as he thought fleetingly of Ilana.

Mhari laughed. "Good, because we don't have the time." She fingered around the base of the leaves. "Look," she said, revealing split seedpods. "Never harvest a plant that does not have ripe seeds."

"Does that detract from the potency?"

"No," replied Mhari. She dug a small hole and planted the seeds, taking care not to touch them. "You should never harvest the root of a plant without giving back, preparing for its future. The earth could not sustain our plunder otherwise."

Mhari wrapped the root in burlap. "We'll dry it before you leave and share the bounty."

She hugged the bundle. "Men went to war over such a root, over land where the danseng grew. Danseng gatherers made a lot of money from selling old roots to kings and lords. But they became greedy, as men often did, and now it is very difficult to find and keep an aged plant."

"Am I going to drink it?" Seanchai asked.

"Yes. You will need it for the replenishment it provides after you've wielded the energy. This plant may end up being of great importance to you. Danseng and stamina will help you through the trials ahead."

"What does it taste like?"

"Very bitter, Seanchai, but it has an immediate and startling effect. It can make your heart beat very fast. But if you're to follow the path I think is before you, the danseng will be of great help. And you are going to need all the help you can get."

TWENTY-SIX

Shayth's pulse was racing. He had known they were being followed. How could he have let these men slip past him? He was foolish to think he could stay awake for the whole night. He peered around a rock and saw four men cornering Ilana, who crouched defensively with the rock face behind her.

She had her long knife held in front, but the men had not drawn their own weapons.

They were big, imposing men with shaggy hair and beards. Their clothes were thick layers of no recognizable style, and their weapons were primitive and looked to be old. Shayth was puzzled. These were not soldiers or scouts.

One of them stepped forward and put his hand out to touch Ilana's wounded arm. She pressed herself even tighter against the rock, and Shayth quietly strung his bow and took aim.

A throaty *tut* came from behind, freezing him. Sitting on a rock just a few feet away was another man. Shayth stared at the man as he shook his head and held up his hands to show he wasn't armed. Shayth slowly took the arrow from the bow and returned it to his quiver.

The man nodded and stood, signaling for Shayth to follow him. They joined the others, and Shayth and Ilana were fascinated to discover they spoke with a series of clicks.

The band parted, and the man who had accompanied Shayth clicked and pointed to Ilana. Shayth seemed to understand what was being asked of him.

"Ilana, it's alright. I don't think they're a threat to us."

She rubbed her head and muttered, "I don't do well being woken like that," but she sheathed her long knife and forced a smile. The men relaxed and smiled back. The one who had reached for her wounded arm before stepped toward her and caressed it gently.

He clicked to another and a conversation ensued. They headed back toward the main path, signaling the others to follow. The strangers took the horses' reins and picked up all of Ilana and Shayth's traveling gear. Shayth offered to carry a bag, but the man he addressed held out a hand, smiled, and shook his head.

They walked out of the mountains and went west into the dry plains. Shayth worried that they were moving away from Galbrieth.

Several hours later, they entered a camp that had been set up between two rock faces. Clearly they had been there awhile. There was a built fireplace with a drying area, where meat was being smoked and animal skins tanned. This looked like a hunting party, a very large hunting party. They were probably stalking herds that crossed the plain. Shayth struggled to think. He had heard of a nomadic people who clicked, but could not recall who they were. Still, he had a nagging feeling that there was something very important he should remember.

He and Ilana were escorted to a fire pit and invited to sit. A youngster, with no facial hair, brought them water and some cooked meat on leaves.

Then he crouched down and examined them, his head cocked to one side. Ilana had pushed back her hood to eat. The young man clicked and reached slowly with his hand to touch her left ear. She instinctively jerked her head back and an older man clicked what

Shayth interpreted as a rebuke to the youngster, who began clicking in response and feeling his own round ears.

"I think he's never seen an elf," Shayth said, and Ilana relaxed. She beckoned him forward and, taking his hand, directed it to her ear. He touched it gently and looked closely. He turned to the older man who had rebuked him and clicked. Then he faced Ilana and put her hand on his own round, hairy ears.

"Thank you," she said with regained composure.

Another man came forward with water in a bowl. He undressed Ilana's wound, carefully cleaned it, and then put some leaves in his mouth and chewed hard.

"Is he—" Ilana glanced at Shayth. He shrugged his shoulders, doing a terrible job of not grinning.

The man laid the chewed leaves on her wound and rolled another bandage around her arm. He clicked at her as he worked, making continual eye contact. Though they understood nothing, Shayth was sure the man was trying to reassure her.

Shayth finished eating and walked over to the horses. They were with the hunters' horses and he was pleased to see that they, too, were being well cared for. On his way back to Ilana, he saw an old man, his hair gray and his beard thin and white. The others treated him with great deference and he held an air of reserved authority.

Shayth saw that the man was watching him and walked over. He extended his hands to his sides with palms facing the man and bent his head in deference. When he raised his head he said "Thank You" slowly and clearly. The man wouldn't understand the words, but Shayth wanted him to understand the intention.

"You...very...welcome," the man replied. His voice was quiet and the words clearly did not come naturally.

Surprised, Shayth pointed to the rock next to the man. The man nodded and he sat down.

"Who are you?" Shayth asked. "You and your people?"

The man took a moment to speak. "Not easy speak your way. Me Targs, people are Tutan. I no know how say. We people from desert," and he pointed to the south.

"I don't think I have ever heard of a people who communicate this way," Shayth felt guilty not telling the truth, but wanted to keep the conversation focused on the Tutan and not his past. "Is your home far? Are there many of you?"

The man laughed showing a mouth full of yellow teeth.

"What's so funny?" Shayth asked.

"So many askings," the man said. "Northerners always need know. Why? Why? Why?" Again he laughed. "I come north long time before. Work in city with silver tower? Name hard to say? Long time before."

"Galbrieth?" Shayth suggested and the man nodded.

"Galbrie...yes. Work as horseman. Take care of horses, make food for big man. Was nice before army. People think I stupid. Is good. Leave stupid man alone."

"Why did you leave?"

The man chewed on a stem of a plant. "Want home, want people. When army come to Gal—"

"Galbrieth."

"Yes. When army come, no good. We no fight here. Hunt meat, no people. Very bad in city. Very sad. Soldiers see stupid man, no good. I leave. I go home. Many of my people, no come home. Killed by soldiers."

"How many Tutans are there?" Shayth asked.

"Here, you see," and he extended his arm before waving toward the south. "Home, many, many. Live in desert. Live as one with desert. Desert hide and protect us."

"Why have we not heard of you? Don't you trade anything?"

The man shook his head. "After big meeting many killings. We no want be near you people. Sorry, but some very bad, want only with swords."

Shayth nodded. A few of Targ's men had come and sat on the ground to listen and watch, though they could not understand the exchange. Ilana and the young boy came and sat together, though he seemed more interested in her and her ears, rather than the conversation.

The man clicked to those seated and then turned to Shayth and explained. "Tell them what we talk of." Then he continued. "We no like fight. Here people angry, we talk. Tutans help each other. There, no so quick with help. People good in family but no more. We no want fight. You understand?"

Shayth nodded. "So you wanted to get away from the men here and your people went deep into the desert?"

The old man nodded. "Happened, yes, when I young. We tell stories. Once all live good. Was man and elf. Also…" he mimed a shorter creature with his hand. "Go under earth."

"Dwarves," said Shayth and the man nodded again.

The young Tutan with Ilana rose on his knees and clicked. He made a flapping movement with his arms and snorted from his nose. Others clicked at him and laughed.

"Aah yes," said the old man with a big smile. "Also big flying, with fire in nose and tail like many sword."

"Dragons?" Shayth raised his eyebrows. "You don't believe in dragons, do you?"

The old man looked at him, surprised. "Oh, yes. They live, and they no happy for what man do."

"Dragons are a myth," said Shayth. "Humans don't believe it. What about your people, Ilana?"

"The elves have stories that we tell around the campfire," she said. "But they don't exist, do they?"

"Yes, yes," the man raised his voice. "They live. I see. Like us, but hate other men."

"Wow," said Shayth. "I wonder…" But he kept the rest of his thoughts to himself.

TWENTY-SEVEN

Since there hadn't been any signs of soldiers, Mhari and Seanchai hiked in the mountains. Building stamina and long conversations were the order of the day. Mhari spoke of the history of the land and lectured him on ethics. Seanchai treasured these times and as his endurance grew, he loved even the most strenuous hikes. With his sharp elf eyesight, he could see in the distance another snow-capped mountain range and a long valley with a bright blue river winding through. It was beautiful and only lacked, in his opinion, a forest. He guessed he would always be a wood elf.

Mhari drew maps on the ground with a branch and described the lands and people. Later, she would ask Seanchai to relay the information back. This improved his ability to retain knowledge and taught him that everything she told him was a lesson.

During breaks, they practiced their exercises. Seanchai had also begun calisthenics to complement his running and energy training. This resulted in a rapid improvement in his poses as his body adjusted to the physical aspect, allowing Seanchai to focus more effort on gathering energy.

They often stopped to examine herbs and trees. Mhari would explain properties and applications; what herbs could be used in a combination; and how to make a tea, salve, or poultice. Next time they came across the plant, she would ask Seanchai to relay this information back to her. From then on, Seanchai was expected to point out the herb when next they passed it without prompting. At night, they mapped the stars, refining the rudimentary understanding that Seanchai had gleaned during his childhood.

At the end of the third day of one particularly grueling hike they reached the snow line. Seanchai had never seen snow and was excited until he felt the cold, penetrating wind that kept the snow from melting.

He was relieved when Mhari led him into a cave and they began to descend inside the mountain. There were long, noble stalagmites and stalactites some almost meeting each other, like lovers stretching to touch fingertips.

"They are so close," Mhari said. "Yet it'll take several more centuries for them to join together."

"Wow," Seanchai said, as he gazed into the cavern.

Their lit torches revealed shiny, diamond-like mineral deposits in the rocks. The air was chilly in the caves, and Seanchai could smell the moisture all around him.

He lost all track of time and direction, though he could tell that Mhari was navigating a specific route that took them at once through tightly squeezed tunnels and then into great echoing caverns. When they rested, he asked how she knew the way.

"I have been here before," Mhari replied. "This mountain contains a great source of power and I want to share it with you. It's quite honestly far too early for this, but we don't have time to wait. We're nearly there. Hold your questions for now."

Seanchai reflected on how much and how quickly he was learning as they continued deep into the mountain. Mhari was pushing him to gain physical strength and build an energy reserve inside his body. He enjoyed learning to use herbs to heal and strengthen, and remained convinced that it should have been his vocation. Here under the mountain, he even discovered several varieties of mushrooms. Mhari told him that they had grown unusually large from the rich mineral deposits, but there was no time now to study them.

"I would love to be able to spend more time with you," Mhari said, in what was becoming a mantra for her. "There's so much I could teach you. But out of necessity, we must remain very focused."

On this hike, Mhari had concentrated on teaching stealth. She constantly tested her student and almost, though not always, found him. A forest elf grows up learning how to walk silently, and Seanchai had applied many of the techniques when he had gone hunting. When he succeeded against his teacher, he felt a wave of satisfaction.

"You're proficient, Seanchai, but you need to know how to avoid being noticed by those seeking you out. This is very different than stalking an oblivious deer or rabbit. If you can perfect such techniques, they might prevent you from having to fight and kill people."

Many times, despite the acquisition of these practical tools, Mhari did not provide explanations on why she was teaching him certain things. Seanchai was learning to acquire energy, for example, but not how to use it. He had so many questions for his teacher: How much would he learn, and what for? Where had his talent come from? And maybe the biggest question: Who was he and what was his destiny? So far, Mhari had refrained from answering his questions.

Seanchai came out of his musings when he realized he was sweating. Mhari had stopped and, after drinking some water, folded her cloak into her bag. Seanchai followed suit. When he finished, Mhari was smiling at him.

"We are almost there," she said. "Come, we will stay in this place for a few days."

Soon, the steep path began to flatten out. They turned a corner and walked along a ridge. Seanchai could not see down through the darkness. At the end, Mhari stopped where two rocks stood parallel with what seemed like a very narrow corridor.

"Wait a moment, Seanchai," she said, holding out her hand. "This is your first test. You must seek out that warm energy with which we fill our bodies. You must do this now and do it well. Only when your body is full of the energy can you enter the cavern beyond. Let us begin."

They both assumed the first position. It felt natural and he began to feel the familiar sensation resonating though his feet. The elf directed his breathing up his legs and channeled it into his stomach. He imagined storing it there and then summoned more. Intuitively he began to direct it into his chest and arms. His whole body vibrated as the energy coursed through him and he involuntarily sighed. Mhari spoke softly.

"Hold the ball, Seanchai."

Seanchai's hands moved in front of his chest, and he directed the energy to his fingertips. Then he imagined the ball and, in his mind, it began to appear. In his expanding state of consciousness, he could clearly see the ball though his eyes were closed. It was in his hands, against his chest and in his head.

"Now, holding the ball, open your eyes. Keep the energy around you."

Mhari was several feet in front of Seanchai, beyond the narrow corridor. When she spoke, her voice carried with gravitas. "Step forward, Seanchai of Morthian Wood, and enter."

Seanchai entered the cavern, and his life changed forever.

TWENTY-EIGHT

It seemed to Shayth that the Tutans genuinely enjoyed hosting Ilana and him that night. They were generous with food and drink, and as it got dark they passed around a sweet, rich liquid in a large horn that was held over expectant mouths with great reverence. There was also drumming on hollow wood of all shapes, covered with animal skins, and other forms of percussion.

Targs was the only one who could talk with them, but it didn't stop the ear-infatuated youngster from trying to tell Ilana many things. She smiled at him and spoke warmly even though they did not understand each other.

"My people not like this far north," Targs explained. "Like deep in desert. Only scouts come and see what happening. But this year buffalo and cow herds not come south and tribe send us out for track and hunt."

Shayth noted many bundles that he assumed to be dried meat or skins. There were also carts and a tall, thin breed of horse that he had never seen. Though he could discern the animals' bones, they seemed muscular, efficient, and hardy.

Targs pointed to the shiny horn being passed round. "Drink little, very strong," he warned. The liquid burned Shayth's throat and he coughed, causing the Tutans to laugh.

Ilana, saw how Shayth had reacted to the strong liquor and was relieved that he laughed along with their hosts. She declined to drink when it reached her, but the man who had dressed her wound clapped his hands for silence. He clicked to Targs, who turned to Ilana.

"Healer says you drink. If bad inside body from wound, it kills. Drink please, but only little."

Ilana drank and everyone cheered her. She shivered and let out a small burp, which made them all laugh again. A little while later as there was a lull in the drumming, Shayth turned to the leader.

"Targs. Can you show us the best route to Galbrieth?" When the old man frowned, Shayth continued. "We don't want to go there, but we must."

He nodded and began drawing a map in the sand of different routes to the city. Ilana interrupted him.

"Targs. We're only interested in the shortest route. We have a friend, a good elf, in terrible danger and need to get there quickly."

"Fast way, most dangerous."

"I don't care," she said with conviction. "Please show us the fastest way."

Targs shrugged and drew a line and, as he did, some of his people began to click and shake their heads emphatically. Targs responded, pointing to Ilana. One man got up and took the stick from him. He drew two people by the path, indicating Shayth and Ilana. With his boot, he rubbed them out.

Targs turned to explain, but Shayth spoke first. "That was pretty clear."

"Often fast way not fast way if want reach end way." Targs replied.

"We understand," Shayth said, nodding to the man who had drawn and erased their figures in the sand.

Then the young boy who had attached himself to Ilana stood. He took the stick and drew first two figures and then a third, pointing to himself. A cacophony of clicks erupted from around the circle. Shayth rose and walked over. He patted the boy on the shoulder.

"That's very nice of you to offer," he said. "Thank you." Then he erased the third figure.

The ensuing conversation among the Tutans was accompanied by hand gestures and frowns–they were arguing. The boy rose again and drew the third figure. Shayth sighed. He did not want to start jumping up and down in a weird children's game.

Then another man stepped forward and added a fourth figure. Now the argument was more measured. People looked stunned, but neither Shayth nor Ilana could follow the discussion. Another man rose, took the stick, and then there was a fifth figure.

Shayth turned to Targs. "You must stop them. They don't know what they're headed into. This is a fortress. You've seen Galbrieth. These soldiers are brutal. They will show no mercy for your people and you said Tutans don't know how to fight."

Targs looked at him and frowned. "I say we no like fight. I no say we no know how fight." He sighed and turned to his people. A long discussion began, and Shayth felt his frustration rising.

Ilana rose and quietly left the Tutans to their discussion. Shayth followed. She took a skin of water and drank while Shayth paced in front of her.

When she finished, she said, "I don't think these people are as delicate as you think, Shayth. As Targs said, the fact that they choose not to fight does not mean they are not able to. To survive and thrive in the desert, you must be tough. To live there, you must value life. I don't think they will act recklessly or impede us."

Shayth was not pacified. "It's crazy. I'm used to working alone, not looking out for others."

"But you work together with Seanchai, Rhoddan and myself."

He nodded. "But that's different."

"How?"

He didn't clarify, but continued pacing and passing his hand through his unruly hair. "People don't put themselves in danger like this unless there's some serious personal gain or they're simply idiots."

"The Tutans are not idiots," Ilana snapped.

"No, no, I didn't mean to imply they were."

"Listen, Shayth. Mhari asked me why I had requested from Uncle to accompany Seanchai. I told her I felt strangely compelled from the very beginning. She said that it wasn't strange; that good people with a strong sense of right and wrong will often be attracted to someone special like Seanchai. Look at yourself—"

"Ha!" Shayth spat. "You think I'm a good person."

When she spoke, Ilana's voice was firm and measured. "I don't care what you *were*, Shayth, I only see who you are now. You're drawn to Seanchai, Rhoddan and me because of friendship. It's striking a chord deep inside of you. So you're ready to put your life on the line for us."

Shayth looked at her. Would she still feel that way when she discovered his past? "You're a good pers...a good elfe, Ilana. You really are. But I'm..."

He heard footsteps approaching and stopped. Targs and the young boy joined them. The boy's face was flushed, and he looked at the ground as Targs spoke.

"We decide. Three men go with you to Galbrieth. The three they um...they want go. They show you good way, fast way. They go in city, they not go in city, they choose then. They not go, it good. Yes?"

Ilana nodded. "Thank you. We appreciate the help your people are offering."

"More," Targs said and he addressed Ilana. "In Tutan way, we say two people together, they touch hearts." He moved his hand to his heart. "Touch heart very, very good. Two people. Boy asks if you touch heart with other?"

The young boy was staring intensely at his feet. Ilana gently raised his head so that he looked up at her.

"Thank you, I'm honored," she said, and her voice quivered. "But yes, my heart is touched by another. It belongs to another elf."

She turned abruptly and walked away, tears welling up in her eyes.

TWENTY-NINE

Seanchai gazed into the huge cavern at a dark, shimmering underground lake. Shiny rock walls rose around the perimeter, and there were huge cracks higher up, letting in light that illuminated the mineral deposits. But dominating everything was a huge stalactite reaching down toward the middle of the lake. Water rhythmically dripped from it into the lake, echoing off the walls. Seanchai felt such intense energy in the air that he stood with his mouth agape.

"Close your mouth, boy," Mhari said. "You'll swallow a bat."

"Bats? Really?"

Mhari smiled. "No. I will teach you many things, my young elf, but a sense of humor you'll have to learn elsewhere. Let us eat something and then sleep. Tomorrow will be a very long day."

Seanchai unpacked their bags and bedrolls. He cut some bread and covered it with a nut paste then added cut vegetables and a block of cheese to the meal. He could see the old woman was tired, and she seemed content to let him serve her. It was a sign of respect, and he knew it was appreciated.

"Seanchai," she said, suddenly serious. "You must not go near the lake or touch the water until I tell you to. Is that clear? It could kill you."

Seanchai nodded. "What is this place?"

"It's a ley junction. We believe that the world is crossed with lines of energy called leys, and the places where they intersect hold great power. Throughout history, they have been used for many magical events and ceremonies. They are places where people such as us come for rejuvenation and transformation.

"Tomorrow I will answer as many of your questions as I can, but for now we'll finish eating and then sleep." She yawned. "We often have powerful dreams here. Be prepared. If you do dream, enjoy the ride."

The warrior saw them all as he flew above, and he let out an exuberant cry. The magnificent beast he rode raised its head and billowed fire before it curled its great, scaly wings and dove. Cold air hit the warrior's face. It was exhilarating. As they neared the ground, the warrior raised a shining broadsword above his head.

All eyes rose to meet him. Elves raised handsome wooden bows in tribute. Men thrust mighty swords into the air, and helmeted dwarves banged battleaxes against their shields.

Next to the dwarves stood massive trolls who shook the ground with their stomping feet. In contrast to the trolls' gray, bulky bodies were tall, thin green creatures from the mighty forests of Miden. All hailed the warrior and the great beast under him roared with joy.

The beast headed for the hills, soaring over a sea of aqua-skinned creatures riding huge, gray four-legged mammals with long trunks and even longer horns. They let out high-pitched cries when they saw him, and raised their own curved swords while their animals raised their trunks and trumpeted.

The warrior sheathed his mighty sword, checked his own two-horned helmet, the straps of his armor and saddle. Then, oblivious to the height and speed at which he flew, he leaned forward, careful of the creature's scales and adjusted the armored helmet and mask that his winged steed wore.

He was ready. His armies had gathered in greater numbers than even he had dared to imagine. He turned the beast towards the east and saw a mighty host of foe, similar in number gathering across the plain.

Let the battle begin!

Seanchai woke, breathing hard. He sat up and found that he was damp from sweat and humidity. He looked around for his teacher. Mhari was neck-deep in the lake with her back to Seanchai.

Seanchai sat and watched her, trying to both slow his racing pulse and force himself to remember every detail of his dream so that he could share it with his teacher. The elf looked around for some wood, hoping to make a warm drink, but there was none, and they were too far into the mountain for him to go out and collect some. Why hadn't Mhari thought of this?

He chewed some dried meat instead. Mhari finished her exercise and stretched her hands around and up in slow circular movements, exhaling loudly. Then she ducked under the water, surfacing a minute or so later.

When Mhari turned and began walking out of the lake, Seanchai gasped. She looked twenty years younger. Her wrinkled face was now almost smooth; her white hair a speckled mix of vibrant black and gray. Her muscles looked tight and defined.

Mhari poured water into her clay bowl and added an herb mixture. She sat cross-legged, cupped it in her hands and closed her eyes. Soon her cup was steaming. Moments later, Seanchai could hear the water beginning to bubble. Mhari slowly opened her eyes, blew on the tea, and took a sip.

"So, Seanchai. How was your night?" Her smile told him she knew what he was bursting to ask her.

Seanchai decided to play along for now and come back to the lake and boiling water later. He recounted his dream and Mhari questioned him at length. Describe the helmet. What color were the beasts' scales? The aqua-colored creatures—how many did he think he saw? Was there a figure flying above the enemy's army, too?

Finally Seanchai began to feel frustrated. "Mhari, why have you brought me here? Am I going to take some sort of test? Is something going to happen in the water? Am I going to undergo some kind of change like you have?"

He brushed his hair back. "You counsel me not to be impatient, but also constantly warn that we don't have time to dally. I want to walk out of here understanding what is happening to me and where I fit into everything."

His teacher nodded. "I understand, Seanchai. I know this is very difficult for you. But for transformation to happen, you need to understand the stories and their power. To take the test, you must understand why you are taking it. You will enter the water. But there is a process, and understanding it will go a long way to helping you walk out of here alive."

THIRTY

The Tutans accompanying Shayth and Ilana were ready at first light. As they waited for the healer to check Ilana's wound one last time, it suddenly occurred to Shayth that there would be a problem with communication. As far as he knew, Targs was the only one who knew how to communicate using words.

But for the moment they rode away from the camp in single file with no need to talk. Shayth appreciated the help guarding at night and carrying supplies. They would also be most welcome if they needed to defend themselves.

He dug his heels gently into his horse's side and moved alongside Ilana. She rode with her back slightly arched, staring mechanically at the man who led the way. Her eyes were red and puffy.

"Hey, you okay?" he asked eventually.

She nodded, but kept facing forward.

"I miss Seanchai, too," Shayth said. "I wonder what he's going through and if he will be different when we see him again."

"Has it ever occurred to you that we might *not* see him again?" Her voice was impassive. "We're about to take on a fortified garrison. We: an impulsive and unpredictable young man with a huge chip on his shoulder and a wounded elfe. I'm not sure the odds are particularly in our favor."

Shayth tried to laugh, but sighed instead. "You don't have to do this, Ilana. You are wounded and...well, you don't have to do this. I will go on. I owe Rhoddan, and I'm not afraid to die."

"I've never been afraid to die," Ilana replied. "It just seems different now. I don't understand why."

"It *is* different now," Shayth said after a moment's contemplation. "Before, when you fought in the resistance cell, your only concern was completing whatever task you were given without question. Now there's someone special in your life and it's not so easy to be that self-sacrificing."

Ilana kept looking ahead, but Shayth heard a loud sigh escape her .

"You're very world-wise, my sage," she said and smiled to show she wasn't being rude. "I've also wondered how Seanchai will be different. It is disconcerting. I think he'll become very focused on whatever his destiny reveals."

Shayth nodded. "Yes, but Seanchai's greatest qualities are his humility and his humanity, or whatever you elves call it. I just can't believe he'll go through such a big transformation that there'll be no room left for you. In fact, he may need what you can offer him all the more in order to fulfill his destiny. Have you thought of that?"

"A lot must happen before we find out," she replied. "Do you have a plan for when we reach the garrison at Galbrieth?"

"Oh, yes," he said. "I have several. And each is as hopeless as the next."

Ilana looked at him. He wasn't smiling.

"Have you even been there?" she asked.

"Yes," he replied, his voice still grim. "It was actually a nice town once, and if the army wasn't there, you might enjoy your visit. But the fortifications, while not as extensive as those in other places, are still going to be difficult. Tall, thick stone walls surround the city and within that is a fortress just for the army. But that's not what's worrying me."

"What is, then?"

"If they don't believe that Rhoddan is the special one, then they'll torture him to find out who is. The battalion commander, General Tarlach, is a sadistic swine. He is also very ambitious and will no doubt see the capture of the special one as his quick ticket into the Emperor's good graces.

"He'll be very angry when he discovers that he doesn't hold the right elf, especially if he has already sent word to the Emperor of the capture. It doesn't bode well for Rhoddan."

They rode in silence for some time. Then Ilana turned to her companion. "There is another possibility."

"What's that?"

"Mhari said that the general might need to keep Rhoddan alive," she said, "even after he discovers that he isn't Seanchai."

"Why would he do that?"

"If he discovers that Rhoddan is Seanchai's friend, then keeping him alive would serve another purpose. He could wait for Seanchai to come to Galbrieth to rescue his friend."

Shayth turned to her. "So we could be walking into a trap?"

She nodded and Shayth shrugged.

"Could be worse," he said, looking forward.

"How's that?"

"I'm not sure, but knowing our luck, we'll probably find out."

A few hours later as they were eating lunch, the Tutan on guard clicked a warning. They melted behind rocks, taking defensive positions rather than trying to hide. Their packs were undone and their horses nearby.

Two men rode up, perched on a wagon. When they saw the remains of the camp, they froze. Shayth jumped out, his bow ready. Both men put their hands in the air, clearly scared.

From her position, Ilana started to speak. "They are no th–"

"Quiet," hissed Shayth and he approached them. "Put your hands down slowly but on your legs where I can see them."

"W-we be simple f-farmers," the older one began. "W-we wuz in Galbrieth, selling vegetables from our village. We be poor men. What you take from us might kill our families. It be the very food from their poor little mouths."

"Get down from the cart," Shayth ordered them. He pointed at the cowering younger man. "You hold the horse still. I have a half-dozen men surrounding you. Is that clear?"

The young man nodded. Shayth turned back to the older man, who was alighting stiffly.

"I don't want your money. I want information, and I want to make it clear that I will hunt you down and kill you and your families if you ever tell anyone of our conversation."

The old man nodded and breathed a sigh of relief. "You not be soldiers, so I reckon you ain't good friends wiv that General Tarlach, eh?" he asked. "We'll answer your questions as best we can, sir, though we be simple farmers. Please, can you lower that there bow and let an old man sit?"

Shayth nodded and lowered his bow. The old man sat heavily and looked at the remains of their interrupted meal.

"Help yourself," said Ilana as she approached them.

They stared at her and Shayth glared but let it go. Instead, he turned to the farmers, who were stuffing themselves with bread and dried meat.

"You seem surprised to see an elf," he remarked.

"There be none where we live," the farmer replied, his mouth full of food. "And in Galbrieth they be hunted down right now. You might not want to take her there if that be your plan."

"Why are they being hunted?" Ilana asked.

The younger man answered. "Have you ever been there?" When

she shook her head, he continued: "They've never treated elves too good if you know what I mean – mainly they be slaves and servants. Now they's afraid of elves. I dunno why for certain, but word is that it has something to do with one particular elf who was captured, like. He wuz chained. We saw him."

He looked to the older man for validation, and received a nod. No longer afraid they were in danger, he continued.

"See, he arrived just 'bout the same time as we did. Them soldiers had him in chains and wuz shouting and boasting that they'd caught a mighty warrior. Looked like a young and scrawny elf to me, begging your pardon, miss. That night, there wuz a lot of soldiers out drinking and in a fine mood. Horace here drank with a few. Soldiers they be happy to buy drinks for them who listen and fluff up their egos."

Horace drank some water from the skin and nodded. "I know how t'get the buggers to buy me drinks. They says the elf has special powers and all."

The younger one continued. "Anyways, yesterday, it all changed. Lots o' shouting and grabbing elves off the street. Weren't nice. We figures best be getting out and left."

"We heard they be pulling in soldiers from patrols and the like. Mebbe they'z 'specting a fight."

"Yeah," said Shayth, nodding slowly. "Seems like that's exactly what they're expecting."

THIRTY-ONE

Seanchai's entire body filled with vibrant energy. He was becoming increasingly proficient at maintaining his standing exercises, but this time the energy felt more intense. He followed a free form, allowing the energy to move his hands, and was only vaguely aware that his body was transitioning between the different poses.

Usually while practicing free flow, Mhari would allow him to continue until Seanchai was ready to stop. But this time, she softly talked him through the stretching ritual with which they concluded their exercise.

"Sit down," said Mhari, when she had finished her instruction. "We must talk."

She handed Seanchai a cup of hot tea, and he winced at the bitterness. The last two days, Mhari had prepared higher concentrations of the danseng herb for Seanchai to drink. He assumed her intention was to build his stamina in preparation for the trials that waited. As he sipped the tea, she began to speak.

"When you were little, your parents and teachers told you stories. You remember these stories, treasuring them as the beautiful and imaginative tales they are.

"But these stories were told to you for a reason. They are ancient tales, created and preserved because of the power they possess. Words, Seanchai, are very potent. You know this because you have already used them to summon magic in times of great danger.

"A storyteller is usually chosen at birth, often because of a hereditary line or certain religious signs. Often the choice is not clear. But in those first few years she or he learns to remember the stories and store the words in the same way we store energy when we stand. All the words are kept safe within them, like precious jewels locked in a chest.

"But strong emotions can often release a word to come to the aid of the storyteller. This is what is happening to you.

"We have come to this powerful place of energy so that you can release the words from your subconscious and utilize them at will."

"How do I do that?" Seanchai asked. He could feel a knot of fear in his stomach rather than a well of words.

"Submerge yourself in the lake. Do your standing exercises and see what happens." Mhari smiled. "I cannot tell you much beyond this, as it is different for each of us."

"You want me to stand in the water like you did earlier?"

"No. You will walk out to the middle of the lake."

Seanchai frowned. "How will I be able to breathe when I'm under the water?"

"You just will," Mhari replied. "This isn't ordinary water, and you aren't an ordinary elf."

"When should I do this?" Seanchai asked, feeling a rising wave of anxiety.

"Finish your tea first. Every drop of danseng will help. Listen—not just with your ears, but also your heart. Be prepared for the unexpected."

"Like what?" Seanchai frowned. "What might go wrong?"

His teacher shrugged. "You might not be able to breathe underwater."

"Then what should I do?"

Mhari couldn't help but smile. "Then you should probably swim to the surface."

Seanchai screwed up his face, trying to understand her sense of humor. Realizing this was a lost cause, he took a deep breath, undressed, bowed to his teacher, and walked to the underground lake's edge. His feet touched very cold water, and he paused.

But it wasn't going to get any warmer, he reasoned, and tentatively began to walk in. By the time his shoulders were submerged, he wasn't sure he could feel his feet. He glanced up at the glistening stalactite and felt very small.

He continued until his head was submerged. Underwater, all he could hear was his own breathing. He felt truly alone and was acutely aware of each breath. He closed his eyes and focused on the water flowing through his body. It was not choking him and tasted metallic from the minerals in the rocks. As the pressure built around him, he realized the water felt considerably denser than normal lake water, and he no longer felt too cold.

Focus, he thought. *Concentrate on taking one step at a time.* He planted his right foot on the bed of the lake, deliberately digging his toes into the sandy gravel. Then his left foot: a rhythm, a reason. He thought of his parents; of Mhari, Shayth and Rhoddan; and then an image of Ilana the morning she and Shayth had departed. There were many reasons to continue, many reasons to succeed.

Seanchai continued until he felt the stalactite directly above him. He planted his feet in the gravel and began his exercises. Within moments he felt the energy enter his body and begin to circulate. But this time, it came not only from his feet, but also through the top of his head. Its familiarity helped to calm him and warmed his body.

All at once a blinding white light engulfed him. He felt totally consumed by it and at the same time sure it came from within his body. It felt as though his insides were churning. The water swirled in front of him and a portal opened through which he saw images of mountains, lakes, desert, forest, and ocean.

Herds of animals raced past him: white horses; brown humpers from the desert; and the big, horned gray beasts from his dream the previous night. Flying above his head were shining dragons, giant eagles, and ospreys large enough to carry a small elf.

Rows of wood elves marched past alongside bigger, dark-skinned elves in white cloaks. Next came human men of all types: white with blond hair and blue eyes, black with large muscles, wild men from the north with beards. Seanchai saw those with slanted eyes like Mhari had, as well as the aqua green-skinned men. Behind them came dwarves, stout with long beards and fine metal buckles on their belts. Seanchai gasped as huge rock-like creatures thundered past. They were twice as big as a grown elf and after them came even bigger creatures seemingly made of red clay, with massive limbs and dull red eyes. Finally, rows upon rows of pictorians marched with huge axes, shinning armor, their horns gleaming in the light.

Seanchai strode forward, watching playful dolphins and huge whales. Large ships sailed past him. He walked on, past great war towers on wheels with turrets and flags. He saw farms, villages, towns and cities. He passed huge stone castles and fortresses, all with banners flying proudly in the wind.

Seanchai transported into a room full of all sorts of bladed weapons: ornately carved knives, jewel-encrusted axes, and every size and shape of sword he could imagine. There were beautifully crafted bows, pikes, lances, and spears of great elegance. On the wall were shields, helmets and chain mail of all kinds.

It all gradually faded except for a pair of thin handled swords with black blades engraved with runes and intricate symbols. Seanchai examined them with wonder. He had never seen such swords, and yet they looked so familiar.

Every time Seanchai stretched out to touch them, they floated out of his reach. But he doggedly followed, convinced these were meant for him. He entered a large hall where the swords hung on the far wall. He felt he had arrived at a crossroads. If he crossed the hall and took the swords off the wall, there would be no turning back. This was the moment. He took a deep breath, strode forward, and reached up.

The young elf held a sword in each hand. He felt the perfect balance of the blades and slowly swung one in an arc, and then the other. There was a whoosh from each as though they were cutting through air rather than water.

Seanchai reached back to the wall and took the swords' double sheaths as the room began to fade. He swung it over his shoulders as the room disappeared and he once again stood on the bed of the lake, testing the swords.

Seanchai only possessed rudimentary knowledge of swords, yet he moved his new weapons smoothly. They had become as one, he and the swords. He was exhilarated at the fluency and energy. Somewhat reluctantly, he sheathed the swords. They were a part of him now. Perhaps they had always been so.

Seanchai moved beneath the stalactite, and a beam of white light engulfed him. His body lifted off the lake floor, stretching and contracting. He lifted his face in the light, and a burning sensation reverberated through his body. Seanchai screamed with pain.

Slowly he drifted down to the bed of the lake, where he fell to his knees, utterly exhausted. He knew he needed to stay awake and leave the water, but his desire to rest was strong.

From far away, the voice of his teacher called him. "Come, Seanchai. You cannot stay in the lake. You must leave the water. Come to me again and finish your training. Seanchai. Come to me."

Seanchai forced himself to stand. Step by heavy step, he began to walk, shoulders sagging from fatigue and the weight of expectation. He plodded along, Mhari's voice in his ear. He needed to focus. Left foot, right foot, left, right, Ilana, right, Shayth, right, Rhoddan, right, Mhari, right, left, right, Ilana, Ilana, Ilana...

As Seanchai emerged from the lake, he found Mhari, usually so composed, staring with her mouth open. Seanchai dragged his body to his bedroll and collapsed onto it. Void of support from the water, he felt so heavy, so weary. He was vaguely aware of his teacher holding his head up, forcing him to drink the hot tea, and the words Mhari kept repeating: "Seanchai. Seanchai. What have you become?"

THIRTY-TWO

It was getting warmer as Shayth, Ilana and the desert people entered the Vale of Galbrieth, a narrow valley of farmland. Cows and sheep grazed in fields edged with fences or untidy hedges.

They passed families; men on their way to work; and creaky wagons packed precariously with food and livestock. People furtively got out of their way and kept their eyes on the ground, determined to avoid any kind of contact. No one stopped them or asked questions. Fear and intimidation permeated the air all around them.

Shayth's big bow, intense black eyes, and shabby clothes were enough to get him the service he required when they stopped for supplies without any discussions. The one time he tried to get some information, the shopkeeper refused to talk to him and retreated hastily to the back of his shop as soon as he had received his money for the goods that Shayth had purchased.

As the valley stretched out, so did the frequency of hamlets and villages. Shortly after leaving one such village, Shayth pulled off the road and moved under some trees. He dismounted from his horse and the others followed suit.

"I'm going on a bit to check something. I'll be back soon." He made a series of hand gestures to the Tutans that seemed to get his message across.

Shayth returned to the road and walked around a long bend. He stopped a stone's throw from a checkpoint with barricades across the width of the road. Behind one was a small hut. Shayth counted four guards on post and assumed there were more resting in the hut. He observed how they stopped everyone and searched any supplies being brought in. One man with a donkey and cart was forced to hand over a skin of wine.

Shayth returned to their camp and called the others over. He drew two parallel lines in the sand and pointed to the road. The Tutans nodded. There had been no need for conversation until now and, apart from working out the order for guard duty at night, they were fine to just smile and nod at each other.

Then he drew a castle tower. He looked at the men to see that they understood. On the other side, he put a cross and pointed at himself, Ilana and the Tutans. Again, they nodded.

Shayth put up a finger to signal that the next part was important. Close to where he had drawn their company, he drew two small lines and a helmet. When his audience didn't immediately understand, he stood to attention and then put out a hand to stop people approaching. He also produced a credible salute. His expression was comically stern, and Ilana burst out laughing.

"You are not helping," he said, failing to suppress a smile, himself.

"No, but at least I understand you," she replied.

"We have to get past the checkpoint here. I have a plan," he said and looked at the desert men. "But I've no idea how to explain it to you."

It took time and a lot of pantomime for Shayth to explain what he wanted to do, but finally he felt that the Tutans understood his plan.

As the sun began its westerly descent, a line of horses and riders approached the guards. These guards were about to go off duty from a long day and were tired and bored. They also had trouble seeing the group coming out of the direct sunlight.

The leader was heavily armed and wrapped in a cloak. Behind him rode three scruffy men, hands tied and eyes down. A final rider, also armed and cloaked, brought up the rear.

"Trader," said the leader, his tone gruff. "Got an agreement with Taben for these slaves."

"Taben?" one soldier said. "Not sure I know him."

"Do you know all the merchants in Galbrieth?" the man snapped. "I've traded here for years and I only know a select few."

"And do you have a contract with this Taben? Some document?"

"I have his word," the trader said.

"That's all? Not sure I would be so trusting in your trade."

Shayth tapped his sword and nonchalantly adjusted his bow. "I have an understanding with merchants. I have never tried to cheat them, ever. I agree on a price and bring them whatever I promise. And no one has ever let me down...twice."

There was something in the man's dark eyes that unsettled the officer. He laughed uneasily.

"You should get them housed by dark," the officer said and handed Shayth a board to sign. "Move along."

They passed through and all breathed a sigh of relief.

"Is this Taben for real?" asked Ilana.

"I hope not," Shayth replied. "If we succeed and they remember this exchange, he won't be in an envious position. We'll go on for another hour and find a place to camp. We're only a few miles from the town and I imagine the gates will be locked until morning."

When they had settled down and eaten, Shayth turned to the three men. Again he took a stick and drew a path. He signaled their camp with a cross and then the town and castle, saying Galbrieth over and over. He drew two figures and a line into the castle. Then he drew three more and waited.

The three men spoke to each other. The clicking continued for a few minutes and then one of the men turned to Shayth and Ilana.

"We go in, too." He said each word deliberately.

"You can understand us?" asked Ilana, raising her eyebrows.

"Why did you make me dance around like crazy trying to explain everything?" Shayth asked, clearly exasperated.

The man turned to speak to his friends. Their conversation was accompanied by considerable nodding. Then he turned back to Shayth.

"You scare us. We not used to your ways. When you dance and move hands around," he did a credible impression, "we feel better with you."

Ilana burst into laughter and the men joined her. Only Shayth stood there, his hands on his hips, the smiling butt of their joke.

THIRTY-THREE

Seanchai sunk into a deep sleep. He would learn later that Mhari kept close watch over him, leaving his side only to prepare food and do her own exercises.

He woke in one of the rare moments she was away. He lay for a long time, probably trying to piece together what had happened. Had it all been a dream? He started to sit up, but his head spun and he groaned. Mhari heard him and quickly came to his side.

"Welcome back, my young student. How do you feel?"

"Like I've drunk a barrel of very potent ale," Seanchai replied, rubbing his head. "I'm not sure I even have the strength to stand."

"It's natural that you feel this way after what you have been through," Mhari said. "You slept for at least two full days. You were in the lake for two days before that. Let me make you some tea. I think you might need it."

"Four days have passed? Wow!"

Seanchai laid his head back on the bedroll to doze. When Mhari returned, he needed help to sit up, and sipped the tea she brought him slowly. It was difficult for him to swallow, but he drank two cups of the resuscitating brew before declaring he was hungry.

"A good sign," said Mhari. "I baked a tasty peach pie while you were gone." She threw back her head, and her laughter bounced off the cavern walls. "Oh, Seanchai. I have been in such places as this for many days, even weeks, all alone. But this was the loneliest time I have ever endured."

Seanchai smiled gratefully and munched the cracker bread and cheese offered. He devoured a couple of apples and some nuts, noticing how his teacher kept glancing at him. Mhari often made jokes, but now they seemed strained.

"You were worried, weren't you?" Seanchai asked as the realization hit him. "You doubted whether I could make it."

"I doubted whether I had prepared you well enough. We have had such little time together, and I knew it would be intense. Usually a student trains for at least two years before the teacher even considers such tests. But you've come through it successfully."

"How do you know how it went?" Seanchai shot her a look. "Apart from how long it took."

The old woman hesitated. "Well, to begin with, you're alive." She nodded at the swords that Seanchai had brought out of the water. "While it's not unheard of that the lake offers up gifts and visions, it's very rare. None of my past students have walked from the lake with something physical. You are different, very different. Are you strong enough to walk? There is something you need to see."

Seanchai nodded and rose unsteadily. As he followed Mhari, his muscles protested, each movement awkward and alien. They went downward, and Seanchai rubbed his arms as the temperature dropped rapidly.

"We will not stay long; I only need you to see something," Mhari said. "It is just around here."

They rounded a corner and Seanchai saw a towering black rock behind a sheet of ice. Mhari stopped and faced him.

"Seanchai. I want you to look into this ice sheet. It makes for a nice mirror. Be prepared for what you will see."

Seanchai creased his brow, not understanding what Mhari was getting at. But no warning could have prepared him for what he saw. He stared. He leaned forward and moved his hand to his hair and then his face.

His shoulder-length, mousey hair was now white. Not blond, but a clean white. He thought it might be a trick of the light, so he glanced at Mhari in the ice sheet. The old woman's reflection was accurate. Seanchai leaned forward and stared again–this time at his once brown eyes. They were now a bright, piercing blue.

The elf took a step back to look at the rest of his body. He removed his shirt to find muscles that were defined and taut. His arms looked impressive, his chest and stomach lean. Seanchai had seen elves like this, but their bodies were toned by years of hard training or physical labor.

He looked at his teacher in puzzlement. But Mhari had already turned to go back up to the lake. He followed, putting his shirt back on as he went. His prior discomfort had only partly been fatigue. He had felt like his body was not his own, and now he understood why.

Back in the cavern, Mhari made more tea. When it was ready, she poured two cups and signaled to Seanchai to join her on a ledge overlooking the lake. They sat with their backs supported, in a silence that was at once comfortable and heavy. After a few moments, Mhari turned to the young elf and smiled.

"What? No questions?"

"I don't know where to begin," said Seanchai, shaking his head, and he heard how small his own voice sounded.

THIRTY-FOUR

Shayth led his "slaves" unhindered into the city of Galbrieth. There was only one other checkpoint, and the guards seemed happy to let them through. They were so busy and had been told to watch out for elves. As he passed through the thick stone gateway, he looked up and marveled at the thickness of the great walls.

Shayth negotiated with ease, clearly familiar with the streets. He evaded the alleyways and shot furtive glances down their dark holes as he passed by. Nearer the center of the city, the bustle intensified and Shayth felt that they blended well into the crowd. But he also noticed many sixers of soldiers patrolling. Shayth had advised Ilana to keep her hood on and be assertive with the desert men. She pushed them to keep in line, though Shayth knew she derived no pleasure from it. There were very few elves wandering around and those he saw were scared and scampering from one place to the next.

They stopped at a small inn with an adjacent stable. Shayth directed the slaves into the stable and pretended to tie them to the wooden beams that separated the horses. After confirming they were alone, he whispered to the one who spoke his language.

"I'm sorry for treating you this way. We will bring you food soon, then you should try and sleep. We will come for you during the night."

The big Tutan just nodded. As Shayth left the stable he heard quiet clicking among them. Ilana would bring them food and then stay in the room. She was nervous enough in a human city, but seeing how elves were being treated had made it considerably more intimidating.

Shayth wandered the streets, noting that the town looked worse for wear since the last time he had seen it. Many shops were closed and boarded up. There were more alehouses, and when he poked his head into one, the rancid smell and noise repelled him.

He made his way to the graveyard at the eastern end of the city. Before he entered, he looked carefully around. There was no one in sight. Shayth moved silently through the rows to the oldest part where the stones were smooth, the inscriptions indistinguishable, and the weeds overgrown. Behind a large tomb, he removed a small, crumbling corner stone and pulled two bags of coins from behind it. He had such stashes scattered around this region of Odessiya, ready if he ever had a need. He did now, but he shook his head to himself. Using it to rescue an elf, a friend, at that, was not something he had anticipated when he had hidden the money. He pushed the stone back in and replaced the weeds as best he could.

He needed to buy information. He had been in the garrison before, but that was many years ago, and he didn't have a good picture of the layout anymore. He left the graveyard and made his way to the shadier part of town, continually checking that he was not being followed. Then he ducked into a dark alley and hugged the wall. A couple men staggered past, laughing wildly and holding each other up.

When he found the door he wanted, he knocked with two quick raps and then a third rap after two more seconds. A peephole opened and a bloodshot eye peered out.

"Who goes there?" the voice that came from behind the door was rough.

"A simple traveler," replied Shayth.

"What will you have with us?"

"A meal. Some Grampton mead if you have it."

He heard whispers inside. Shayth closed his eyes, hoping that the passwords had not changed. Then he heard the locks being scraped back and the door opened. He walked in, his hand on his hilt, though he knew there were unseen bows aimed at him.

A voice, deep and hoarse, came from the end of a long wooden table. "Oh look! What a guest we have. I'm surprised you're willing to show your face here, my young prince."

"I am no prince," Shayth snapped back.

Laughter came from the shadows. Shayth was furious with himself for reacting so easily.

"No, you're not," the man retorted. "Or at least, not any more. So you would do well to guard your tongue. If you are here, then you endanger us all. What is it you want?"

"I was once told of a tunnel that led into the garrison, possibly to the prison cells. Is this true?"

"Maybe."

"I need to know and I need to use it."

"You want to get into the dungeons? That's ironic. I'm sure the venerable General Tarlach would allow you to enter without problem, if you asked nicely. Probably don't even need your manners, come to think of it."

Laughter swept around the room, but this time Shayth bit his tongue. He knew he must keep his cool. "I also need to get out of there."

Again there was laughter, but now he smiled, trying to show that he was enjoying the banter. The man at the end of the table spoke.

"Who are you trying to rescue?"

"Does it matter?"

"I guess not. What is this information worth to you?"

"I have a little money to offer you." Shayth patted a bag of coins.

"I doubt it is enough," the man said. "How about you join me on a little business venture first?"

"I can't. I need to get this man out and home so that I can get paid. I owe a debt and I would rather pay it off with draktans than my blood. I will receive sixty draktans if I bring him back. I owe thirty-five and I am offering you twenty."

Again he rattled the bag.

The man leaned back and stroked his beard. "Anyone want to take him?"

"I will," said a young voice from the corner.

"Very well," said the leader. "Give me the money."

Shayth tossed the bag onto the table. The seated man did not touch it. A grunt opened the bag and counted it out. He nodded to his leader. The man turned to the one who had claimed the job.

"Rowan. How much do you still owe me?"

"Six draktans," the young man answered. "I will be happy to receive four and a clean slate with you."

"Very well. Go with the young prince, but know that he is trouble. Wherever he goes, blood is spilt." He turned back to Shayth. "It would be best if you didn't return here for further business."

Shayth turned to go without acknowledgement.

"The elf is alive," the leader said from the end of the table. "You're going through a lot of trouble for just an elf."

Shayth hesitated. So he had known all along why Shayth had come. This man was way ahead of anything that Shayth had anticipated. He gathered himself. You don't lie to someone like him, and Shayth was already disliked in this company.

"Yes," he said and turned slightly to look at the man. "But he's worth the trouble."

"Maybe. But I can't imagine the Shayth I know doing anything for anyone but himself. That is even harder to believe."

Shayth could not stop himself. "People change."

THIRTY-FIVE

Seanchai and Mhari remained in the cave for two more days. Seanchai's strength slowly returned until he felt better than he could ever recall feeling. On the third day, they packed up and followed the path out of the mountain. Seanchai wore both swords on his back, but had not drawn or tried to use them. He knew Mhari was worried that the lake had yielded this gift.

The climb out of the cave was hard for Mhari —not so much physically, as the waters had invigorated them both. Rather, she had to refrain from constantly looking back at her apprentice.

"You will trip if you keep glancing back here," Seanchai quipped. "I'm right behind you."

"I've had three other students go through the ritual," Mhari mused, "and I see my own changes each time I enter the lake. We have all been impacted in different ways, but none as drastically as you.

"The speed with which your powers are evolving is remarkable. Either you have an exceptional talent, or the ancient world knows you must prepare quickly. Either idea frightens me."

She turned around and started walking, but stopped again almost immediately and looked back over her shoulder. "I have told you that I won't be able to complete your training. Events are falling into place that won't allow us to spend much more time in each other's company."

"Mhari?"

"No, don't ask. Just listen." The old woman sounded forlorn. "It's this transformation that you've gone through. I am more convinced than ever that you will face great danger in the very near future. I must impart as much as I can in whatever time we have left together."

Mhari continued walking, leaving Seanchai to focus on his own thoughts. He walked slowly and felt a greater confidence in his body with each step. He barely noticed the rocks, stalagmites and stalactites that had so intrigued him on the way in. He would leave the mountain a different person than the one who had entered. He felt increasingly vibrant as he walked, and when he saw blue sky through a crack in the rock face ahead, he had to contain himself from running on. Seanchai was ready to introduce his new self to the world.

When they exited the tunnel, they stopped to eat while their eyes adjusted to the light. The sun was high in the sky and everything seemed to Seanchai to be so bright, so vivid.

Mhari had instructed him to remember the way back to the mountain and through the tunnels. "I should have liked to test you, to send you back inside alone. But there's no time for such luxuries. I intentionally followed the same trails out that we used to go in."

As they walked, Mhari tested her apprentice on every herb and plant she could find. She forced Seanchai to recall every detail about each one and snapped whenever his answer was not perfect. Seanchai was sure her relentlessness was mostly an attempt to curb her own growing tension.

She lectured Seanchai tirelessly on the art of stealth, of moving without leaving a trace, and made him practice until it became second nature to the young elf.

"You should be able to stand so still, be so at one with your surroundings, that even if a person looked right at you, they would not see you."

When they set up camp that night, Seanchai made a watery stew of roots they had collected as they walked. He listened as Mhari lectured him about eating nutritious food, keeping his body hydrated, and conserving his energy. After they finished their meal and had cleared it away, Seanchai prepared his bedroll. Mhari, however, had other ideas.

"The time has arrived for me to tell you the story, Seanchai. It will not be short, but it's what you've been waiting for."

Seanchai settled in opposite his teacher, positioning a small log to support his back and keep him sitting straight. Inside he felt jittery and full of anticipation. Mhari made herself comfortable and prepared her dwarf pipe. Once it was packed correctly, she lit it and slowly inhaled and exhaled, sending smoke floating into the night. After a few minutes she spoke.

"A long time ago, this land was settled by elves who came out of the Western Isles. It was a beautiful land, green and lush, with mighty trees and forests. The land was good to them and they thrived.

"In time, the elves opened themselves up to their neighbors in the Lakelands, called the Azuri. Their skin had an aqua-green hue, and they lived primarily along the waterways, comfortable in the water as on land. The elves fished and hunted, and were happy to trade meat for vegetables and fruits. They also made fine wines and cultivated plants whose leaves could be dried and smoked." She tapped her pipe. "I am particularly grateful for this.

"From the Midan Mountains came delegations of dwarves, perhaps the most ancient of races. They were stout, quick-tempered, and armed with axes and pikes, though they did not come to fight. The dwarves lived and worked in huge mines that went deep into the mountains and brought with them pieces of fine craftsmanship: armor inlaid with precious metals, ornate jewelry from gems and stones, and art carved from rocks.

"In return for the wares, they sought an alliance against the wild men from the north. Elves had not seen men before, and they were curious. They agreed to send soldiers to aid the dwarves. The elves were trained to fight and had magnificent horses, called Shieldhei, which is an ancient word meaning 'creatures of battle.'

"The battle was easily won. The dwarves stood at one end of the Plains of Penryn while the tribes of men massed and charged. After the men had crossed the river, confident in their sheer numbers, the cavalry charged out from the forest."

Mhari paused to sip her drink. "It was a rout until a great horn was blown. The surviving men and dwarves stood frozen while the elves surrounded them. The Elf-Lord Markwin spoke to them of the peace enjoyed in the Western Isles.

"He counseled them to make their own peace. They listened, and though it took the best part of a century, a peace held. They began trading food and supplies, then swapping stories, art, and culture.

"When the wild men were attacked from further north by the pictorians, the elves and dwarves allied with the humans. Again, once victory was assured, the Elf-Lord proposed peace."

Mhari stopped to puff her pipe. "And so began the period known as The Great Alliance. On the Plains of Penryn, where the first battle had taken place, a mighty city was built.

"It was not owned by any one race. The city was called Flywyn in the Elven tongue, Dur-Rhustan by the dwarves, and City of Many Colors in the tongue of man. A High Council of representatives from all the races ruled over the city and the alliance.

"Every race pledged to the defense of the city and it became a great center of wealth and intellect. An enormous library collected ancient texts from all corners of Odessiya and beyond. A school that studied and passed down the lore of all races to new generations flourished. There was a faculty of medicine, another of letters and, one of science. Great tomes were written on astrology, weather, agriculture, and culture."

Mhari stopped and glared at her student, who was yawning.

"I am totally listening," he said defensively as he sat up straighter.

Mhari frowned, puffed her pipe, and continued. "With the success of the school of lore began an experiment. Each race had its own magic. These disciplines were gathered and taught to select students.

"The magic of each culture fused with the others, as well as with the powerful earth magic. Those who mastered these arts and disciplines became known as the Wycaans, or wise ones. They helped to heal using herbs, energy, and good counsel. They were revered, and people told tales for generations of when one of the white-haired Wycaans visited their village.

"Some of these Wycaans learned the great stories of the ancient times and recounted them when they visited, teaching the people to live by an ethical code of conduct."

Mhari took a deep puff from her pipe, followed by a long exhalation, before she continued.

"These Wycaans became known as the *Seanchai*, the storytellers, and they would go on to change the course of history."

THIRTY-SIX

Ilana yawned as she trudged through the streets of Galbrieth deep in the night. The guide, Rowan, led Shayth, herself, and the three Tutan tribesmen through a maze of alleyways. He didn't stop to explain directions or engage in conversation. Shayth scrutinized his every move, and Ilana focused on remembering landmarks so that she might lead them out if they escaped.

Abruptly, Rowan stopped and turned to them. "This passage is known only to our organization," he said, his voice low. "People pay us to bring food and medicine to prisoners. It's all that keeps them alive. You must swear never to reveal it."

The Tutan who understood turned to the other two and clicked. They shrugged. Rowan stared at them in wonder and then at Shayth.

"Don't ask anything you don't need to know," Shayth snapped.

Ilana looked at her friend. His voice was cold and bitter, as it had been when they had first met. All of his armor was internal. When she had questioned the integrity of the man that Shayth had dealt with, he had growled back.

"There is a code between scum like us. Retribution is clear. Once we agreed on a price and I paid him, he became duty bound to help me."

"And the man who'll guide us? This Rowan?" she had asked.

"If he betrays us, then we have a right to his life—to both of theirs."

Assuming we *are still alive,* Ilana thought.

As they walked, Ilana began to recognize landmarks she had already seen and frowned. She touched Shayth's shoulder and made a circular motion with her hands before pointing to a balcony.

Shayth nodded and moved behind their guide. With one swift movement he had Rowan against a wall with a knife at his throat. "You're leading us in circles. Do you plan for us not to leave?"

The man shook his head frantically. "No, no. I'm being cautious in case someone's following. I swear. Here, I have a map ready for you."

He moved his hand slowly to a pocket in his jacket and held it up. Shayth nodded to Ilana who took the map and scanned it. She walked back to check street names and nodded at Shayth who glared back at the guide.

"When were you planning to give it to us?" Shayth snarled.

"When we reached the entrance to the dungeons. I swear it." Two beads of sweat dripped down Rowan's face.

Shayth lightened his grip and felt Rowan relax. Just as quickly, he tightened it again, and Rowan gasped. "Just so it's clear: If this goes wrong, I'll come after you. You won't know when. You won't know where. But I will come, and I will absolutely find you. Pray then that I choose to finish you with a solitary arrow and not torture you with more. I don't miss, so if you get an arrow anywhere but in the heart, know it's not an accident and that more will follow."

He let go and Rowan took a moment to compose himself before continuing. A few moments later, he led them into an old stable with a pungent, disgusting odor. After a furtive glance up and down the narrow street, he closed the door behind them.

He told Shayth to watch through the holes in the wood to see if they had been trailed, then signaled to one of the Tutan that he wanted to move a table and chairs and clear hay from underneath. The Tutan just nodded and turned to his friends with instructions.

"Maybe the little elf-girl should stay here out of the way?" Rowan addressed Shayth nodding at Ilana.

Ilana's fists bunched at her hips and her cheeks began to glow. Shayth grinned.

"Maybe you should let her show you how good she is in a fight?" Shayth suggested, and Ilana drew her blades as Shayth continued. "I've seen her take down several soldiers at once without breaking much of a sweat."

Rowan quickly raised his palms. "Okay, okay. Just a suggestion–a very, very bad suggestion." He quickly produced three unlit torches from a corner of the stable. "I will take you as far as the sewage drain under the dungeon. Then I will leave you. That is our agreement. The way is clear from that point."

Shayth nodded. "Draw out the route in the dust so that we can all visualize it on the way back."

"You're coming back this way?"

"No," Ilana retorted. "We thought to take on the whole garrison and then march out the front door."

Rowan stared at her and noticed her hands grasping the handles of her knives. He drew the route and noted different junctions and landmarks. Ilana asked questions and kept repeating what he had said. Then she recounted the whole route to him without fault.

"That's very good," said Rowan, nodding too vigorously.

Shayth rolled his eyes. "Let's go. We're wasting time."

They eased themselves down into the passage. The mud under their feet smelled like sewage. They lit the torches and followed Rowan.

Ilana tried to focus on remembering the route, but all she saw was dark, slimy stones, packed in with mud. With her knife, she notched the second cornerstone of each tunnel they entered. Shayth watched her, his expression suggesting he thought it was useless.

They heard muffled voices nearby and waited until they receded. The passage descended into much colder dank air. They stopped in front of a large metal cap built into the wall. Rowan handed his torch to Ilana and signaled to a Tutan for help. As they twisted, rust fell from the screw thread.

When it was off, Rowan whispered to Shayth. "I'll put the cap back but not screw it on. I'll return in a few days to tighten it if I don't see you again. If you come back out, make sure that you screw it on and hide any footprints on the other side."

Shayth nodded. They extinguished the torches, and all but Rowan slipped through the hole into a large stone tunnels. Wall torches lighted the passageway.

They moved silently, hugging the walls, until they reached a junction. They saw cells in one direction and an alcove in the other. Shayth slipped over to the cells, and there was harried whispering. He returned and pointed toward the alcove.

They approached the opening carefully. Shayth looked up, though he could not see ten feet beyond where the torches ended.

Two men were chained to the alcove wall. One was clearly dead and emaciated. The other was Rhoddan. He was stripped to his waist, his feet bare and his body covered with bruises and cuts. Dried blood clung to his cracked lips.

Shayth approached and put his hand quickly over his friend's mouth. He gently woke Rhoddan. It took several seconds before recognition spread across the wounded elf's face.

Rhoddan shook his head, and a solitary tear dripped down his cheek. An order was barked and a ring of torches lit above them. Ilana drew her long knife and felt Shayth assume a defensive crouch with his back to her. The two Tutans backed up into a square.

As Ilana's eyes adjusted to the torches, she saw above them a narrow ridge where a dozen archers stood poised, bows strung and taut. Their short-range weapons were useless.

Soldiers entered the alcove and surrounded them. One spoke. "I suggest you submit quietly. You are surrounded and outnumbered."

Shayth hissed under his breath, his head jerking from side to side, but Ilana put a hand on his arm. "There are archers above us," she said, forcing her voice to remain steady. Her weapons clattered eerily on the stone when she tossed them away.

The soldiers took no additional action. Reinforcements arrived, followed several minutes later by a tall, uniformed man in boots that clacked in staccato on the stone floor.

"Well, well," he gloated. "We didn't catch the prize the first time, but the elf proved to be good bait, after all. Now, which one of you is the so-called Special One?"

The officer stepped forward and swept back the captives' hoods, one by one. "Tutans," he said in surprised recognition. "I'm impressed."

The two Tutans stared back at him impassively. Ilana noted that the officer evidently knew who the Tutans were. He now turned to her.

"An elf! We're getting closer, I think. But alas, you are apparently female." He leered at Ilana's body and she pulled her cloak tighter, making him laugh.

Shayth's hood was last.

"General Tarlach," he drawled with as much disdain as he could muster. "What a pleasure."

The general frowned and stroked his chin. "Very familiar," he said, clearly intrigued. Shayth drew back his own hood, and General Tarlach's face lost its composure.

"Well, now," he said after a few moments. "We don't have the elf that the Emperor wants so much, but you make for a close second."

THIRTY-SEVEN

Mhari stretched. "That's enough for tonight. I'll continue tomorrow. We're both weary."

She lay down and was snoring almost immediately. Seanchai, however, couldn't sleep. Though he was tired, his mind raced. He rose and sat on a rock nearby to think. The moon had risen and was poking out from behind a cloud.

Seanchai's thoughts raced between what he had just learned about the past and how what he had become would impact the future. Somewhere in between was a lot of knowledge that he needed in order to connect the two.

There was so much to digest and so much to learn. He needed time and wasn't sure he would have enough with Mhari.

Time. How long had he been with the master? Seanchai realized that he had not kept track from when Ilana and Shayth had left. He grew uneasy. If they were in trouble, how would he even know? He shifted on his rock and sighed.

"What is worrying you?" Mhari's voice made him jump. She was standing just behind him.

"You're not sleeping?" Seanchai said.

"Neither are you. I, at least, can't be faulted for not trying. Why such long sighs?"

"I'm sorry if I woke you. I was wondering about my friends. I don't know how long it has been since they left. I don't know if any of them are even still alive. What if they are in trouble and I'm sitting around here studying?"

"What would they tell you to do?" his teacher asked.

Seanchai snorted. "Oh, that my life is more important, that they are willing to sacrifice themselves for me–stuff like that."

"Have they told you that in the past?"

"Yes."

"And did you listen to them then?"

"Generally not."

"So," Mhari asked as she smiled broadly. "Why listen to them now?"

Seanchai turned and faced the old woman. He had assumed she would agree with his friends and try to keep her student studying with her.

"What motivates you, Seanchai? When you acted in battle or when you cast a spell, what gave you the power? Was it a higher moral code? A philosophy? Was it a superior's orders?"

"No," Seanchai replied after a moment's consideration. "Whenever I did anything like that, my friends were in danger. I guess I was driven by friendship and loyalty."

"And these run deep within you. You should not fight them, for I suspect they are your strongest weapons. Just know that, even with such strong loyalty for friends, sometimes you will need to make difficult decisions that contradict everything you hold so dear.

"Tomorrow, we will rise early, walk faster, and camp earlier. Then I will finish the story. The day after that, we will stop near a small hamlet where I am known and trusted. I shall seek information. That night we will scry so you can try and see how your friends fare. Now, let's go to bed so that we can be fresh in the morning."

She returned to her bedroll. Seanchai followed and, as he settled in, he spoke again to his teacher.

"Thank you, Mhari."

"For what?"

"For understanding and accepting what is important to me."

"Hmm," said the old woman. "I do because we are very similar."

"You have had to make difficult choices?" Seanchai asked.

"Yes, too many times." Mhari was despondent. "And one hurts more than the others."

"What happened?"

"Look at me. I am alive, but I'm also very much alone." And she turned her back on her student.

"No," Seanchai replied. "You are not alone. Not anymore."

Seanchai woke to the enticing smell of food cooking and scrambled to his feet. His teacher had made danseng tea with grain.

"What have you added?" Seanchai asked as he sniffed the broth in his cup.

"Even the blandest of food can become special with the addition of a few spices," his teacher replied and pulled out a small bag. "This is cinnamon, a bark that warms us in the morning."

They ate quickly and Seanchai felt the tea, warm in his stomach. Once walking the descent was slower than Seanchai wanted with Mhari determining the pace. Since leaving the lake, Seanchai was ready to do everything faster than before.

At the bottom of the mountain, they followed a narrow river. Seanchai saw some bubbles emerge where the current was quelled and would have liked to catch some fresh fish, but there was no time. He used to enjoy fishing and wondered if he would ever have the time to fish again. It was something he had done with his father. That would surely never happen again. He felt terribly sad.

They rested at midday, snacking on stale bread and tough dried meat. Even river water couldn't save it.

"Will they have food at the hamlet?" Seanchai asked as a road come into view.

"Only a little to spare for us. Their food is sparse. They make some money as an inn, but not much. And anyway, I think you had better stay out of sight, or in the mountains."

"Why?"

"You have become very … distinguishable. Word will get around soon enough. I would prefer it be later rather than sooner. We should cherish any time left for you to remain anonymous."

They found a small cave secluded from the road. Mhari went on alone while Seanchai settled into his standing exercises. With those completed, he practiced summoning energy and tried to move nearby stones. He was still not very good at this. It required an iron temperament, and he still found it difficult to attain such focus.

Mhari returned in the evening with a sack that had Seanchai licking his lips in anticipation. As they prepared a feast of fried eggs, soft bread, and vegetables, Seanchai tried to quiz his teacher.

"Let me rest and eat, Seanchai. There was no news about you. It seems they have caught someone near Galbrieth. A trader passing through last night said that there were many guards out on patrol. The captive is someone important–a high-ranking rebel or criminal. This might work in our favor."

"Why?" Seanchai asked.

"It's a distraction for the army. They might lower their guard for a while and make it easier for Shayth and Ilana to rescue Rhoddan. I think this is good news."

They ate the rest of their meal in silence. Seanchai thought of his friends and the news Mhari had delivered. And he became increasingly despondent.

THIRTY-EIGHT

General Tarlach paced the length of his office. It was a sparse room with thick, bare walls, and a huge, imposing desk and chair. Anyone sitting on the opposite side was dwarfed by his presence. There was a smaller table where he met with his officers to look over maps and models.

General Tarlach had moved up through the ranks of the Emperor's army. He was not the son of a rich noble, nor had he caught the attention of the Emperor with some daring, random feat. He had earned his place with an astute tactical mind, an unfaltering obedience to orders, and a ruthlessness many feared.

He rarely spoke, never boasted, and had self-serving connections with anyone who could influence his advancement and the future of the Empire. He was respected, feared, and generally given a very wide berth. He never raised his voice, preferring instead the quiet fury of a man not to be trifled with by anyone—even his superiors.

He was pacing now because he was unable to make a decision—something he was very unused to. It had been ten days since they captured the boy and his elfe friend. Tarlach had sent messages to the capital for the eyes of the Emperor alone, requesting direction. Now that he had received the answer and read his orders twice, he was still not prepared.

General Tarlach had sent thousands of soldiers to their deaths. He had indirectly killed tens of thousands of enemy soldiers, razed villages to the ground, and murdered countless women and children. He was not squeamish.

But this was different. In another ten days, it would be the Emperor's fiftieth birthday, and the whole kingdom would celebrate. Tarlach's staff was preparing a huge feast for the nobles of all the neighboring provinces and another in the streets outside the garrison for the commoners. They had procured fireworks from the East and circus performers the likes of which most had never seen and never would again.

Now there would be an additional event. An hour before dusk, the boy and his elf friends would be hanged on a stage for all to see. To the ale-drunk, full-bellied peasants, as well as the nobles of the Galbrieth region, this would drive home an unforgettable point: The Emperor is benevolent to those who serve him. Now they would cheer as the enemies of the Emperor were publicly hung.

And Tarlach would ensure that everyone saw how the Emperor's own nephew, for so long the heir to the throne, received the same punishment for treason as anyone else in the kingdom.

General Tarlach summoned his secretary. A rotund middle-aged man shuffled in almost immediately. Tarlach turned to him from the window as he entered. "Mr. Bortand, what is happening with the preparations for the Emperor's birthday?"

Bortand nodded emphatically. There was nothing he enjoyed more than a complex set of instructions to implement such as these celebrations. He had an amazing propensity to remember even the smallest of details, and he was fiercely loyal to General Tarlach.

"Um, everything is going to plan, sir—um, right on schedule. The fireworks will arrive the day after tomorrow from our supplier."

"Very good. Please send him a crate of our finest ales in appreciation."

"With your permission, General Tarlach, I think he would prefer, um, wine. May I send him a crate from your cellar?"

"Of course," Tarlach waved a hand to indicate he was unconcerned with the subject. Bortand had probably already selected the vintage.

Bortand sensed his superior had something on his mind. "You have something else that needs to be added to the preparations?"

"Yes. It concerns the prisoners." Tarlach handed his secretary the scroll with the Emperor's orders.

Bortand read the order and frowned. "Um, my Lord, are we sure these orders are genuine?"

"It bears the Emperor's seal."

"With your permission, I will send an, um, trusted aid to verify in confidence. The Emperor's secretary and I are old friends. Just in case, sire. The Emperor trusts and values you as one of his closest confidants. There are many who would like, um, to loosen the ties between you."

"Very good," said the general. "In the meantime, however, make the necessary plans. Have the scribes prepare scrolls to hang on every notice board in every village throughout the land. "

"My Lord. By doing this, we will be alerting those who might be, um... *sympathetic* to the traitor. They might get ideas—"

General Tarlach nodded. "I believe that is intentional. Would you not otherwise expect the Emperor to send for his nephew to be executed in the capital? Doing it here may bring to light the special one that we are hearing rumors about."

"The Emperor is wise," Bortand said.

The general turned to him and frowned. "You don't have family, do you, Bortand?"

"Yes I do, sir. But they are scattered and I, um, serve only the Emperor."

Tarlach stared. Bortand was being serious.

"Very well," Tarlach said. "You know what must be done. Order my officers to a meeting in an hour. We must plan for every possibility."

"You don't believe in this special one, do you sir?"

"No. But I am expecting some kind of insurgency, maybe from the elves."

"The elves? But they are so weak and subservient."

General Tarlach turned and looked out the window. "Don't be deceived, Bortand. The elves were once the noblest of races. They were proud and wise. The same blood flows through these elves. The stories have been passed on, and the memories survive. Never underestimate an elf."

Bortand nodded. "And if he exists, this, um, special one might be an elf?"

Tarlach hesitated and this was more telling to his aide than any words. "Possibly just a charismatic young ideologue. But…"

The sentence was left unfinished and as the general stared out of his window, the secretary knew his master's mind was far away.

THIRTY-NINE

Mhari woke to the welcome aroma of food. Seanchai had been busy making porridge with the danseng root, and the old woman smiled at the extremely pungent scent of cinnamon. She had a feeling that she was about to eat a rather spicy breakfast, but she was pleased her student was trying.

She found Seanchai practicing his standing exercises. Mhari took a few meditative breaths herself before focusing on the periphery of her student. There was a strong light emanating from the young elf. He looked so different, with his white hair, deep blue eyes and chiseled upper body. He was definitely not the scrawny youth who had come to her only a few weeks ago.

Mhari helped herself to the hot breakfast and flinched, as she tasted the spicy cereal. When she was finished, she left the cave and found four branches. She peeled the bark away and cut each to the approximate length of a broadsword.

Upon her return to the cave, she found Seanchai concluding his exercises. The young elf stretched and yawned. Mhari served him a portion of the hot grain. He caught her watching him eat.

"A bit spicy," Seanchai admitted.

"A bit," his master responded and they both laughed. "Remember, Seanchai, that you can always add more of an ingredient to a dish, but it's very difficult to take out when there's too much. It is the same with plans and strategies. Move slowly and surely, a little bit at a time."

Seanchai nodded.

"But thank you for breakfast," Mhari said. "Come, we will begin a new practice."

"Are you not going to continue the story?"

"We will talk in a while. But first I want to begin teaching you the art of Bushido Dao. It is a form of martial fighting from a region in the east, one not far from where I was born. Bushido means warrior, and Dao means two swords. They live by a code, and students usually learn with curved swords with blades thin at the hilt and thick at the tip.

"The swords you have are Win Dao swords. They're very rare and we know them primarily from pictures. I have only seen one other warrior with such swords. He passed through my village a few times when I was young and put on exhibitions for money.

"I will teach you Bushido Dao, as this is what I know. You will need to adapt it for your swords. Perhaps your next teacher will be able to show you more, but the foundations for swords are the same, and for Dao swords, doubly so."

She laughed at her own pun, but Seanchai was too excited and focused to find much humor. "Oh, Seanchai! I can teach you many skills, but I'll never have enough time to teach you a sense of humor."

Mhari shrugged and stood. She picked up the four branches that she had prepared earlier and gave two to Seanchai. "Come stand behind me and follow what I do. Pay attention to the way my arms move, the way my feet move, and the shifts in my body weight."

What happened then was like a slow dance. Two swords and two arms became one. The body leaned in harmony with the feet. As Mhari drew one sword over her head, so did her student. When she thrust with one sword and parried with the other, so did Seanchai.

Mhari let him practice alone while she gently pointing out subtleties. "Do not lock your elbows. Lean with the legs but keep the upper torso straight. Bring your weight to the back foot. Anchor your right foot so that you can kick with the left."

They trained all day. Eventually, Seanchai stood in front of Mhari to lead, a juxtaposition of where they started that morning. She was impressed. Seanchai performed the form again and again with Mhari occasionally stopping him to correct his pose or footing. She did this less and less as the lesson progressed.

Finally, Mhari faced Seanchai, and they sparred very slowly. Seanchai was gradually able match his teacher.

Two hours later, they stopped. Seanchai looked like his arms might drop off. When Mhari asked him to fetch some water to cook with, he had to hold the full pot against his body to compensate for his exhausted muscles.

"I'm sorry," said Mhari as she watched him return. "I shouldn't have asked you to do that."

"It's my job to carry water for my teacher," Seanchai replied with reverence.

"I wish we had time for such civilities. Come, I want you to lie down and rest on your bedroll. We need to train again in the afternoon. I will make us food, but I want you to listen.

"The sword is an extension of the arm. The arm is an extension of the body. The body takes power from the legs pushing or kicking, from the hips that can flick even a pictorian over by harnessing the other's momentum. Even the arms take their power from the shoulders and hips."

Mhari bustled around the soup pot while continuing to talk about weapons and combat. Seanchai found it difficult to concentrate on what she was teaching him once the smell of food wafted over to him.

"If you rely solely on your own strength and power then you will tire quickly and be unable to sustain your form in battle. If you use only your own strength, then you'll lose to the stronger opponent. Does this make sense? I'll show you what I mean when we train again.

"Remember, the world is made up of opposing forces: one unyielding and brittle and the other supple and flexible. One male and the other female; one hard and the other soft. You must learn when to use each, and how to switch from one to another in an instant."

She checked the soup. "Come. Let us switch from the talking to the eating. I believe our lunch is ready."

They ate in silence. Mhari saw that Seanchai was still exhausted and suggested that he rest for a while. She woke him after two hours, and Seanchai insisted he was ready to train. They spent a couple of hours working back up to sparring, Seanchai settling quickly into a comfortable rhythm.

After a break for water, Mhari instructed Seanchai to charge at her. He was apprehensive at first, but complied when she insisted. The old woman threw him down using his own momentum against him. Next, he was to punch her in the face. This resulted in him squirming with pain from the arm Mhari had pinned behind his back.

She explained each scenario and how the move correlated to the form she had taught him. They swapped roles and, though Seanchai sometimes mistimed—or missed entirely—his teacher's attacks, he began to feel confident in the rudiments of the method. Seanchai told Mhari this with a proud grin on his face, and she responded by spinning round and kicking him in the stomach, sending him rolling along the ground.

"Practice the form, Seanchai," she corrected tersely. "When it becomes second nature to you, so will these moves. Until then, be ready for the unexpected. And know there is always someone better than you out there."

When he recovered, they resumed sparring. Mhari attacked

slowly at first, as she talked the young elf through the moves. But as time passed, she gradually stopped providing verbal instruction and sped up her attacks.

It wasn't clear to Mhari when her student's moves became fluent and independent. Seanchai was blocking his teacher with confidence and natural fluidity. They sparred faster and faster. He repelled her with an increasingly greater ease, and Mhari became incredulous as to just how good Seanchai was becoming so quickly. She soon found herself sparring as fast as she could.

The next time they stopped, it was Mhari who needed to rest. She looked at her student, who was trying not to burst with excitement.

"What is happening to you?" she asked in awe.

"I don't know," Seanchai replied, wonder in his voice. "It felt strange at first, but now it's like second nature."

Mhari stared at him, contemplating. She reached a decision. "Give me the sticks and go fetch your swords."

As Seanchai climbed the hill to where Mhari was waiting, he swung the swords around him in eerily perfect synchronicity. Mhari checked the swords. They were sheathed in thin leather training guards. "Leave these on when we train, though you must remember to remove the safety clips at all other times. Come, let us spar. We shall begin slowly."

They dueled without words, Mhari again increasing speed incrementally as Seanchai became comfortable. As the red fireball of sun set in the west, she called Seanchai to attack once more. They fought faster and faster in a graceful, lethal dance. One wooden sword snapped as the blows came faster. Then a second broke. Mhari picked up the other two sticks, but a third soon cracked and she threw it away. Seanchai stopped.

"What's the matter?" Mhari roared. "Do you yield?"

Seanchai laughed and then attacked. His blows hailed down on his teacher, and her single sword blurred as she parried. They stopped only when the sun set and there was not enough light to continue. They returned to the cave, dripping sweat and feeling exhilarated.

They stopped at the stream to wash. Once she had dowsed her face, Mhari opened her eyes to see the young elf silhouetted in the failing light, long white hair flowing in the breeze and eyes bright blue. He smiled and held his swords high, then turned to face her.

"Thank you, my master," he said and bowed low. "Thank you."

FORTY

Ilana woke and gasped. She thought something had crawled over her legs, but she couldn't find anything. She stood up, taking a moment to stop panting and, realizing there was nowhere she could go, returned to her pallet. She was in a straw-strewn cell by herself with a cot and a bucket. Every other day she was handed a broom and ordered to sweep the floor so more straw could be thrown in.

Though the human guards were rude and insulting, they never touched or physically intimidated her. But females around here, she was warned, knew their place. Ilana kept her head bowed and worked hard to keep her temper in check. She knew she was vulnerable as an elf, a female, and a rebel.

There were two other cells in her alcove. Both were empty. She should be relieved to have some privacy, but she felt very lonely. When the guards were not watching, she exercised to keep her body strong and fit. If the opportunity to escape presented itself, she wanted to be ready.

But she could only exercise for so long. Most of the time, Ilana lay on the cot staring at the stone ceiling. She wondered who Shayth really was. The general had recognized him immediately, and Shayth had almost seemed relieved to be caught, instead of afraid.

She wished she could talk to him. He was so complex and short-fused; she both admired and feared him. Very much like most human leaders she had known.

But Ilana's thoughts did not dwell on Shayth for long. She missed Seanchai. What was he doing? Was he safe? Had he learned enough to fulfill his destiny? And she could not help but wonder: did he ever think of her?

She hoped he was away on an important quest or somewhere far away to complete his training. Then maybe he would not hear that they had been captured. She knew he would drop everything to come after them and feared what might happen if he did. He was so innocent, so inexperienced.

But he was ferociously loyal to Rhoddan; he had already proven that on numerous occasions, and she recalled how he had charged the soldiers who had caught Rhoddan on the plain. That had been the first time she had met him. He had advocated for Shayth as soon as they had met, and she could see how Shayth was affected by his faith and friendship. Seanchai, she thought, possessed a unique quality for recognizing the potential in people and binding them to him. The problem was he also bound himself to *them*.

And what about her? She had immediately felt something for him that she had never felt for another elf. Her father had recognized this, and she was sure that was why he had allowed his only daughter to leave on such a dangerous mission.

Ilana's father had known true love. Since her mother had died, he had never even considered being with another elfe, though there were plenty interested in him. Her father was a bear of a leader, but when it came to matters of the heart, he was strangely fragile. Ilana smiled as she recalled how willing he always was to share how he and Ilana's mother had fallen in love the first time they met. She realized that her father had almost certainly recognized and understood his daughter's feelings toward Seanchai long before she herself had.

And Ilana wept. She had grieved before for friends when the army had killed them, but this was different. For the first time since dealing with her mother's death, Ilana cried for herself. Not because she feared death, or because of the way she was treated, or even because of her captivity. She cried because Seanchai had a part of her, and she might never see him again. She tried to keep her sobs quiet, but there was no other noise in the dark.

"Stay strong, Ilana," Shayth whispered from one of the cells outside the alcove.

She was embarrassed she had been heard. "I'm fine," she whispered back after a moment. "Are you and Rhoddan okay?"

"Yes," he replied.

"Shut up," a voice yelled, and something metallic was thrown at the bars of the mens' cell.

Silence. Darkness. Ilana sniffled a few times and then, thankfully, fell asleep.

It was daylight when Ilana woke to gruff voices and keys rattling. Her cell door opened and a human girl was tossed, sprawling, to the floor. When she stood up shakily, a blanket was thrown at her and she fell again, whimpering. The guards roared with laughter. Ilana rose to help her, but a guard stopped her in her tracks by banging his club against the bars. Ilana had never been hit by one, but she had seen men with swollen faces when she walked past the male prisoners to empty her slops bucket.

"Let her learn for herself, the trollop," the guard sneered.

The girl remained on the floor. She was a few years younger than Ilana. Her black hair was wild and unkempt, and she was shaking and moaning quietly. The guards quickly got bored, locked the cell, and left. When Ilana saw they were alone, she bent over and put her hand on the girl's shoulder.

"Come on," she soothed. "The cots aren't much more comfortable, but they are still better than the stone floor."

The girl let herself be guided to the straw pallet. She was much shorter than a lot of humans and definitely most elves, Ilana thought, as she picked the straw out of girl's thick, matted hair. The girl's eyes were closed and one side of her face was bruised and swollen. Ilana wanted to say something encouraging, but could not think of anything, so she instead hesitantly stroked the girl's hair while she cried silently on Ilana's shoulder.

A while later, the girl sat up. She whispered her gratitude as she straightened and looked at Ilana. She took in Ilana's pointed ears and jerked backwards.

"An elf!" she said, wrinkling her nose.

"What of it?" Ilana snapped. "I'm a prisoner just like you. I'm not sure there's much room here for status."

"I–I'm sorry. I've never been close to an elf like this." Then she waved her hand around the prison cell. "Well, I guess technically I've never been close to *anyone* like this." Her eyebrows rose and fell while she thought what to say next. "So...you're an elf?"

"We're not that different," said Ilana, forcing a smile. "In my village, we grew up together, humans and elves. I have friends who are humans, good friends."

The girl stared wide-eyed. "Really? Oh. I grew up hearing... things... about elves, and they were never really very, um..."

"Complimentary?"

"Yeah, you could say that," the girl ducked her head, embarrassed. "Still, what can you say about humans who treat anyone like this?"

Good point, Ilana thought, and asked, "Why have they arrested you?"

The girl shrugged. "We are poor. My mother is sick and my

father rarely has work. He has fallen behind on his taxes because he uses what little money we have for my mother's medicine."

"Why did they take you and not him?"

"They beat him, but if they put him in jail, then he can't earn money and they don't get their taxes. He loves me very much. I'm afraid that he and my mother might decide to stop buying her herbs in order to get me out, and then she might die."

The girl bent her head into her lap and began to sob again. Ilana reached out, but the girl flinched so she quickly withdrew her hand.

"No," the girl whispered. "I'm sorry. Please…" Ilana pulled her close.

FORTY-ONE

When Seanchai woke the next morning, he could barely lift his arms. Mhari must have noticed, for she fetched the water from the stream and left her student to rest in the sun. She insisted that Seanchai not help with breakfast, either. The tea strengthened the elf, and he ate two bowls of the grainy gruel that his teacher had prepared.

"It's sweeter than usual," Seanchai commented.

Mhari nodded. "I added some Drovas honey. Drovas are bees that live in the mountains near here, and their honey is particularly strong. You can dry it on a wound to protect from infection. I picked up a jar in the village. It'll help sustain our energy through so much physical work and long journeys."

After Mhari cleared away the meal, she moved over to her student. "Let me work on your body to try and stimulate some energy into those muscles. We must train again today." She poked at various places on Seanchai's arms, chest and back, searching for specific points in the cleft of a joint or between two bones. When she found one, Mhari pressed gently and held her fingers there. Each area she touched seemed to vibrate, and Seanchai felt waves of warm energy flood through his body.

Seanchai dozed until Mhari woke him to share some more tea. Seanchai flexed his muscles and told her that the soreness had subsided. "Thank you," the young elf said. "That's great. I'm ready to train."

"Good," Mhari nodded. "I wish I had time to teach you these techniques. Wherever you go, Seanchai, seek out healers and learn whatever you can. Seek to balance the violence by learning to save lives. Most Wycaans learn the healing arts.

"Remember, the body always seeks to heal itself, but sometimes, it needs a little help. Healers do not heal people. They merely help the person's body to heal itself. The energy that we draw from the earth flows through our bodies. When it flows too quickly, we say that there's too much or that it is too hot. When it is too slow or gets blocked, then we say there is not enough. This is the essence of healing."

Seanchai nodded. "So, when you press a point on my body like that, you are adjusting the flow of the energy?"

"Yes, exactly," Mhari beamed, thrilled Seanchai understood. "Do you remember me explaining in the cave about the energy lines that surround the earth?"

Seanchai nodded again, and the old woman continued. "Our bodies are similar. There are channels flowing through our bodies, and there are points of power along these channels. Those points are where we adjust the flow of energy."

"Can you feel the energy in someone else's body?"

"Yes," Mhari replied. "But it takes practice. Today, we'll do our standing exercises and then eat lunch. The morning has almost gone. After lunch we'll practice sparring again. Then I'll tell you more about the age of the Alliance and the Wycaans since we did not get to finish yesterday. This will give us a chance to rest. We will need our energy to scry tonight and try to find your friends."

"Thank you," Seanchai said, grateful and relieved.

As Seanchai assumed the first stance, Mhari reflected on how natural the interactions were between them. Students were often too impatient or arrogant. Only the best put their trust totally in their master without allowing ego to take over. Seanchai could have defeated her yesterday when they sparred, but he had not sought to dominate or embarrass his teacher and Mhari felt very proud of him. Her emotions were mixed: glad for the opportunity to train Seanchai, while also sad her time with him was fast coming to a close.

The afternoon passed quickly and they didn't rest until the sun began its descent and the land was cooling. When they both had steaming cups of tea in front of them, Mhari began to speak.

"When we last spoke, I told you of the Great Alliance, of the city Flywyn, and of the Wycaans. Centuries passed and the people and land flourished. The city was magnificent. It expanded to encompass several hills and its gold-capped domes could be seen from far away, glimmering on a sunny day.

"As time passed and men sought new adventures, they traveled beyond the borders of the Alliance. They discovered a rich land, far to the west. They mined there for gold and other precious metals and they shipped it back, earning great wealth. The men consolidated their riches, building castles and assembling armies, all of which they carefully hid from the Wycaans.

"But that wasn't all they hid. In this land already lived men, elves, and dwarves. These were simpler people, who had been cut off from the great progression of civilization elsewhere. They were not happy with the way their land was invaded and pillaged.

"The miners became even greedier, forcing the restless natives to work the mines and increase profit. It became a slave nation."

Mhari stopped and lit her pipe, smoke pluming above her head. "Over time, the High Council became aware, through taxation, of wealth coming into the land, though they did not know where it flowed from. As greed bred more greed, the cities of man resented their tithes more and more.

"The head of the High Council changed every five years and ensured equality among the people by mandating that the same race could not serve two terms in a row.

"When a human stepped down to be replaced by the dwarf, Thoran Hydrensson, many of the wealthy men refused to send tribute to Flywyn. At one rowdy electoral celebration, a man climbed onto a table and spoke loudly.

"He questioned the right of either elf or dwarf to rule over man. He boasted of his mining slaves —there were more than a thousand elves and dwarves, mainly dwarves as they were better miners, under his control.

"The mood shifted radically. At first, fists flew, and then blades were drawn. Most elves and dwarves around the city did not carry arms, and the overwhelming casualties were members of the local populace."

Mhari coughed and Seanchai quickly replenished their tea. She drank and drew on her pipe for a few moments, her eyes looking off into the distance.

"The High Council met for many days, sending scouts and then troops out to the Western lands. Anger crackled among the dwarves and elves, and the land quickly segregated.

"When the High Council at last decreed that all slavery was illegal and drafted a charter of rights for all races, there was open rebellion. Fights broke out between men and dwarves, men and elves, and even between men."

"Between men?" asked Seanchai.

The old woman sipped her tea. "Not all humans are greedy, Seanchai. Not all elves and dwarves are good. The world isn't so simple.

"Anyway, many of the rich men had amassed great armies in the West and trained their slaves to fight by pitting them against each other. It was horrific, a tragedy.

"Even as it all came to a climax on the Plains of Penryn, the High Council thought it could prevent bloodshed. The Wycaans dispersed, to talk with the leaders of all races, clans, and tribes. Many were scorned or even murdered, and the great battle began. The end result is what you see now. Man rules, elves are virtually a subclass, and the dwarves have disappeared under the mountains."

"What happened to the elves?" Seanchai asked. "I grew up hearing stories of countries far from here where elves live free."

"Indeed they do. Ironically, after man had mined all the gold, they abandoned the West and returned to Flywyn. The elves fled to the land man had left and, hidden by a great forest, began to thrive again. Also in the East, near my own land, there's a mighty range of ancient woods. It's said that dwarves reside in the mountains there and cultivate their own magic."

"You mentioned the Western elves," Seanchai said, feeling a wave of excitement. "But do they really exist, do you think?"

"Yes, I do. In fact, I know they do, though I am sworn to secrecy and only share this with you because—"

"Because what?"

Mhari sighed. "Because if all this fails and you still live, that is where you should flee to."

"If it fails, what will you do?"

"I won't live to see it all end in failure. I'm an old woman and my only concern is to help you as much as I can. It's what I have trained for all my life, and I will pay with my life if it helps you onward."

Seanchai looked at his teacher as she puffed her pipe and stared out across the plain. Though she had shared so much with him, she was holding something back now, something she would not share with him. He followed her gaze and fell into deep contemplation.

FORTY-TWO

Ilana woke early, again convinced something was crawling on her. She immediately rose and brushed herself off, but couldn't see anything. As she crouched awkwardly over the bucket in the corner to relieve herself before her cellmate woke, she noticed Shayth lying on the floor in the middle of the adjoining alcoves.

"Shayth," she whispered after finishing on the bucket. "Shayth."

She tried to stretch through the bars and touch him, but he was just out of reach. She bunched some straw together and threw it. It barely missed, and she cursed. She was thankful a few minutes later when he did stir. His face was swollen, his clothes torn, and he blinked a few times to focus.

"What happened?" she said.

"Oh," he rubbed his head. "A few of our cell mates didn't like sharing the cell with an elf. We had a…a *discussion* on the matter. Then the guards decided to add their opinion, which was considerably more emphatic."

"Is anything broken?"

"Doubt it," he didn't move to check. "They seem to want us in one piece—for now, at least."

"Where are the Tutans?"

"In a different cell, thank goodness. They would have killed them."

"Shayth. What happened to the third one? Only two got caught with us."

"I've been wondering too. Probably dead. Best we don't talk about him. There were only two, Ilana. Understand?"

She didn't get a chance to respond as two guards dragged Rhoddan into the alcove. Shayth pretended to be unconscious as they opened the cell door and tossed both limp bodies inside.

As one guard locked the door, the other sneered at Ilana. "You ain't gonna have no privacy now, she-elf."

The other guard looked over. "Elves don't need no privacy," he said. "Shame for the girl, though." He regarded her sleeping cellmate, then spoke to Ilana once more. "You don't say much, do you, little she-elf? Smart. Best way to stay alive."

Ilana retreated to the back of the cell and the guards lost interest. One of them made a derogatory comment about she-elves' hygiene, and their cruel laughter echoing through the stone corridor hurt all the same.

"I'm sorry," said the girl, who had woken. "They were brought up that way. Don't know any better. Me neither, I guess."

"There is not much difference between a bad elf and a bad man," Ilana snapped.

"Nor a good one, I guess," the girl replied.

Her tone mollified Ilana and she took a deep breath, sat heavily on her cot, and put her head in her hands.

"Why you all here?" the girl asked.

"Doesn't matter," Ilana mumbled.

"Sure it does," the girl said. "You listened to me last night. Now it's my turn."

She sat on the cot beside Ilana and put her arm around her. She impulsively touched Ilana's ear, causing the elfe to jerk away.

"I'm sorry. I've never touched an elf's ear. Suddenly wanted to. I'm sorry. I shouldn't have."

"It's okay. Guess it has the same feeling as a human's ear, no?"

"Let's check," the girl said, and smiled. After they had touched each other's ears and realized there was nothing interesting about it, the girl continued. "So, why are you in here?"

"We tried to rescue our friend, the elf over there." Ilana nodded at the prone Rhoddan.

"And you know the boy, too?"

"Shayth? Yes, he was helping us."

"Really?" This seemed very interesting to the young girl. She paused. "He was helping you rescue an elf? Is he your friend?"

"Yes. Listen. What's your name?"

"Maugwen. People usually just call me Gwen."

"Okay, Gwen, listen. Outside of Galbrieth there are many places where man and elf live and work together. That human has saved our lives a number of times and we have saved his. That's how it works when you escape the clutches of the Emperor."

"You're rebels?" Maugwen's eyes grew large, and she shrank against the wall.

"I'm not going to hurt you. We think of ourselves more as freedom fighters, but yes, we rebel against an evil empire, where the rich treat us all like slaves."

"And that elf there—is he your boyfriend? Is that why you tried to rescue him?"

"No, he is a dear friend, but not *the* friend."

Despite her fear of being with a rebel, the idea of a boyfriend seemed to intrigue Maugwen. She returned to sit beside Ilana, curiosity replacing the fear.

"Tell me about him, your boyfriend. Will he come to rescue you?"

"I hope not."

"Why? If he really loves you…"

"I don't want to put him in any danger," Ilana explained. "When you love someone, you don't want to see them harmed."

Maugwen absorbed this. "Does he know you came here to rescue the other elf?"

Ilana nodded.

"Then he will come," Maugwen said confidently. "And when he does, he can rescue me, too. That is, if you don't mind."

They both laughed. Then Ilana spoke. "I'm glad you're with me, Gwen, though I wish neither of us were in this predicament."

A guard appeared. "You girls used the bucket yet?"

"I haven't," said Maugwen quietly.

"Use it," he ordered. "We don't want to stink out the place." He turned and smashed his baton on the bars of Shayth and Rhoddan's cell. "And if either of you peek, I'll let you have it."

The guard returned a few minutes later and unlocked the cell. He beckoned to Maugwen. "Bring the bucket, girl, and don't spill it, or else."

Maugwen rose and picked up the bucket. She moved slowly and kept her head lowered. When they were gone, Shayth called softly to Ilana. "Careful what you say," he said. "I don't trust her."

"She's just a little girl," Ilana replied, "and so scared."

"Ilana, listen to me. I know the system." Shayth glanced to the entrance, where footsteps were returning. "Don't share anything you shouldn't." Then he melted back into the darkness of the cell.

When Maugwen returned, there was fear on her face.

"What is it?" Ilana asked.

"Guess your boyfriend isn't going to be rescuing you. Or if he plans to, he had better show up real quick."

"Why? What did you hear?"

"They asked if we had spoken. I said yes and that you were nice, and they told me that you and your friends will be dead soon. They plan to execute you on the Emperor's birthday and make a big show of it. It's being announced in all the towns and villages so that all will know what they do with rebels and traitors. Each town has to draw a big picture of the hanging and display it in the square for everyone to see."

Ilana put her head in her hands and began crying quietly. Maugwen watched her cellmate's shaking shoulders. She came over and put her arm around Ilana.

"I'm sorry," she said. "I shouldn't have told you. Maybe the Emperor will pardon you at the last minute 'cause it's his birthday." She was silent for a few minutes while Ilana sobbed. "I'm sorry I made you sad telling you that you'll die soon. Now I've scared you, and you've been so nice to me."

Ilana shook her head. "I'm not afraid to die. It's not that."

"Then what?"

"It's the posters," Ilana sniffed. "He'll see them and he'll come. I know he will."

FORTY-THREE

Seanchai played with his food as they ate their evening meal by the fire. It was clear that this period of his life was fast coming to an end, and that Mhari would not be around much longer. Seanchai had become accustomed to having her with him when he did not know what to do. Even though he possessed the power and strength, he needed her knowledge and wisdom to guide him.

When everything was cleared away, they settled near the fire, preparing to scry First, Mhari wanted Seanchai to drink more danseng tea and plenty of water.

"Remember," his teacher said, "so far every time you have yielded magic or scryed, you have fainted or felt weak. While practice and energy-gathering exercises are critical, drinking lots of water will quicken your recovery. Generally eat and drink carefully, keeping your body clean so the energy can flow unimpeded. Maintain a diet of fish or light meat, and eat primarily grains, fruit and vegetables. Beware alcohol and anything else that can weaken or compromise you."

Seanchai felt again that Mhari was passing on as much as possible in the short time left together. They settled near the fire where they had earlier planted rocks that would support their backs while meditating.

"Remember the map I showed you earlier?" Mhari asked.

Seanchai nodded. It had outlined the routes to Galbrieth, similar to the map she had drawn for Shayth and Ilana.

"I want you to visualize that map when we scry to find your friends. I am going to lead you to them, but as soon as you see them, or their trail, tell me to disconnect. Is that clear?"

"Yes," Seanchai replied.

"Then let us begin."

They sat in silence, emptying their minds and relaxing their bodies. Seanchai had become increasingly proficient with these exercises and, despite the tension he felt to find his friends, his body instinctively knew what needed to be done.

Mhari began to speak in a low monotone. "We are leaving this place, entering the valley below, and following the road that cuts through the valley. See the beginning of villages and agricultural land. See the bridge at the village of Cositos and the junction that directs you left or right. We will travel to the right."

As Mhari described their journey, Seanchai felt like a bird gliding above the terrain, without physically needing to propel himself forward.

The towers of Galbrieth appeared on the horizon and became taller and more ominous as they neared the city. Great stone walls surrounded the city, and several caravan of wagons laden with supplies were traveling along a human river into the city. Galbrieth was preparing to celebrate.

Seanchai and Mhari glided above the checkpoints and city gates. Ilana and Shayth had evidently not prevented Rhoddan from being taken into the garrison. He felt he could sense Ilana and Shayth's trail.

Seanchai felt compelled to choose his own direction now and heard his real self tell Mhari that he was going on alone. Mhari's voice echoed in his head. "Be careful, Seanchai. I will be close by, gathering my own information. Call to me when you are finished and listen for my voice in return."

Seanchai floated into a dark alley and entered a room through a closed door. It was dark, but he could make out a table and men standing in shadows.

The man sitting at the head of the table was talking to Seanchai. No ... not him. He was seeing through Shayth's eyes. Shayth was negotiating and a bag of coins was handed over.

A moment of static, and then he was in an alleyway, following a hooded man. Next to him was Ilana. Ilana! He reached out for her, but there was no contact, no recognition. He felt sad as he realized that he was not really with them.

Three others accompanied them. Seanchai didn't understand when they clicked to each other instead of using words. Was it a code?

They entered a dilapidated house and slipped through a hole in the floor. They crept through stone corridors and found Rhoddan chained to the wall. Now they were surrounded. A tall, authoritative man—an officer—stepped forward into the light. He pulled back the hoods of the two clicking men and then Ilana. Seanchai shuddered when the man leered at her body.

Shayth pulled back his own hood. He saw the shocked expression on the officer's chiseled face. It was clear that the man recognized Shayth.

From a long way off, he heard his master calling him. "Seanchai, Seanchai, leave the garrison. Come into the streets. You need to look at the posters hung all around."

Seanchai rose out of the garrison and found himself in the street. He looked around and saw on every third pole, there hung a notice. It announced the Emperor's fiftieth birthday. There would be a great celebration, and the people would feel the benevolence of their ruler.

Further down, Seanchai read about the execution of the Emperor's nephew and his elf companions, and Tutans, also traitors to the Emperor. There would be a great display in the evening following the executions. The Emperor had ordered something special to happen in every city shortly after sunset.

...following the executions!

A shiver went through him.

...the execution of the Emperor's nephew and elves, all traitors to the Emperor.

"Seanchai, hold fast; control your emotions." The voice was distant but demanding. "I am going to guide you home. You must follow me."

Seanchai felt himself connecting once again with Mhari and being led beyond the mighty walls of Galbrieth into the valley. He wanted to pull free and go back. He needed to know more.

"Let me go," he called out, frustrated.

"No," came the reply. "You must return to your body."

"My friends…"

"I know."

"I must go to them. They need me."

"Yes, but not this way. There is still time."

"I might be too late."

"No there is time. Return to your body. We must make a plan."

"ILANAAAAAAA."

FORTY-FOUR

When Ilana woke from yet another hapless, shallow sleep, she caught Maugwen staring at Rhoddan, who was exercising in his cell. Ilana remembered Shayth's warning as she observed the girl, who didn't look quite so young as she had before. She was probably closer to their age. She had arched her hips a bit, though Ilana wasn't sure if this was intentional, and was chewing on a piece of straw.

Ilana sat up and stretched. Maugwen heard her and turned around. "How are you feeling?" she asked.

"I'm okay," Ilana replied, wincing at the stiffness in her lower back.

Maugwen came to sit next to Ilana and whispered, "Tell me about him," she nodded towards Rhoddan. "He looks kind of cute."

Ilana laughed. "He's sweet," she replied. "He is a brave warrior, though he is convinced he should be better and is always training."

"Brave?"

"Oh, yes. He has pulled us out of a few tight situations. He is driven by the strict moral code of a warrior. I think it makes him a bit wooden sometimes, but when he is not thinking like that, he can be funny and quite creative."

She was about to compliment Rhoddan's acting abilities, but stopped short, thinking of Shayth's warning.

"That's cool," Maugwen said. "Tell me. You said that elves and humans live and work together. Do they also sometimes, you know, become couples?"

Ilana thought for a while. "I don't know any, but I have seen a few when we have joined with other groups."

"I guess they can ... you know?"

Ilana stared at her for a moment before understanding. "Make love?"

Maugwen giggled. "Shush! Actually I was thinking about babies and family."

Ilana laughed. She realized it had been a very long time since she had spent time with other females her age. She was the only young elfe in Uncle's group. The others were older by eight or ten years. There had been a dark-skinned elfe in a neighboring group that had been her friend. She wondered what was happening with Sellia.

"Does he have any magical powers?" Maugwen asked, and Ilana abruptly tensed.

"What do you mean?"

"I've heard the guards talk about an elf they're chasing. They're scared of him. He has some kind of power. I thought that maybe Rhoddan could be this special one."

Ilana thought for a few moments before answering. "Sounds like wild rumors. A magical elf? Really?" She laughed flippantly, but saw Gwen wasn't smiling. "Look, even if there really was a magical elf—and I doubt there is—and even if it was Rhoddan, and it wasn't being kept a secret, and I really did know," she hesitated, "then I still wouldn't tell you."

"Oh," Maugwen pouted. "You could trust me. I hate General Tarlach after what he did to my father and me."

"It's not that," said Ilana, now with more confidence. "If I told you a secret and the guards asked you, they could probably sense if you were lying. You would be tortured."

The girl's eyes widened at the prospect. "I wouldn't tell them anything," she said unconvincingly.

"You wouldn't be able to stop yourself, and it wouldn't be your fault."

Maugwen nodded and then sighed. Her cheeks puffed with air, and she exhaled. "You're right. Thank you. But I still want to think he is the special one."

Ilana smiled. "He *is* special. Each one of us is. You are special, too, Maugwen."

Maugwen snorted. "Me! I doubt it."

"Of course you are. Perhaps you just haven't figured out how yet. That's okay. You're still young. Or maybe you haven't been around people who appreciate you."

"Do you really think so?" Maugwen's eyes widened. "Thank you, Ilana. That's the nicest thing anyone has ever said to me."

She looked over at the other cell. Rhoddan had finished exercising and was talking with Shayth very quietly.

"That one is quite a mystery, too, from what I've heard."

"Shayth?" Ilana asked, suddenly interested. "What about him?"

"He's the Emperor's nephew and has been really bad. Apparently he thought he was going to inherit the throne until one of the Emperor's wives bore an heir. Then he went off killing innocent people and—"

She stopped abruptly. Shayth was squeezing the cell bars, his knuckles white, and glaring at her. His dark eyes scared even Ilana. She felt a chilling tension fill the alcove of cells.

"Do you believe every worthless piece of gossip you hear?" Shayth snarled.

Maugwen wilted and sidled closer to Ilana. She didn't say anything and Ilana wasn't sure what to do.

"Steady, Shayth," Rhoddan murmured. "She's just a kid."

"Yeah, but even kids spread lies," Shayth rounded on the elf, his voice still icy. "And lies can become as powerful as the truth when they're repeated enough times."

Rhoddan was lost for words, but Ilana stood up and came to the front of her cell. When she spoke, her voice was quiet.

"Shayth. We have never insisted that you tell us what you've been through, and we won't now." She felt herself using considerable effort to keep her tone steady. "But it is difficult learning to trust you when we don't know anything."

"How much do you know of Rhoddan here?" Shayth snapped. "You only met him a few weeks ago, and he isn't being forced to stand before an inquisition."

"Okay," she replied, forcing a smile. "We can drop it. And for the record, Shayth, I *do* trust you. And I also believe that people can change who they are if they really want to."

"Maybe I don't want to."

"I think you do. I think that is why you are with Sean—with us. I believe we have come into your life to help you make that change."

There was silence from Shayth's cell—a brooding, ominous silence—and Ilana felt sorry for Rhoddan being stuck in there with him.

"Ilana?" It was Shayth, but his voice had lost its edge.

"Yeah, Shayth?"

"It's true, what she said, more or less. There is more to it, but it still doesn't paint a pretty picture."

"Okay."

"Do you believe what you said, Ilana? About people being able to change?"

"I do, Shayth. I really do."

"Good," he said. "I want to believe that you're right."

FORTY-FIVE

M hari was adamant that whatever conversation Seanchai wanted to have that night would have to wait. They were both exhausted, and she insisted they drink some resuscitating danseng tea and go straight to sleep.

"We must plan this carefully," Mhari said, the tone of her voice firm. "Right now you lack the strength and clarity to talk this through rationally. Is your head hurting?"

"No," Seanchai replied. "I can—"

Mhari shook her head. "We are both tired. Drink up."

As soon as they had finished their tea, they both fell straight to sleep.

When Mhari woke the next morning, it was already daylight. She heard her student's heavy breathing. Seanchai usually started the day with his standing exercises, but today he had both swords out and was exerting himself using movements that Mhari had not taught him. His form was tense and slightly erratic, and he glistened with sweat in the crisp morning light.

Mhari sighed to herself as she rose and went to start a fire. This conversation would not be easy, and the old woman was not sure she would be able to persuade Seanchai not to charge off to Galbrieth. She glanced his way again. The young elf was furiously fighting his invisible opponent and needed to get it out of his system. Breakfast could wait.

The sun was considerably higher in the sky when Seanchai finally stopped for a drink. He took great gulps of water before picking up his shirt to mop the sweat off his face and body.

Mhari offered him a bowl of the thick oat gruel they ate each morning. Seanchai nodded his thanks and sat, waiting to start the conversation. Instead, after they finished eating, Mhari stood. "I need to think about our next steps. I want you to do your standing exercises." She turned and walked off.

Seanchai glared at his teacher's departing back, impatient to take action. He realized he had no choice but to wait, and did as he was told. As his stomach filled with warm waves of energy, he felt the tension drain from his muscles. He sighed and fully embraced the energy. When he finally opened his eyes, Mhari was sitting in front of him.

"I only wanted a short walk," she smiled. "You've been standing for two hours."

"Wow, I had no idea," Seanchai replied, then stretched, his body, which vigorously emphatically confirmed the long time spent in the poses.

They sat down and drank water. Mhari spoke. "We scryed together, but I'm not sure we saw the same things. It's important to correlate even insignificant details and not assume that our experiences were the same. Understand?"

Seanchai nodded.

"I will begin," said Mhari. "Interrupt me if I miss anything. Your friends are prisoners in the garrison. Ilana is there, and the boy, and they are now together with the elf, who we can assume is also alive. Am I correct so far?"

Seanchai nodded. "Yes. Rhoddan is alive."

"Did you see Ilana and Shayth enter Galbrieth?"

"Yes."

"Were they alone?"

"No. There were three others with them."

"Did you see Shayth negotiate with someone for a guide into the garrison?"

"Yes," said Seanchai. "But I couldn't make out much in the dark."

"Did you follow them into the garrison?"

"Yes."

"How many were caught? This might be important."

Seanchai thought for a moment. "I'm not sure. There was the guide, Shayth, Ilana, and two others. There was something strange about them. They didn't talk, but clicked to each other."

"Two? And they clicked as a means of communication? Are you sure?"

Seanchai thought for a moment. "Yes. I saw when the officer pulled back the hoods. There were definitely four including Ilana and Shayth. The guide had left them."

Mhari nodded. "So we know your friends are together. We're not sure whether the general thinks Rhoddan is you, but we should assume that by now they know he isn't. What else?"

"The Emperor plans to have them executed on his birthday as an example to everyone." Seanchai said. This was really what he wanted to discuss.

"Is there anyone else with them in the cells?"

"I don't know," Seanchai snapped. "Is it important?"

"Possibly. I felt a presence; a power I didn't recognize."

"Well, we're going there, right?" Seanchai's voice rose. "They could be executed any day."

"Not any day. Remember, the execution is planned as part of the

Emperor's birthday celebration. We read it on the notices that were posted."

"But if the general knows I'm not one of the prisoners, why wait to kill them?" Seanchai was becoming increasingly agitated and took a deep breath.

"The Emperor wants to make an example of them," Mhari replied. "He must have given specific orders. You saw the posters. Anyway, there's still a big piece you are not aware of."

"What is that?"

"What do you know of your friend Shayth?"

Seanchai shook his head. "You asked me this once. I told you I don't know much. He's very closed about his past."

"But you said you would vouch for him, right?"

"Yes, but that was...I guess that was instinct. Why?"

"Instinct can go a long way, so allow me not to reveal what he hasn't told you yet. Just trust me that Tarlach will keep the company alive, and that he'll follow the Emperor's orders exactly. If that means keeping the prisoners alive and unharmed until the Emperor's birthday, then that is what will happen."

Mhari took a moment to eat some of her meal before continuing. "Now, this is what I suggest we do. You will go back to our base camp in the morning and pack everything up. Hide what you cannot carry in the back of the cave where I sleep. Leave no evidence that anyone was ever there. Perhaps one of us can return some day.

"There is a bag of herbs there, including danseng root. Take it all with you. I will keep the danseng that we have here. There's also a small bag of money stowed away there. It's not much, but use it to pay for information, as you need it.

"There is a book with the herbs." Mhari leaned forward and spoke fervently. "Listen, Seanchai: this book is very, very important. It is something for you to keep, to treasure. You must look after the book. When you read it, you will hopefully understand. Read and reread. Memorize every word. Do you understand?"

"Yes," Seanchai replied, "but—"

"No, no buts." Mhari's voice had risen and she took a moment to compose herself. "Sometimes things are not what they seem. Listen to me. Whatever you might think of it, memorize every word in the book."

"I understand," Seanchai replied. "You are my teacher and I will follow your instructions."

"Thank you," she whispered and took a moment to eat some more of her meal.

"Now, stay at the camp for two days. After the full moon, take Snowmane and ride to Galbrieth. Keep your hood up at all times. Remember, you are physically very distinctive. People will remember and talk about you, and we'll lose any element of surprise. Take your time. You shouldn't enter the city until a week has passed. It will be two days before the celebration, and the place will be swarming with people. Lose yourself in the crowd.

"Go to a hostel called The Galbrieth Arms and ask for Jalkieth. When you mention my name to him, he will deny that he knows me. You must let him see your hair and eyes, but *no one* else can see you do this. Tell him you have something under your hood to show him. He will know what to do. He'll take care of you and your horse. And *always* leave the inn with your hood up, or you'll endanger a rare friend. Understand?"

"Yes, but—"

"No *buts,*" Mhari's voice became firm. "Wait for me as long as you can. In the meantime, scout out the main square and its surroundings. Do not go near the garrison or the jail. Formulate a plan to break them out in case I do not come. Be ready to change it on a moment's notice."

"Where will you be?" Seanchai asked.

"I'm going to look up some old friends."

"Do we have any?"

"Let's hope so," Mhari grimaced. "What you saw through your scrying gave me a glimmer of hope."

"Which part?" Seanchai frowned.

"You referred to the two men who were caught with Ilana and Shayth. They clicked as a means of communication."

"Yes. Who are they?"

"I'd rather not say for now, as they are in hiding. General Tarlach tried to wipe them out some years ago when they refused to submit to the authority of the Emperor."

"Who is this General Tarlach you keep mentioning?"

"He's the officer in charge of the garrison. He has a sordid, violent history, especially with these people."

"Do you know how to find them?"

"Maybe."

"It's a bit of a wild card, don't you think?"

"More than you can imagine," Mhari said, her voice grim. "But you told me that Ilana and Shayth were with three others when they entered the city. When they went underground and got caught, there were only two of them."

"So? How might that help us?"

"I hope one escaped," the old woman said. "But only after he saw the man who massacred so many of his people. Even if he missed who the general is, I will be sure to let them know."

"That sounds hopeful," Seanchai said.

"Not really, my dear pupil. You may very well find yourself alone, in a crowded city, with no time and very few options."

"Then what should I do?"

"Grab your friends and bring the mighty stone walls of Galbrieth crashing down. Then run like hell and don't stop running."

FORTY-SIX

General Tarlach stood on the thick, gray wall of the garrison at Galbrieth looking at the main square below him. The chilly wind ruffled his cloak, but he stood straight, oblivious to the elements. He held his hands loosely behind his back absorbing every detail of the bustling activity below.

There, workers were erecting huge circus tents, building a stage, and assembling a sheltered area with seating for the traveling nobles and the ambassadors sent from the Emperor's court.

Tarlach reflected on his position. He had been part of the army that had conquered Galbrieth twenty years ago. For many years the army had remained on alert to the threat of rebellion. This was why the garrison was so large, so formidable—to keep anyone and everyone out.

Though most of the rulers from those days had now passed on, there was always a potential threat of usurpers. Hosting the land's nobility at the Emperor's celebrations, and showing them considerable honor, would help woo the younger generation of influential wealth to become allies. The execution would also ensure they understood what would happen to them if they didn't *act* as trusted associates. They would, after all, have front-row seats for the hanging of Shayth and the elves.

Earlier that day, the young man that Bortand had sent to the capital to verify the orders had returned. He had appeared nervous before the general and Tarlach soon understood why. He was supposed to verify the orders to execute Shayth were legitimate with the Emperor's aides, but that had not happened.

"My lord," the messenger said, shuffling his feet. "I was brought before the Emperor. He commended your decision to verify such a sensitive issue, but also wanted to…"

The man swallowed hard and Tarlach grew impatient. "What did he say, man? Don't be afraid. You're the messenger, nothing more."

The man glanced at Bortand and then up at his general. "He said to tell you to be on your guard, sir. And to expect the unexpected."

This perturbed Tarlach and he was unable to put it from his mind. That the Emperor was uneasy was understandable. He was making a grandiose display of authority and Shayth was still family, despite all that he had done.

But *expect the unexpected*. What did he mean by that?

A soldier patrolled the walls to his left, making an obvious effort to show how thoroughly he was searching for the enemy while on duty. No doubt he usually rushed past this exposed area before finding shelter further along the wall, Tarlach thought. Now he was certainly not thrilled at the prospect of the general watching him. It was about to get worse for the sentry.

"Come here, man," Tarlach commanded.

"Yes, sir. What can I do for you, sir?" The soldier snapped to attention.

"Look down at the square. Do you know what those areas of construction are?"

"Yes, sir, General Tarlach. The stage, the pavilion, and the stand for the special guests, sir."

"Good man. Are you aware that we are planning an execution on the stage?"

"Yes, sir. The traitor and some elf scum, sir."

"Now look around and imagine that you wanted to save them. What would you do? How would you go about it?"

"Sir?"

"How would you attack the celebration and rescue your friends?"

"I wouldn't, sir. I'm loyal to the Emperor and I've served under your command for five years, sir."

The general sighed. A good soldier required discipline, fitness, and a single-track mind. Creative thinking was not part of the job description.

"Just try to imagine yourself in the shoes of the rebels. What would you do?"

The man stared around and creased his brow in concentration. "Sir. I wouldn't try here. I'd try to break into the garrison. Like they did before."

"Yes, so would I," Tarlach replied. "But we found their passage and sealed it. We haven't found any more. What else?"

"Hmm. How many of them are there this time, sir?"

"What?" The general looked at the soldier.

"Well, sir," the soldier gulped. "Are we talking about a small party like last time or a full assault?"

"That's a very good question." The general stroked his beard. "Good work, man. Now go find Bortand, my assistant, for me."

It was ten minutes before the portly Bortand came wheezing up to the general. Tarlach suppressed a smile when he saw that his assistant was winded from climbing the stairs to the battlements and needed a minute to compose himself.

"Any problems, Mr. Bortand?"

"No...sir...right...as...rain," He was panting from exertion and bent over with his meaty hands on his knees.

"You are doing a disservice to yourself if you fail to keep fit. What would you do if you ever needed to defend yourself?"

"Me...sir...I would...bury my enemies...under a pile of memos, sir."

General Tarlach chortled. "Excellent, Bortand. They would have no chance."

Bortand straightened up and took a deep breath. Though his chubby face was red, his breathing was under control. "Aaah. Now, sir, what, um, what can I do for you?"

General Tarlach pointed below. "What do you think the Emperor was telling us when he mentioned to expect the unexpected?"

Bortand considered this for a moment before replying. "He knows or fears something that he cannot communicate to you through, um, normal channels. Something secret."

"The rumors about this special one. Is that it?" Tarlach asked.

"I think it might be, my general. But how would he know something that is happening here when, um, we haven't heard anything, ourselves? Doesn't he get all his, um, information from us?"

The general nodded. "What if it's not information? What if it's a...a prophecy, or something?"

"You think a prophecy would spook the, um, Emperor? He doesn't seem the type to be, um, superstitious."

"No," said the general. "Then what are we missing?"

They stood in silence for a long time, Bortand fidgeting, doing his best to keep warm, and Tarlach ramrod straight and impervious to the cold.

"What are we missing?" General Tarlach mused.

The gathering dusk offered no reply.

FORTY-SEVEN

That evening, Mhari watched her student eat in heavy silence, Seanchai was clearly apprehensive at the prospect of reentering the world, finding his way to Galbrieth, and dealing with more humans than he had ever seen. She thought how, since leaving his parents, the young elf had always leaned on Ilana, Rhoddan and Shayth, or now herself.

Seanchai had said earlier how he had assumed they would go out, two Wycaans together. But instead, he would be alone with the momentous task of rescuing his friends from a heavily guarded fortress. However intimidating his exterior, Mhari knew that inside, Seanchai remained a young, inexperienced elf. And she knew he was aware of this as well.

Mhari sighed inwardly. There was still so much she wanted to teach Seanchai, and the idea that she would not be there to counsel him through his first steps as a Wycaan worried and frustrated her. Her student had no idea how limitless his power was, and if Mhari could not bring reinforcements to Galbrieth, then Seanchai was going to learn a very hard lesson very quickly.

Mhari was not confident that she would find the Tutans. The desert was enormous, and even if she found them, she didn't know if she could persuade them to join her and fight. Last time she had fought with them against the Emperor, Targs, the leader then, had blamed her for not engaging and killing Tarlach. Mhari had counseled them not to fight and then led their escape when everything had gone wrong, saving many lives in the process. But for Targs, this had not been enough. Hundreds of his people were massacred and later, their villages and land destroyed. He wanted Tarlach dead.

They finished their meal, and Mhari had Seanchai recite back their plan. In the morning they would make an early start.

They sat down together on the hill looking out at a sky full of stars and a half-hidden moon, where Mhari imparted her final words of wisdom. "Don't get impatient, Seanchai. Think through every scenario before you make a move. You will prevent many innocent deaths that way." The old woman cleared her throat. "I also want to discuss what you will do after Galbrieth."

"Will we not continue studying together?" Seanchai's voice betrayed his alarm.

"Maybe. But I don't believe it'll happen. You know your training here has been far from complete. There are also things you must learn from the elves—things I cannot teach you. Each Wycaan wields power specific to his or her race.

"We spoke before of the Elves of the West and the great forest of Markwin. That is where you need to seek out your next teacher."

"But what about the Emperor?"

"You are nowhere near the level you need to be to fight the Emperor. And, even when you reach your zenith, you will not be able to complete the task alone."

Seanchai frowned. "Then how will we do this? How can we defeat him?"

Mhari sighed. "Remember how an elf formed the Great Alliance that stood for a hundreds of years?"

Seanchai nodded.

"There is no army of Wycaans. You must forge a great alliance among elves, dwarves and men."

"How?" Seanchai whispered.

She put a hand on the elf's shoulders and said in a quiet voice. "I have known you for only a short time, Seanchai. But I am convinced that it will be your compassion, your ability to make friends–not your skill in battle–that will tip the scales of history."

Neither Seanchai nor Mhari slept well that night, and they rose with the first hues of dawn. The young elf saddled Snowmane and tied his bags carefully. When Mhari was ready to go, he hugged her tightly. "Be careful, my teacher," he quavered.

"You too, Seanchai. Remember to keep yourself covered. You have yet to see yourself in a clear mirror. Cultivate your energy whenever it is safe to stand. Practice your Bushido Dao, but never think of yourself as invincible. Remember, there is always a better swords master out there than you. And Seanchai–"

"Yes?"

"If I fail to come to your aid, you may have to make a choice between your friends and your destiny."

"My friends share my destiny," Seanchai retorted.

"Such an answer," Mhari replied, shaking her head as she mounted the horse she had been lent from her friends in the hamlet. "That is what I fear the most."

"Then let's hope we meet in Galbrieth," Seanchai replied. "Ride well, Mhari."

"You too, Seanchai. You too."

As Seanchai watched Mhari ride southeast a wave of anxiety rose in him. He was anxious to move on and try to save his friends, yet afraid to put distance between himself and his teacher. He sighed and turned Snowmane towards the mountains in the north.

The road back to camp was one that led into Galbrieth. Seanchai was tempted to follow it and go straight to the aid of his friends, but the endless stream of people traveling to Galbrieth kept him adhering to his teacher's plan. Many of the travelers were families or merchants hoping to sell their wares, and all spoke with great anticipation about the Emperor's birthday.

Seanchai kept himself hidden inside his hooded cloak. He distanced himself from the travelers as best he could and longed for the solitude he had enjoyed with Mhari.

On the outskirts of a small town, the road crossed a river that flowed through the Vale of Galbrieth. Seanchai stared into the current for a few moments, deciding whether to heed Mhari's plan or deviate from it, and then left the road to follow the river upstream into the mountains, as he had been instructed.

For the next two days, he rode steadily and watched the river become a stream as it neared the mountain range. He was generally alone and able to practice his standing exercises, but he never drew his swords for fear that he would be noticed. Mhari had warned him that the duel swords were not known in this part of the empire and would stand out if he practiced with them.

He was an alert traveler and scryed often as he tried to see if anyone was following. No one gave him any trouble, though a hooded rider, heavily armed and traveling alone, while not uncommon, was often best left alone.

Still, Seanchai breathed a sigh of relief when he entered the mountain range. Though the paths were narrower and the possibility of ambush greater, he was relieved when he ceased to pass anyone else traveling. At the end of the second day, he stopped within eyesight of the lake.

As soon as Seanchai finished cooking his meal, he extinguished the fire. He ate, and went through his standing exercises. He stretched upon finishing and looked around. In the anonymity of darkness, he drew his swords and practiced without regard for time.

FORTY-EIGHT

Rhoddan and Shayth watched as both Tutans, apparently unconscious, were thrown unmercifully into the third prison cell in their alcove. They had clearly been beaten, but since neither was the Tutan who could speak, Rhoddan was not worried that they had given away information. It occurred to him that he was not sure what secrets they could reveal.

"Shayth? Why is Tarlach interrogating them at all? Is there any information that the Tutans might give up?"

Shayth shook his head, "I'm sorry these peaceful nomads got involved in this mess. I shouldn't have allowed it."

Rhoddan lay on his cot and yawned. He often slept during the day, as he exercised at night when the guards almost never patrolled. Even if they did, he would see their torches long before they would see him doing strengthening exercises, stretching or running on the spot. Rhoddan was a warrior; he would be ready to fight if he got the opportunity.

Something bothered him about the Tutans' involvement. He turned to Shayth. "I had no knowledge of the Tutans before all this. Did the general know of their existence?"

"Oh, yes," Shayth replied. "Tarlach led the army that massacred their people before they fled into the desert. But that doesn't explain why he's interrogating them. He must know he can't communicate with them."

"Perhaps it's to serve as a warning to us," Rhoddan suggested. "They worked me over pretty badly before I became your bait."

"Yes. I'm worried that they'll go after Ilana next. I doubt they'll harm me too much. At the gallows, all eyes will be upon me. They won't want people to see me beaten and feel sorry for me. How come you never broke when they tortured you?"

"I decided not to try and be the...you know." Rhoddan's voice quivered. "I knew I couldn't keep it up. So I stayed silent as long as possible. When I finally did speak, I had a story planned. I told them I was part of a small group of wannabe rebels who stole, more than anything else, because we were always hungry.

"When they told me they had been hunting a special one, I told them that I had heard rumors but assumed he was a human. My story sounded plausible enough and they would've lost interest completely if not for the fact that I'm an elf."

Shayth nodded thoughtfully. "We should make sure that Ilana has the same story," he said as he closed his eyes for yet another nap.

It was nighttime when the scrape of boots on the stone floor woke Shayth. The rock alcove glowed with the burning torches of at least six soldiers. Keys jangled in the cell door, and the officer pointed his baton at Shayth.

"General Tarlach wants to see you."

"How convenient," Shayth sneered, daring them to punish him for insolence. "I just so happen to have an hour open for him right now."

The soldiers did not react, and Shayth was mildly disappointed. If any other prisoner, especially an elf, had cheeked up to a guard like that, he would have been beaten to a pulp.

Shayth walked out of the cell and was immediately engulfed by the guards. Another sixer waited at the edge of the alcove to march him up to the General's office.

One soldier knocked on the heavy oak door and a small plump man opened it. Bortand, General Tarlach's assistant, smiled at the young prisoner and invited him inside as if he were a guest at a dinner party. When the guards tried to follow, the general's deep voice stopped them.

"Post guards outside my door and at regular intervals down each corridor. I also want guards beneath my windows. Otherwise, we're to be left alone." He turned to Shayth. "If you try to escape, I will kill the she elf, and I'll do it slowly. The Emperor won't care if you are down a couple of friends on his birthday. And I can always find more elves."

Then Tarlach dismissed Bortand. "You can go to bed, old friend."

"Thank you, General. Send for me if, um, the need arises."

Tarlach waited for the door to close before he continued. "Please, sit. There's food and ale on the table. Help yourself."

"So what's the joke?" Shayth had not moved.

"Joke?"

"The food, the wine, the hospitality. It's laughable." Shayth pushed his hair back from his face.

"Well, I could do this the unpleasant way, but there seems no point. The Emperor doesn't want you messed up, and, while we have your friends in the dungeon, we have easy ways to ensure you cooperate."

Shayth mulled this over and ultimately rose to take some food. He picked up two plates and offered one to the general.

"I have eaten," Tarlach said. "Thank you."

"Then me too," Shayth responded, and tossed everything back down on the general's desk. The plates spun for a few moments and made the only sound in the room. Then Shayth spoke. "What do you want? And please, don't offer me a pardon."

"There is no amnesty," Tarlach replied. "So unless the Emperor himself intervenes, my hands are tied."

"I know that feeling," Shayth responded wryly.

"What I need to know, Shayth, is whether *he* will come?"

"The Emperor?"

"No, your friend," Tarlach leaned in. "The one we call the special one."

"I have no special friend," Shayth replied. "I have no friends, period. Those elves might have actually become friends in time. But I guess we're not going to find out."

"Making friends was never one of your talents," Tarlach observed, and Shayth inadvertently stiffened. "Now, what about the Tutans?"

"Probably hoping to meet you. Maybe they came for a cultural exchange since you have visited their people in the past. I'm sure the Tutans don't exactly hold you in high esteem…or many others, come to think of it. Making friends wasn't one of your talents either, was it?"

Shayth was pleased to see Tarlach's hand flex into a fist. He was going to enjoy himself since Tarlach was instructed not to hit him. The general was a finely trained and disciplined soldier. He would not disobey orders.

"How many of these desert men were with you and how did they join you?"

Shayth yawned and tried to sound nonchalant. "That was the strange thing. They just kind of attached themselves. Maybe they understand better than they let on."

"How many?" The general demanded.

"I'm not sure …" Shayth thought of Rhoddan's advice to have a believable story. He was amused by the growing irritation on the general's face. "Two entered the tunnel with us. But they could have been switching in and out with others and I wouldn't have known. They all look the same to me."

"Are they linked with this special one?"

Shayth shrugged. "I don't know. I don't even know if there *is* a special one. I've heard rumors, like you. When I met the elves, they were sniffing around. But they were easily distracted if they picked up the scent of ale or gold."

"What I want to know, Shayth, is if they will come together?" The general leaned forward, his voice low and intense.

"What? Who?" Shayth was suddenly interested. What was worrying Tarlach?

"Is there some kind of alliance between the elf and the desert men?"

"Rhoddan? No, he's a kid. And you would know after what you did to him."

"You know who I mean."

"This special one?" Shayth parroted Rhoddan's script. "An elf? I assumed he's a man, if he exists to begin with."

"Maybe. But our sources suggest he's an elf."

"I really wouldn't know."

There was little else to say. Shayth rose from his chair and turned to go. But Tarlach stopped him at the door.

"Shayth?"

"Yes?" Shayth turned, wary.

"Just for my own personal curiosity: Do you regret what you did?"

Shayth stared intently at the general, debating at length how to answer, or if he should at all. "I regret many of the people I have killed," he said eventually. "Is that what you mean?"

"No, I meant betraying your father's name and how you left things with your uncle, the Emperor."

"Uncle?" Shayth spat the word venomously as he turned and slowly walked to the general's desk. "Yes, I have regrets. I regret that I'm to die here and will never get the chance to slit his miserable throat or drive my sword through the place where his heart should be. Is *that* what you mean?"

Shayth leaned forward, his fists on the desk. When he spoke again, he struggled to keep the rage under control. "What about your regrets, Tarlach? Do you have any? Can you even sleep at night? My father was your best friend."

The general's face tightened and he stared stonily into Shayth's eyes. When he did not reply, Shayth turned and walked out.

FORTY-NINE

Seanchai woke at dawn. He was stiff from his training the night before but credited the strenuous routine with easing his anxieties and allowing him to fall asleep. Without waiting to eat, he led Snowmane down to the lake. Seanchai reminisced when he had come here with Mhari in the early mornings and watched the wisps of mist rise from the water as the sun warmed it.

He smiled to himself as he recalled the first time Mhari had brought him here. She had instructed him to bathe and, when he had protested about the cold water, had thrown him in, together with his clothes. This reminded him that he should probably bathe again while here.

About an hour later, he arrived at the small grove, where they had harvested the danseng root. Seanchai guided Snowmane into the trees and unsaddled him. The horse seemed happy to graze. Seanchai looked up and down the shore of the lake for signs of life and, seeing none, he left the glade and walked down to the water.

He undressed, cut some soapwort stems, and entered the water to bathe and wash his clothes. This was the first time that he had been in the water since his initiation in the cave. He began his exercises and submerged underwater. It felt safe. Chilly water rushed through his body, and embraced it into his lungs as he walked out into the lake.

He hadn't been under long when he sensed distress on the surface. He walked back toward the shore and cautiously peeked above the water. Snowmane stood at the edge neighing, having seen his rider go under and not resurface. Seanchai hugged the horse's neck, enjoying the warmth emanating from the steed, while Snowmane vocally chided him.

"Alright, alright, I'm sorry. Next time I'll warn you first."

Seanchai dressed in the grove and looked at the earth where the danseng root had been harvested. He wondered if he could scry for the plant. He didn't need any now as Mhari had a supply in her camp. But it might be useful to learn for the future.

He sat and closed his eyes, summoning the energy to fill himself. He relaxed his body and, after filling himself with energy, began to reach out with his mind to the young plants near him. When he recognized their signature, he began to reach out further.

He could see into the gorges that entered the mountains nearby and followed them with his mind seeking plant life. The plant signatures he found were weak and definitely not that of the danseng.

His mind began to follow the path that he would take to Mhari's camp and was about to withdraw when something red and hot caught his attention. His natural reaction was to retreat, but he took a moment to collect himself and then probed cautiously.

There were several figures, neither human nor elf, but rather wolfish: heavy-boned and covered with fur. They were unarmed, bipedal and wearing tattered clothes and boots. Weapons or not, Seanchai had no doubt they were dangerous. As he watched in horror, the pack attacked one of their own, viciously ripping it to pieces. Seanchai watched the carnage with horror, the vivid images filling his mind.

Thank goodness Mhari had gone south, or she could easily have walked straight into her death. Seanchai would have to pass these creatures one way or another, but at least he knew what was ahead.

They devoured their dismembered pack mate while the biggest

one gave orders. The creatures fell quickly into line and moved out—heading straight for the lake, and Seanchai.

He withdrew his mind and decided he would wait in the grove and wait for the pack to pass him by. There was a faint breeze coming from the lake, so they shouldn't pick up either his or Snowmane's scent. He just had to keep his horse quiet.

He didn't wait long before he saw the pack enter the basin and approach the lake to drink. Seanchai felt a chill rise up his spine as he suddenly realized that he had left a trail of footprints from the lake where he had bathed back to the grove.

He took a deep breath and focused his mind on the sand between the grove and the lake. A calm feeling went through him and a word seemed to appear in his mind. He began chanting *Moriarhtur, Moriarhtur, Moriarhtur.*

As he did he felt the breeze pick up and move in an easterly direction. Grains of sand tumbled across and began to cover over his tracks. He continued to whisper the word with increasing intensity. *Moriarhtur, Moriarhtur, Moriarhtur.* The breeze became a wind and more grains moved across the footprints he had left. In moments, he had created a sandstorm.

The pack leader looked up, puzzled by the sudden change in weather. They tightened their formation and all moved on four legs. The pack passed right in front of Seanchai. He was shielded from sight by the sandstorm his chant had created, but they stopped too close for comfort to sniff around the now-covered tracks.

Seanchai kept murmuring *Moriarhtur, Moriarhtur,* but the pack's attention was diverted away from his tracks to further down the lakeshore. Something, or someone was there.

Seanchai hurriedly reached out with his mind, balancing his scrying and holding the sandstorm. He saw three figures on horseback headed toward him and the beasts, hoods drawn over their heads to protect them from the whirling sand.

Though he could not see them with his mind, he was sure that they were elves. They were riding into a trap; oblivious to the danger because of the windstorm he had created. A wave of panic rose inside of him as he realized he would be responsible for leading innocent elves to their deaths.

FIFTY

General Tarlach could not sleep that night. He had known that Shayth would not give up information easily–definitely not without Tarlach being able to use torture. He could have broken him, he could break anyone, but he had a feeling that even then Shayth would take quite a beating before relenting. Still it was only theoretical. The Emperor wanted Shayth to look physically fit when he walked to his execution.

He should not have summoned the boy. Nothing good could have come from it. He had known that and yet was driven to speak with him alone. He had known Shayth since he was a baby crawling. Tarlach had trained in the academy with Shayth's father, Prince Shindell, and they had been close friends with sons around the same age. The boys grew up together much to the delight of their parents. General Tarlach was a young officer then and didn't know or understand the politics of the time. Or perhaps he had allowed himself to be oblivious until tragedy had forced him to put the pieces together later.

None of the Emperor's wives had bore him a child, so he showed great interest in Shayth–his potential heir–as he grew. But the Emperor was known for his temper and when Tarlach returned on leave from a very successful campaign in the Galbrieth region, he had sensed the growing tension in the capital.

Prince Shindell would never share anything with Tarlach concerning palace politics, and that was as much for Tarlach's safety as traditional loyalty among royal families. But Tarlach's wife had told him that she and their son, Ahad, had not been invited over as often as before. When she did spend time with Shayth's mother, the beautiful woman seemed depressed and distant. There were also rumors that the Emperor had sired a son with another woman and this was a source of tension within the royal family. But Tarlach was loyal to his Emperor and his best friend. He would not listen to the whispers and suddenly wanted to be back with his troops, something he understood.

On Shayth's fifth birthday, a party was held, first for children and then in the evening for the adults. Tarlach's wife had taken their son and later, she and Tarlach were invited to the evening festivities.

Though there were many guests, the Emperor was not one of them. He had surely been invited, but chosen not to attend. Neither, from what they could discern, had he sent a gift, as it would surely have been the most opulent.

The next morning, Tarlach received orders to return to the Galbrieth passes. He was surprised as he had just led a great victory there, and had crushed any resistance. The Emperor himself, only a few years older than Tarlach, had decorated him. Now he wanted his general to return with some of the Emperor's own regiments. Though Tarlach was perplexed, he could not ask questions. Still he was happy for these reinforcements meant Tarlach's own troops would be relieved and they certainly deserved a break.

What excited him, however, was that the Emperor's brother was to lead the company. He and Tarlach rode side-by-side, exchanging stories around the fire at night and smoking their pipes together. Away from the formalities of court, Tarlach found his old friend to be the same funny and raucous companion he had treasured during their time in military academy.

Four days after arriving at the fort, Shayth's father led a routine patrol. His lifeless body returned with two arrows protruding. The soldiers, all members of the Emperor's regiment, swore they had been ambushed. Three of them had returned lightly wounded, though none had been killed.

However, along with the Emperor's brother, Tarlach's two scouts had been killed in the ambush. He found this disturbing since his scouts were so accomplished. In ten years of service, no scout had ever lost his life in this way.

Tarlach was furious and led his own troops out from the fort to find the renegades and kill them. But they found no resistance or even tracks. Tarlach terrorized the already broken villages, but gleaned no information. He tapped the smugglers and the men of commerce. Usually it was just a matter of price as the businessmen, in particular, would not risk the comfortable arrangements they enjoyed with the Emperor's lieutenants.

Tarlach decided to tell the Emperor himself what had happened. He bore responsibility for the Emperor's brother and feared for his career and maybe his life. But he was a man of honor and fiercely loyal to his Emperor. He would face him and suffer the consequences.

He had ridden through the night and was brought straight before the Emperor as dawn was breaking. He recounted all that had transpired. Only two generals were present and they asked many questions. Tarlach was a good officer and had taken all the correct steps: the right number of scouts, enough soldiers in the patrol, the follow up. There was nothing he could be faulted for and the generals both told the Emperor this in front of him.

Tarlach had stepped forward before the Emperor and went down on one knee. "Your Majesty. Though the generals exonerate my actions, I have failed you. Know that I was a close friend of your brother, that we trained together in the academy, and that our sons play together. I wish I had taken his place and that the arrow had found me.

"I'm sorry for failing you, my lord. I will accept any punishment you deem appropriate."

He lowered his head and waited. The Emperor sat on his throne, his head resting on one arm. There were black rings around his eyes and his pallor was gray. Tarlach felt even more wretched. At length, the Emperor sighed and spoke.

"Get off your knees, Tarlach. Stand up. Though I mourn the loss of my brother I can see no way to blame you. He was a fine warrior and knew what he was doing."

The Emperor rose and walked to a window. Though his back was to Tarlach, the latter was sure his liege was wiping away tears.

"My brother was a good man, Tarlach. We had our differences but I will miss him. The generals here speak highly of you as a soldier and an officer, but my brother spoke highly of you as a friend and a father."

The Emperor turned, his face now composed. He came and stood opposite Tarlach and put his hand on the young officer's shoulder. Royalty usually never touched their subjects, and this was not lost on Tarlach. The Emperor's face was sad and drawn.

"As your Emperor, I order you to grieve for my brother but not to blame yourself. My brother believed that you would rise through the ranks and my advisers here concur. Let us be bonded by my brother's memory.

"But I will ask a favor. I have no experience or time to father his son, Shayth…"

A sharp knock rapped on the door and the Emperor withdrew quickly from Tarlach. One of the generals opened the door and a woman pushed past him and threw herself on the floor at the Emperor's feet.

"My lord," she cried. "Your brother's wife…"

The woman wailed. The other general stepped forward and pulled the woman effortlessly to her feet. He had to hold her to stop her collapsing. "What is it?" he boomed. "What has happened to your mistress?"

The woman was shaking her head. "My lady is dead. She hung herself during the night." She screamed into the air and her voice echoed from the high ceiling.

There was a blur of shouts, orders given, and the woman was dragged out. Tarlach stayed where he was as a flurry of activity swirled around him. When things quieted down, he went back onto one knee. The Emperor stared at him, his face an impassive, blank page.

"My lord," Tarlach said, his heart tight. "Let me go to the boy. I will take Shayth into my house. He knows my son and wife. We can be a comfort for him. Let me serve you in this way."

The Emperor nodded and then looked at Tarlach. His stare was icy. "Never forget, Tarlach, that until such time as the Gods give me my own son, he is the heir to the throne of Odessiya, of this entire empire. Train him well."

Tarlach nodded, he had nothing to say. As he exited, he glanced at the general by the door. The old man's face was impassive, void of emotion, but Tarlach caught a furtive look in the direction of the Emperor.

Stunned at the scene he had witnessed, Tarlach walked down the long corridor from the throne room. Something was missing, but he couldn't put his finger on it. Suddenly he stopped in his tracks, a cold shiver went through him. When the woman had burst in bearing the news of Shayth's mother's suicide, the Emperor had not appeared shocked or surprised.

FIFTY-ONE

The pack crouched close to the ground, ready to spring as one unit at their leader's command. The ungainly creatures were single-mindedly focused during the hunt. Muscles strained, claws dug into the sand, and they waited.

The elves stopped uneasily when their horses began simpering. A dark-skinned elfe took two arrows and latched them onto her bow. The others drew long knives and moved out to flank the archer. They continued forward slowly, bracing themselves for an attack.

It came when they were only twenty yards away, still blinded by the sand. The pack leader was at the forward horse's throat when a long knife javelined into his side. The elfe quickly brought down another attacker with her bow before she fell, trapped with her leg under her wounded horse. Her two companions each fought and slew another beast each.

A white-haired warrior leapt into the fray, two long, curved swords held high. He fell upon the remaining four beasts as they charged the fallen horse and elfe. His swords were a blur and it was all over within seconds.

Stillness. Only the heavy breathing of the survivors could be heard. Steam rose from the hewn bodies of the beasts, and Seanchai ensured each was dead before turning to the travelers. Her companions were helping the trapped elfe out from under her fallen horse.

Her horse struggled to rise, but its gaping wound kept it on the ground. The elfe walked unsteadily and then knelt by her baying steed. One of the elves gently helped her rise and offered her his horse's reins.

"Move away," he said softly. "Let me."

"Head over to the grove," Seanchai pointed in the direction. "My horse is inside. You can feed and settle yours. I will stay here and help."

The third elf took his horse and led the elfe in the direction of the grove. When they had moved away, Seanchai watched the remaining elf nock an arrow and aim at the horse's heart. As he pulled the bowstring taut, he murmured: "Thank you, Amanith, brave steed. You have served us well. May you find green pastures to ever graze on."

His arrow did its job quickly and quietly. Almost immediately, the elf bent over and cut the dead horse open.

"What are you doing?" Seanchai asked, consternated.

"Horse meat is good to eat. It will feed us for a few days. Longer, if we could take the time to dry it."

"But ... that's her *horse*," Seanchai objected.

"Yes, and she will honor him. Eating his meat is not a sign of disrespect, but quite the opposite. He continues to serve us even in death. What honor is there in being picked to the bones by vultures and other scavengers?"

Seanchai looked up and saw the black birds already circling. Still, he didn't have the stomach for this. "I'll head back to the others, if you don't mind," he grimaced.

"Very well. Thank you for coming to our aid. Are there others at your camp?"

"No," Seanchai replied, "I walk alone."

When he reached the grove, the elfe was lying down with her leg elevated on a rock.

"Are you okay, Sellia?" Seanchai asked.

The elfe jerked and stared at him. "We've never met," she said. "I'd remember an elf with white hair and two swords. Chamack must have told you my name."

"No, but you once saved my life and fed me on a number of occasions. Now I repay the debt."

She looked hard at him but then laid back. "I have no idea what you're talking about," she said, her tone terse. "Who are you?"

Seanchai smiled but didn't answer. He was happy to have company, but Mhari had cautioned him about revealing his identity. He rose and watched Chamack dragging a heavy cloth sack toward them. Deep red blood had soaked through and left a trail on the sand.

"I'm sorry, Sellia," Chamack said, panting with exertion. "I did what was necessary. It was quick."

"He was a fine stallion," she replied, her eyes closed. "I will miss him."

The elves sat in an exhausted silence and drank water while they rested. Then Chamack turned to Seanchai. "Excuse our manners. Thank you for coming to our aid. I am Chamack. This is Luvial, and the one lying there is Sellia. Who are you, might I ask?"

"Sharing that would put you in greater danger," Seanchai said. "Be assured we are on the same side."

Sellia groaned as she tried to move her leg, and Seanchai saw that the ankle was swelling up. "May I try ryku on your leg?" he asked. "Maybe I can limit the swelling."

Sellia nodded and Seanchai lay his hands on her ankle. When he finished, she sighed and thanked him. Her eyes were closing and he smiled back.

Then he rose and turned to the two males. "Where have you come from?"

"We've been scouting the Galbrieth valley. We hope to liberate some slave elves from the traders."

"Are you all with Uncle?" Seanchai asked and they glanced at each other nervously. Seanchai continued. "Don't answer that. I'll assume that you are. I need you to get an urgent message to him."

"I'm not sure how well I can travel," Sellia said. "If this message is important, they shouldn't wait for me. We only have two horses now, anyway."

"You can come with me," Seanchai suggested. "I'm on my way somewhere much closer, and you can rest there. If I must, I will leave you there, but I have a couple of days before I must move on."

He rose for a moment and scanned outside the trees, pondering how much he should tell them. If he was asking for their trust, shouldn't they receive his, as well? Then another thought occurred to him. "What were those beasts?"

"They are very ancient creatures called wolfheids," Chamack said. "They were once more humanlike, but they were turned into the beasts you saw by dark magic. They were hunted under the Alliance, but now they are few and prowl the deserts and mountains."

Seanchai could hear scavengers already arguing over the wolfheid corpses. When he returned his attention to his company, he found they were all staring at him curiously.

"Excuse my manners again," Chamack said. "But your ears are pointed. You are an elf, aren't you?"

"Yes I am," Seanchai replied shortly, but he didn't offer any explanation. "I need Uncle to bring his band to the fortress of Galbrieth. I can't give specific instructions, as there is no set plan. We need to rescue a party that's about to be executed and then we'll try and escape. Probably, what I need is that you have people ready to help us if we successfully retrieve them and get past the walls. Maybe you will provide a distraction from outside."

"Are you offering a sum for this? Or weapons, maybe?" Luvial asked. "You are asking Uncle to risk his band for strangers. These are difficult times."

Seanchai glared. "We are not all strangers. One of those we are rescuing is Ilana, one of Uncle's clan and Rhoddan is the other, from Yochai's band. I assume he remembers them."

"I'm sure he does," Sellia said and Seanchai saw them all exchange glances. "Is that clumsy wood elf with them?"

Chamack spoke before Seanchai could answer. "Hey, he may have been clumsy, but remember how he took down a group of soldiers to rescue Rhoddan?"

"I'm not sure he knew what he was doing. It was a stroke of luck," replied Luvial. "He was a lost pup, that one."

"It had nothing to do with luck," Sellia declared. "He could do it again."

Seanchai saw dawning understanding on Sellia's face as she looked at him. Her beautiful brown eyes grew large, but she did not say anything.

Seanchai met her gaze and then spoke again to Chamack. "Can you reach Uncle, organize and be in the area around Galbrieth in five days?"

"It can be done," said Chamack after calculating the distance in his head. "But persuading Uncle to commit will be difficult since he does not know who is requesting his aid, and there is no clear plan of action. I'm sure he will come for Ilana, but may not bring others so near Galbrieth. What can I say that will persuade him to risk the lives of his band?"

Seanchai straightened, his long white hair flowing, his eyes shining blue, his body strong and powerful. When he spoke, his voice commanded attention and respect. "Tell him, and all your people, that Seanchai, a Wycaan warrior, calls them to arms."

FIFTY-TWO

That Rhoddan exercised every night in their cell had never bothered Shayth. He usually fell asleep long before Rhoddan even worked up a sweat. But tonight Shayth did not feel like he was ready to fall sleep.

Rhoddan stood in the shadows at the back of the cell as the guards returned with Shayth. He did not want the guards to know that he was keeping his strength up or give them any excuse to hit him. He was an elf, and they had made their feelings about elves as apparent as those of the prisoners in his last cell. He wouldn't have survived that fight if not for Shayth, he thought.

Shayth went straight to his cot to lie down and glared at the ceiling. Rhoddan waited until he was sure that the guards had gone before he tried talking to his cellmate.

"So, how was the interview?"

No answer.

"You should've let me write you a letter of recommendation. I've seen you in action. I would hire you."

Silence. Rhoddan sighed. "I'm going to continue exercising. If you want to talk, just throw something at me."

He began doing his push ups and then moved to sit ups. He had a whole routine worked out and it was the highlight of his day. It wasn't just about keeping in shape, or passing the time. Shayth had once asked Rhoddan why he continued to train if he was about to die. Rhoddan replied that he was a warrior and not dead yet. He needed to keep to his warrior code, and not just for the physical benefits.

Rhoddan was hanging from the cell bars when a shoe smacked into his stomach. He was momentarily irritated, but then remembered his offer. Shayth was sitting up, his back against the cold stone wall. Rhoddan dropped to the ground, sat next to him, and waited.

"We've got to get out of here," Shayth said.

"I won't disagree with that. But I don't have any ideas. Do you?"

Shayth shook his head. "I expect that when we're taken out, we will have our hands and feet chained. I don't have a clue how to escape."

"Do you think he'll come?" Rhoddan asked, and heard his own shaky voice.

"I hope not," said Shayth. "He doesn't have the ability or experience to get us out of here and would only endanger himself."

"What would you do if you were him?" Rhoddan asked.

"Try and forget about us and focus on what I was being taught."

"Me, too. He's not like that."

"I know," Shayth replied. "But I'm hoping his teacher has figured that out, too."

Shayth tossed and turned on the rough straw bed. Fatigue and despondency were wearing him down. He could feel the long-standing barriers that he had erected begin to crumble. He had suppressed the memories for so long. Why had Tarlach summoned him? Was this his way of torturing Shayth? The walls crumbled and the memories rose, free at last.

Shayth heard the wails from his bedroom. He had heard his mother cry before, but not like this. It was raw, unbridled, and it scared him. He ran to her chamber and saw her sprawled on the bed, surrounded by maids. The elderly housekeeper, shuffled up to Shayth as quickly as he could and swept the little boy into his arms. The man was plump and young Shayth buried his little head in the folds of fat that spilt out of the man's trousers.

"Not now, little one, not now," the man whispered in his ear as he took the boy from the room. His mother's door shut behind them, but her wails slipped through the cracks and lodged forever into his memory.

He remembered going back to his mother's chambers deep in the night, but had heard strange voices, angry male voices. None belonged to his father or anyone else he knew but they scared him and he returned to his room.

He had woken near morning. There was a pale gray light outside his window and it was cold. He had wet his bed but he wanted his mother even though she would chide him for not using his chamber pot. He didn't care. He wanted her to hug him. He wanted to bury himself in her long, soft, black hair. He would snuggle into her and find happiness.

He went to her bedroom door, pushed it open, and screamed.

Rhoddan was shaking him. "Shayth! Shayth! What's happening?"

Ilana called over from the other cell, but fell silent when a guard shouted a warning at them. Shayth was breathing heavily and sweat dripped down his face. There was no towel to give him and Rhoddan doubted an offer of a hug would be well received.

"Leave me alone," Shayth rasped. "I've got to get through this alone. Get away from me."

Rhoddan withdrew. "Go back to sleep then," he said coldly. "I need to finish my workout."

Shayth closed his eyes. He would force himself to sleep and confront the memories.

"Come now, my lad –, we have all your toys and books." The big, powerful hand of Captain Tarlach engulfed Shayth's small, chubby fingers,

and led him from the room that had been his for all his five years of life. "Ahad is waiting for you. From now on, you will be like brothers."

"I want my Mommy. I want my Daddy," Shayth said emotionlessly. He had been told that princes didn't cry countless times, and he believed it.

He was led out of the palace to General Tarlach's house, where he had his own room next to Ahad's and a warm, welcoming hug from Ahad's mother. But it was not his room, and her hug was not like his mommy's.

Ahad and Shayth did not get on after this. When Shayth was a prince at the palace, that had been exciting, but this was Ahad's house and he didn't like sharing his family or his things. Ahad's mother tried hard to smooth things between them. His father, a rising officer in the Emperor's army, was often away. But when the general came home, he would read books to the children and explain his military campaigns using their toy soldiers.

But despite their efforts, young Shayth increasingly withdrew into himself. He found a number of hiding places around the house and in the garden that he kept to himself. One day, five years after Shayth had joined their household, he was hiding near a pagoda that overlooked the palace when Tarlach and his wife approached, mid-conversation and oblivious to the eavesdropper.

Shayth was worried they would see him, as he had behaved badly while Tarlach was away. He and Ahad had come to blows and Ahad sported the remains of a black eye. Shayth knew that Ahad would tell his father, and expected to be rebuked and probably punished. He curled himself into a ball and tried to be invisible.

"I try," Tarlach's wife was saying. "I so feel for him losing his mother and his father like that. Shayth is such an angry little boy. His uncle ignores him. He should have everything, but he has nothing."

"Do not speak of the Emperor like that," Captain Tarlach replied in a sharp tone. "He cares for the boy."

"Ha! Like he cared for his brother?"

"I spoke those words from the depth of my grief. I loved Prince Shindell, as the Emperor did, and all were heartbroken by his death."

"No," his wife challenged. "You were sure his death was arranged. Don't you remember? You were certain the Emperor was behind his...his assassination."

"Quiet, wife!" Tarlach snarled. "You will never repeat those words again. I forbid it. Do you realize what you are saying?"

"And you don't believe his mother committed suicide, either," his wife continued, her temper rising to meet her husband's. "Shayth said he heard male voices in the room. She had no lovers. I knew her well, and she was unequivocally dedicated to her husband and son. She wouldn't have taken her own life and left Shayth. No mother would. She was murdered, too, and you know it."

"What are you saying? Be quiet! This is treason." Tarlach was agitated and pacing. "If he had wanted to kill the family, why let Shayth live?"

"He needs Shayth alive until he has a son of his own. He needs Shayth to be his heir. The rumors of the bastard son still surface regularly."

Tarlach knew this, but he also knew something that his wife did not. He took his wife in his arms and spoke almost under his breath. "The Emperor's new wife is pregnant."

His wife gasped. "What will become of Shayth? Is he safe with us? Are we safe?"

Her husband didn't answer and two days later, a bitter ten-year-old slipped out of the city unnoticed, never to return. His burgeoning reputation after he left would not remain as discreet.

FIFTY-THREE

Seanchai felt Chamack and Luvial's eyes constantly on him while they rested in the grove, and thus was almost relieved when they felt their horses were ready to move off. The Wycaan refused to answer any questions and made them swear they would reveal his identity to no one except Uncle.

To avoid their curious, awe-filled gazes, Seanchai slept. The scrying and the sandstorm had tired him. The actual fighting had felt cathartic, especially as his opponents had not been men or elves, and he was secretly pleased at how easily he wielded his swords after so little training.

Chamack nudged him awake. "Master. We must leave if we want to put some distance in before dark."

Seanchai rose and took the elf's arm. "Ride well, then, my friend. And please, I address my teacher that way. She is a learned and proven Wycaan Master. I do not deserve such a title. To my friends, I am still Seanchai."

"As you wish, Seanchai. I would be proud to address you as my friend."

"Then next time we meet, let it be so." Seanchai smiled.

"It will be at Galbrieth," Chamack replied. "You have my word."

Luvial and Chamack said their farewells to Sellia. Her black skin shone as the rays of the setting sun accentuated her high cheekbones. She was limping and grimaced each time she put any weight on her leg. When they were alone, Seanchai turned to her.

"How is it?" he asked.

"It will be fine. Are we staying here tonight or heading for your camp?"

"My camp is near," Seanchai replied. "I would feel safer there, and we can light a fire and cook hot food."

"That would be nice," she replied, and her smile revealed straight, white teeth. "May I ask you a favor before we go? Could you take me on your horse to the lake? I have not washed for some days, and the cold water might help numb the pain."

"Of course," Seanchai said.

"And while I'm bathing, will you return to the wolfheids and retrieve my arrows? My horse lays there and I don't want to see him the way he looks now. I think arrows spilled from my quiver when he fell."

"No problem. Here, I'll help you onto my horse."

Snowmane allowed Sellia to ride him only when it was clear that Seanchai was coming too. It took a short while to get to the lake, and Sellia slipped as she climbed off the horse. Seanchai caught her and as he held her close, he smelled her musky scent.

She stood up and began to remove her clothes as she walked down to the water. Seanchai watched, mesmerized. Without turning, she called, "The arrows, Seanchai. Now would be a perfect time for you to fetch my arrows."

Seanchai's ears burned as he cleared his throat and leapt onto Snowmane. He made as much noise as he could muster in turning the horse around so she knew he was leaving. He heard Sellia laughing and was quite sure that Snowmane snickered, too. "Hey," he chided his horse. "None of that from you."

Seanchai couldn't resist turning briefly to look. He saw her beautiful, smooth dark skin glowing in the setting sun as she ducked under the water. He felt guilty and confused and hurried Snowmane along.

When he returned, Sellia was wrapped only in her cloak, as she had washed her clothes. He held Snowmane steady as she mounted.

"It would be faster if we both rode," Sellia said as she grimaced from the pain. "You said it's not far. I'll feel bad with you walking while I ride."

Seanchai was tempted, as the thought of being close to her was intoxicating, but that made him feel guiltier.

"No," he said. "I need the exercise."

He put all his gear on Snowmane and then jogged just ahead of the horse. He wanted to work up a good sweat and think of Ilana.

They reached the camp just as it was getting dark. Seanchai helped Sellia down and arranged her bedroll so she could lie near the fire he lit. He filled a pot with water and put it on the fire before going back out to cover their tracks.

When he returned, Sellia had laid out her clothes on the rocks and apparently started to prepare food. But now she lay with her leg elevated on a rock near the flames.

"I wanted to prepare the food," she said, "but my ankle gave out."

"That's okay," Seanchai replied. "It's more important that you rest and your ankle heals. After we eat, I will channel some more healing energy. There are also some herbs we can pack on the swollen area."

"I'm in your hands," she said, raising her arms in surrender. "But be careful. I might begin to enjoy being waited on."

She laughed and Seanchai smiled. He readied a simple meal of potato, onion and some dried meat while he also prepared an herbal poultice for Sellia's ankle. The food was *almost* edible thanks to the herbs he had added. Later, when everything was cleared away and they both had warm tea to drink, Seanchai kneeled by Sellia's feet.

"Stay away from the bottoms of my feet," she warned good-humoredly.

"Why?"

"Because I'm ticklish," she admitted. "And if you ever tell anyone, I'll…" She couldn't think of a suitable punishment.

"That's good information to have," Seanchai grinned mischievously. "I remember you from Uncle's camp. You only ever glared at me. But now I know how to tame the tough girl."

"Elves need to be tough in this world, Seanchai, even more so when you are an elfe. And you were certainly deserving of my glares."

She laughed but stopped when she saw Seanchai's face fall.

"What is it?" she frowned.

"Ilana is an elfe in prison," he whispered, "and I fear, too, for Rhoddan and our friend."

Sellia wanted to ask more, but the pain on his face told her everything she needed to know. Instead she said, "Take care of my wound, please, Seanchai. I want to be ready to ride and help you save Ilana."

He closed his eyes and summoned the energy. When he moved his hands either side of her ankles, she sighed deeply. "That feels good," she said, and her eyes closed.

When he finished, Sellia looked to be asleep. Carefully, he covered her with his blanket, thinking that in the future, he would have his patients open their bedrolls before he worked on them.

Now that he was alone with his thoughts, he could only think of Ilana, and what Sellia had said—*You need to be tough in this world, Seanchai, especially when you are an elf, and even more so when you are an elfe*—and tears welled up in his eyes as he gathered his weapons. The practice might numb his emotions. He removed his shirt, unsheathed his two swords and walked away from the fireplace.

Sellia watched from her bedroll as Seanchai maneuvered his swords in increasingly complex forms, his blades falling faster than his tears. She could feel his pain. Though she was older than Ilana, they had lived close by for a short while and met at gatherings of the resistance. Being the only two young elfes in the camps, they had quickly become friends. She regretted saying what she had said. But she also feared for Ilana, an elfe in a violent world of humans. She was acquainted with the violence of soldiers, especially towards elves and elfes.

And the tears fell from both Sellia and Seanchai, though each hoped the other would not notice.

FIFTY-FOUR

Mhari wiped her brow on her sleeve. She had been riding south for two days and didn't even know if she was going in the right direction. She reached the junction at the southern tip of the Vale of Galbrieth and, though the road headed east, she took a path that continued south.

This brought her to the edge of the Batak desert. Already it was dry and the only signs of vegetation were spindly bushes and shriveled, flat-topped trees. But she knew that when the rainy season hit, temporary rivers would flow down from the mountains through or alongside the plant life and especially the trees. A tree couldn't grow if it wasn't rooted along one of these water channels.

She turned her attention back to the matter at hand. From his scrying, Seanchai had revealed that three Tutans had been with Shayth and Ilana when they entered Galbrieth, but only two had been captured.

She needed to find the one who had escaped on his way back to his tribe. It was the quickest way to the desert people, though she was worried at her chances of actually finding a member of an elusive race of people who were experts at blending in with their surroundings.

If she didn't find him, she would continue south and scry. But once at the camp, she would still have to persuade Targs, if he was leading this hunting party, to let his people accompany her to

Galbrieth. This could prove even more difficult than finding them in the first place after the way their last encounter had ended in many deaths and the dislocation of his entire people. Even if she succeeded in persuading the Tutans, they would still need time to prepare. And time was not something she had much of.

Mhari was frustrated that she could not ride her horse. The terrain here was rough and stony, and it might turn an ankle. She walked impatiently pulling her horse's rein.

A click.

She stopped, cocked her head, and listened. Nothing. She began to walk again, scrying to determine if she was being followed. Yes, there was one man. Another click made Mhari turn and respond in kind to the man standing on the ridge, beaming.

Mhari had exhausted her knowledge of the Tutans' language, so she spread out her arms, palms facing the man in the universal gesture of peace. The man reciprocated and advanced towards Mhari. As she did, the Tutan threw back his hood to reveal gray hair and a withered face.

Mhari relaxed and smiled. She didn't know more than a few of the Tutans, but she knew this man. "Kung, it's good to see you, my friend," she said, and the two embraced.

Kung clicked rapidly, but Mhari just shook her head. "I don't understand you, but I think you might be the one who escaped from Galbrieth."

The desert man stopped and stared. Mhari repeated: "Galbrieth, Galbrieth." Kung nodded understanding, and Mhari felt her heart leap. "I need to find Targs," she said. "Targs," and she pointed at Kung with one hand, at herself with the other, and then moved the two hands together. "Targs," she repeated.

Kung nodded and then spoke. "Targs. We go." Then he beckoned her and they began to walk briskly together. The desert man was looking particularly disheveled, and his clothes were stained and torn. He had clearly been walking for a long time. They continued for several hours before taking a path into the mountains.

A short while later, and through a crevice between steep rock walls, they arrived at the camp. The Tutans were busy skinning animals and drying meat near the fire. As Kung led Mhari through, people stopped what they were doing and followed. A few clicks were exchanged with Kung but he did not stop.

By the time they reached the central fire pit, there were seventy or eighty people gathered. Mhari hoped that there might be others out hunting. Kung clicked to a young man to take Mhari's horse before serving her water and a bowl of stew.

"Thank you," said Mhari and bent her head.

Kung sat opposite her and was also served food and water. The others hovered silently, probably waiting for Targs, but finally a woman clicked to Kung and he began talking at length. Mhari hoped it was about those who had gone with Kung to the garrison.

In the middle of his monologue, Mhari's bowl was suddenly kicked from near her mouth. Targs had arrived. Kung sprang up, angry, but Mhari didn't move. A furious cacophony of clicks ensued between the two elders.

Finally, Kung walked back to the pot of stew and filled another bowl. Glaring at Targs, he handed it to Mhari. Mhari looked up at the leader. She knew Targs hated her and blamed her for the massacre of his people. But the Tutans had a code of honor. Kung had brought Mhari in as his guest and would defend her with his life if necessary.

Targs sighed and shook his head, then sat down facing Kung and Mhari. He had made a serious error in front of many of his people, and judging by the look on his face, he was ashamed. Mhari began to eat again and Kung continued to address the crowd, making sure Targs was listening.

When Kung had finished, Targs turned to Mhari. "I wrong to kick. Not our way."

"Thank you. It is forgotten," said Mhari. "Did Kung tell you about Galbrieth?"

"Yes."

"Did he tell you that our friends will all be executed in three days time?"

"Yes."

"I need your help if they are to be rescued." Mhari continued, her voice slow but strong.

"Last time we help, many dead." Targs raised his voice and then translated to the crowd.

There was a murmur of clicks and nodding of heads.

"Will you tell them what I want them to hear?" Mhari asked. "Will you tell them exactly what I say?"

Targs glared at her but she held his stare. Both knew he was honor-bound to obey. He sighed and nodded.

"Tell them that your people are alive, along with Shayth, Ilana, and the elf they went to save. Tell them all five will be executed publicly on the Emperor's birthday in three days time."

She paused for Targs to translate before continuing.

"Something has happened; something that just might tip the scales and bring about the fall of the Emperor and his evil regime."

Again she paused while Targs translated. A hum of anticipation rippled through the crowd at this.

"But it could all go wrong at Galbrieth. You are the only people I have to turn to for help."

This time a conversation ensued before Targs turned back to her.

"Last time," he said, "you not save us."

"I saved many of you, but no, I could not save you all," Mhari said, her voice low. "I cannot promise that I'll be able to this time, either. But you should know," she looked around at the watching faces and said her next few words very slowly, "the commander of the garrison is General Tarlach, the man who led the massacre of your people." Then to make her point, she repeated, "General Tarlach."

There was another wave of murmurs as many recognized the name. Then a full-blooded argument broke out, a mass of clicks rose in a crescendo, filling the desert air. Mhari remained seated and sipped her water. There was nothing more she could do. The Tutans needed to decide for themselves.

FIFTY-FIVE

Sellia woke disoriented, unfamiliar with her surroundings. The looming rocks were dark brown, ignited at their peaks by a fresh rising sun. She turned on her side and winced as she felt her ankle. It all came rushing back—the wolfheids, Seanchai the Wycaan, and her horse, Amanith. She sighed.

Once up, she looked around and saw Seanchai standing with his eyes closed, breathing deeply from his stomach. She noted his well-built form and decided that now was a good time to take care of herself. She rose as silently as she could and limped over to the small waterfall and washed her hands, teeth and face.

She turned, blinking away water droplets, and found that Seanchai had finished whatever he was doing and was now blowing on the fire's embers. He looked up at her.

"How did you sleep, Sellia?"

"Well enough," she lied.

"I heard you wince in the night. Did your ankle hurt when you changed position? I can work on your ankle while we wait for the water to boil, if you'd like."

Sellia smiled. "Thank you. How can I refuse?"

She lay back on her bedroll and wiggled until she felt comfortable. Seanchai cupped her ankle with his hands, closed his eyes, and began his breathing. Having just concluded his exercises, the energy did not need to be summoned, and Sellia immediately felt wave after wave of warm energy pulsate into her leg. It was far more intense and focused than the day before, and she found herself breathing deeply with him. The warmth swept up through her leg and into the rest of her body, and she felt the weariness that had accompanied her through the night disappear.

Seanchai also felt the intensity. He too had not slept well. He was eager to pack up Mhari's belongings and leave for Galbrieth. He knew there were only a few days left. He wondered if he could travel by night as well as day, using the cover of darkness to move faster than a normal person's speed. He had not done this before, but he was certain he could. He *knew* he could, like he seemed to *know* so much these days.

But for now, he needed Sellia's ankle to heal. He wanted her with him when he went to Galbrieth. He didn't want to go alone. He closed his eyes, thinking of Ilana as he sent out energy with each exhalation.

"Seanchai. Seanchai!" He snapped his eyes open. "It's too much!" Sellia cried, and he swiftly grounded the energy. Her ankle was red, and Seanchai could feel the heat on his thighs where her leg was resting. He took a deep breath and looked up to find her staring at him.

"I'm sorry," he said. "I guess I got–I need–" He stopped, unable to articulate his thoughts.

"What is it, Seanchai?"

"I need you to heal." Frustration poured out of his mouth. "I must leave tonight or early tomorrow for the garrison. I need to have a plan in place, probably more than one. And I've never been to Galbrieth. I've never been to *any* human city."

Sellia stared at him. His muscular physique and piercing blue eyes were impressive. But underneath he was still the scared, young elf she had originally met.

"And you're worried that I'll slow you down." She stated this as fact. "Seanchai, if you want to leave me here, I'll understand. But I can assure you that if I go with you, I will do what needs to be done."

He nodded. "Perhaps. Let me make breakfast. Then I need to pack this place away for Mhari."

"Mhari?"

"She is my teacher, also a Wycaan—a human woman. I must reach Galbrieth before her and be prepared to fight without her. I promised I would wait here for two days and hide what I don't take with me. We lost a day just now, and I'm anxious to scout the city."

He turned away from her collecting supplies.

She smiled. "Seanchai. I *am* coming with you. I know the city and can help you navigate it."

She could see his sigh of relief even though his back was to her. "Thank you," he said, and meant it.

As he prepared their food, Sellia rested but peppered him with questions about everything he knew about where Rhoddan and Ilana were incarcerated. After he passed her a bowl of hot oat gruel, he disappeared under the rock where the fire was and reappeared with a small leather satchel. From the bag, he took out a book and opened it. The pages were brittle with age.

Seanchai handled it reverently and his eyes became large. "This," he said, his voice shook, "is amazing."

FIFTY-SIX

Shayth kicked himself for not trying to escape when he had been summoned to General Tarlach's office. Not that he thought he had any chance of succeeding, but the waiting and thinking were depressing, especially the thinking. Perhaps they might have beaten him unconscious. It would have been merciful.

He looked over at Ilana and her cellmate. He still didn't trust Maugwen and wasn't sure he would try to rescue her. But he certainly wouldn't leave Ilana or Rhoddan. What had happened to him? He was a loner. He tolerated no one and helped no one. But now he felt inexplicably bound to these two elves. He turned to speak with Rhoddan, but found him asleep after exercising for most of the night.

Shayth peered out into the alcove. He could not see any guards. It was possibly their lunchtime, which meant they would stay in their guardhouse for a few hours, eating and drinking. He needed to talk.

"Ilana," he whispered. "You awake?"

She rose and appeared at the bars of her cell, gray and gaunt. She hadn't been beautiful, at least not in the way he measured beauty, but she had possessed a vibrancy that was now absent. Under the insults and blows, Ilana had grown up and it saddened Shayth to see what she had lost.

"What?" she said, looking furtively towards the passageway where the guards might enter at any moment.

"We need to break out of here, and I need you to be ready." Shayth said. "Do you think you can get us back to the tunnel?"

She shrugged. "Does it matter? Even if I could, the cap will be sealed. The guide said he would give us two days and then return to screw it on himself."

Shayth nodded. "That's true. Rowan probably closed it as soon as he left us. I'm sure he set us up. Tarlach was waiting. If so, the tunnel is certain to be already sealed, permanently. If I ever find that weasel, I'll kill him."

"I don't know any other way out." Ilana sighed and hung her head.

"Maybe escaping isn't what's important," Shayth considered. "Perhaps getting ourselves killed is enough to prevent Seanchai from trying to rescue us."

But as he looked at Ilana and Rhoddan, he realized how much he didn't want them to die. An idea sprouted.

"I'll speak to Tarlach," he said.

"Why?" Rhoddan had woken up. "Do you think he might give us a free pass? 'Run along now, my royal prince, and take your young elf friends. Please be good rebels from now on.' Your Tarlach is such a sweetheart."

They made a half-hearted effort to laugh, but had no energy or sense of humor left. After a few moments, Shayth continued his thoughts.

"The Emperor wants me—not you. He knows that neither of you is the one he's looking for. Perhaps I can bargain for your release."

"Then we'll try and rescue you," Rhoddan promised.

"Tarlach wouldn't release you until after my execution for that very reason—and he can't do that without the Emperor's permission. I have to find something to leverage with, but what?"

They all shook their heads and lapsed into silence.

A short time later, Shayth rapped on the cell bars with a shoe, calling out to the guards until one came stomping down the stairs.

"What's the ruckus, scum?"

"Tell Tarlach I want to speak with him," Shayth said his voice strong.

The guard slammed his baton against the bars as a warning, still careful not to touch Shayth. "It's *General* Tarlach to you." Then he turned to leave and muttered over his shoulder, "I'll pass on the message, your highness."

Ilana woke immediately when she heard the guards approaching late that night. Rhoddan scrambled from his workout to his cot just as the guards entered the alcove with their lighted torches and clinking chain mail. They made as much noise as possible unlocking the door to the cell and for good measure a guard smashed his baton on Ilana's and Maugwen's cell bars.

"Come on, you," one said to Shayth with a wry smile. "General Tarlach wants a chat."

Shayth exited his cell silently and was immediately surrounded by six guards. They climbed the stairs and were gone.

Ilana stood up, rubbing her eyes. "What's he doing?" she asked Rhoddan.

"I don't know. If he can, he should bargain his way out."

"That won't help us, though," Maugwen was awake now.

"Still, I would rather he lived than all of us die," Ilana said.

"You're weird," Maugwen said, and smiled.

Shayth was made to stand outside General Tarlach's office until the meeting inside adjourned. A number of voices seeped out but Shayth could not hear any words.

Some time later, the door opened and several officers exited, each glaring at Shayth. One intentionally knocked into him, and Shayth nearly lost his temper. *You would have feared to come within a hundred paces of me if I had…*

It seemed a long time passed before he was called in—perhaps a pointed statement on how unimportant his time was. Shayth watched Bortand clearing papers from the strategy table. He turned and gave Shayth a tight smile. "My apologies, Master Shayth. I, um, I won't be a moment."

Tarlach, who had been standing at the table looking over maps or plans—Shayth could not be sure which—returned to his desk and sat down. He eyed Shayth but never made any move to begin the conversation, and the silence extended. When Bortand finished and made to leave, the general stopped him.

"I think, Mr. Bortand, that a witness to a meeting like this might be protocol."

"Indeed, General Tarlach. I would recommend a third person given the, um, intricacy of the situation."

Shayth contemplated the rotund administrator. "I would threaten to kill you if a word of what's said here ever got out, but given my situation, that's not much of a threat."

The general laughed, the bureaucrat gulped, and the prisoner glared. When Bortand had regained his composure, he said: "I would be expected to reveal whatever I heard in court or, um, to the Emperor. Otherwise, I would, um, out of professional decorum, keep what is said here in the strictest confidentiality."

Bortand was just an aide, Shayth reminded himself, and addressed the general. "I plan to get personal," he warned.

General Tarlach shrugged and signaled for Shayth to continue.

"I have come to bargain for the lives of my friends, the elves and the two Tutans. They're young, foolish, and I think they've learned their lessons. Given that they pose no threat to the Emperor, I ask that they be set free."

"What have you to offer in exchange for this gesture of good will? A single execution makes much less of a statement than all five of you would."

Shayth swallowed. "I'll make a public confession, either here or in the capital. I'll admit to whatever crimes you would like to stick on me."

"You might still be executed after that," the general said.

"I hope I will. It's preferable to rotting in a prison cell."

"So what difference does it make," Tarlach leaned forward, "if we execute you here or there, now or in the future?"

"You'll get the confession. Nothing is as popular as a dead martyr and you can prevent that. Those in the resistance will enjoy playing up my execution. Also the Emperor will be able to put to death all those rumors that abound."

Tarlach looked up and a flicker of doubt crossed his face. "I know not of what you speak."

"About the murder of Prince Shindell and his wife, my father and mother. You remember them, surely? Do you recall your own fears and doubts? How about those of your wife's? About how I had to flee to protect, not just my own life, but also yours and those of your wife and son. Shall I go on?"

"You have no proof," Tarlach snapped, beginning to rise from his chair. "You were just a boy."

Bortand cleared his throat quietly to remind the general where he was and who he was with. Tarlach glanced at him, stood, straightened his uniform, and crossed the room. His heels clicked on the stone floor. He opened a cupboard, took out a bottle, and poured himself something strong and pungent, before returning to his seat, where he sipped his drink.

Shayth continued. "I was there the night you told your wife of the pregnant Empress. I was hiding under the pagoda in the garden when you discussed who murdered my parents."

Shayth saw the general's knuckles whiten as he gripped the desktop. His glass was frozen halfway between his mouth and the desk. He glared at Shayth but said nothing.

"Tell me, General Tarlach," Shayth snarled, "and honestly if that's even possible: if they had come for me in the night and I had cried out to you for help, would you have come to the aid of the ten-year-old orphan living under your roof, under your protection? Back then, before the Emperor corrupted you with rank and power, would you have tried to save me? The son of your best friend?"

The general was breathing heavily, his nostrils flaring. Bortand was quick to intervene. "Allow me, um, with a lifetime of diplomacy, to suggest that calling the impeccable general corrupt might not, um, be the most strategic way to free your friends."

Shayth rolled his eyes and turned his attention back to Tarlach. The general held a scroll with a royal seal on it. He read: "Furthermore, all caught aiding the criminal, Shayth, shall also be put to death, without trial, appeal, or negotiations whatsoever, on the day of my birthday. Let the people understand that hanging is the sole consequence to treason."

Tarlach stared icily at Shayth. "You may go now. Guards!"

Shayth was furious and clenched his fists. "So now your hands are tied, Tarlach? What about *then*? What would you have done to protect the innocent boy under your protection, under your roof? It was me, Shayth. Were you such a coward then as you are now? You never looked for me after I ran away, did you?"

His voice was shaking as two burly guards entered the office, grabbed his arms and began to drag him away. He shouted: "Were you so scared then as you are now? You know who murdered my parents. I heard you admit it to your wife at the pagoda."

"Take him away," Tarlach hissed between clenched teeth. "He's gone mad."

Shayth struggled against the iron grip of the guards and kicked out. A chair spun into the air before crashing to the floor. Shayth twisted and screamed, "WHAT WOULD YOU HAVE DONE IF THEY'D TRIED TO MURDER THE TEN-YEAR-OLD BOY LIKE THEY MURDERED HIS MOTHER AND FATHER? HIS FATHER, YOUR BEST FRIEND, WHO RODE WITH SOLDIERS UNDER YOUR COMMAND, TARLACH, UNDER YOUR PROTECTION."

"GET HIM OUT OF HERE," Tarlach roared, springing to his feet and throwing the glass across the room, where it shattered against the stone wall.

Bortand rose slowly from his chair, but didn't move further. A scuffle broke out outside the office and then more dragging. Shayth's hoarse shouts echoed from around a corner. "THE BOY WAS UNDER YOUR PROTECTION, TARLACH, IN YOUR HOUSE. WOULD YOU HAVE TRIED TO SAVE ME? I WAS SHAYTH SHINDELL?"

And then from further away, almost muffled. "Why won't you answer me? You coward. My father was your best friend."

General Tarlach signaled for his adviser to leave, his chest heaving with rage. Bortand closed the door softly and walked away shaking his head.

FIFTY-SEVEN

Sellia was intrigued with Seanchai's behavior. He sat cross-legged, peering at the open book that crackled with age as each brittle page was turned. His forehead creased with concentration as he read and reread passages. Occasionally he looked up and mouthed a word. Sellia wanted to interrupt him, to ask what he was doing. Why was he reading a book when he had been so anxious to leave for Galbrieth?

Caught in her reverie, she barely saw Seanchai now crouching next to her. "Sellia, Sellia, I need your help. Read this sentence to me."

She peered over at what she now could see was a children's storybook, and read: "He looked out over the valley and called to the wind spirit. *'Wind spirit, wind spirit, I summon you.'* This is a famous children's story, Seanchai. Why are you so excited?"

"What you read are the actual words 'wind spirit', correct? You don't see any other word, any other language?"

"No. It's here in plain Odessiyan," Sellia replied, her exasperated confusion clear. "Why?"

"I see something else." He raised his head and looked across Mhari's camp. "Do you feel the light breeze?"

She nodded.

"*Moriarhtur,*" he whispered, *"Moriarhtur,"*

And the breeze became a wind, whistling through the weathered rocks. Seanchai's palms were facing upwards. He turned them over and brought his hands down, the wind dying to a breeze as they lowered.

"Wow," was the best she could manage.

"Wow is right," Seanchai grinned. "You see the words as they are intended, but a Wycaan sees the words that channel that element. Now that I have become a Wycaan, I can read the magical words."

Sellia couldn't help smiling at his childlike excitement. "Apparently!" she exclaimed. "But finish your packing, and let's go. You can keep reading whenever we rest."

Seanchai couldn't help but lose himself in the book. It was all coming together: the fusion of earth power and the magic of the spoken word. They had all hinted at the power of stories–Mhari, Ilana, Rhoddan, Shayth–and he had always believed in the ancient lore with an inexplicable draw. It had been calling him, and now he suddenly and fervently needed to learn every word. His name was, after all, Seanchai. He was a storyteller, a Wycaan.

A shadow. Sellia stood over him, hands on her hips. She was beautiful, he thought, her ebony skin shining in the crisp morning light. But Sellia was also imposing when annoyed, though her stance only reminded him of Ilana getting angry. He wondered if it was something common to all elfes. He wouldn't know, but his heart felt heavy at the thought of Ilana.

"Yes?" he asked, as pleasantly as he could muster.

"I think we should go. There isn't a lot of time, and I'm not sure reading children's stories is a priority right now." She half-smiled to show she was half-joking, but Seanchai's expression remained intense, and he just nodded.

He rose and disappeared into the cave, retrieving the bag of herbs and a few other items that Mhari had instructed him to bring. Everything else he packed on the hidden rock ridges as his teacher had requested. When he finished and Snowmane was ready, he turned to Sellia.

"Let me work on your ankle for a few minutes."

"It's fine. We should leave."

"No," Seanchai countered. "It's not just about you. I might need you to run, to fight, who knows what."

"I'm feeling much better," she protested, but Seanchai wasn't having it.

"I've seen you wince. This isn't some fairy tale with a brave heroine."

"I'm not the one reading fairy tales, Wycaan," Sellia replied, but obliged him and sat on a rock. She sighed with relief at the healing pulse of energy.

Seanchai led Sellia on Snowmane out of the mountains and down toward the lake. Once the ground was smoother, the Wycaan scryed and, not sensing anyone, began to run so fast that Snowmane was soon galloping to keep up. Sellia watched from the horse's back, an astonished expression on her face.

They rounded the lake in the first two hours and moved through another mountain pass. As they approached the road to Galbrieth, Seanchai slowed to a normal pace. They joined a steady stream of people on their way to the city for the Emperor's birthday, excited by the promise of free food and ale.

Seanchai's frustration grew as the human river slowed his pace. He weaved in and out, keeping his cloak over his head. He looked like a religious eccentric, and where they could, people let him pass with a roll of the eye, an indulgent smile, or a wary glance at their weapons.

When they took a short break, Seanchai stretched and then glanced over at Sellia. "We'll stop early this afternoon to rest. We'll sleep for a few hours and be able to travel faster by night."

There were about two hours of daylight left when Seanchai guided Snowmane off the road and into a treed area. He quickly wrapped himself in his bedroll and closed his eyes. He woke, a wave of panic when sounds from the wave of strangers penetrated his dreams and saw Sellia sitting up, her back against a tree and her hand on the hilt of her long knife. He drifted back to sleep.

It was dark when Seanchai stirred and, despite his fatigue, immediately came awake. He found some dried fish in Mhari's supplies. "Eat this while we ride," he told Sellia, who had only dozed and now looked groggy. "If the road is clearer, I'm going to go fast."

Away from villages and people, Seanchai sped up while Sellia dozed in her saddle. In the villages he stopped only to tear down a few scrolls announcing the execution of his friends. Such notices hung everywhere and he knew his actions were futile. The village scribe had been busy, no doubt being paid for the amount he drew. Seanchai felt a growing sense of urgency and picked up his pace.

As dawn stretched across the valley, Seanchai took them off the road and into another grove of trees. He had his bedroll out quickly, and was about to lie down when he saw Sellia standing and staring off into the distance, her roll of blankets pressed to her chest.

"What is it, Sellia?"

"Nothing. I'm fine."

Seanchai rose and came to stand beside her. On the horizon were the towers rising above the great walls of Galbrieth.

FIFTY-EIGHT

Shayth screamed hysterically as he was dragged all the way from Tarlach's office. Rhoddan, Ilana and Maugwen were all wide-awake and listening to his legs hit one stone stair after another. The soldier leading the sixer glared at Rhoddan.

"Move away from the door," he yelled as he swung his heavy ring of keys. "The traitor has gone nuts."

Rhoddan saw that the soldier's eye had begun to swell. He didn't feel any sympathy, for the man had hit him several times. The other guards were similarly disheveled.

Shayth's black hair was sweaty and standing straight up off his head. His clothes were ripped and bloodstained, and large purple welts were emerging on his body. Shayth, however, still seemed up for a fight. But he was overpowered and unceremoniously thrown into his cell.

He fell onto the floor, facedown, panting. When Rhoddan went to help him up, he snarled, "Don't touch me."

The ferocity in his voice jerked Rhoddan back, and he glanced over at Ilana. She and Maugwen were standing at their bars, staring. Time passed uneventfully, until suddenly Shayth rose and charged the cell door. He howled with pain and fury as his shoulder hit the bars.

"Come and get it over with, you worms," he yelled. "If you're too scared to fight me, then bring your scum of a general and let him face me! He's a coward! Your general is a coward!"

He charged the door of the cell again, this time recoiling in pain with his arm clutched to his body.

"He was too scared to protect a little boy in his care," Shayth's voice was becoming hoarse, but still he yelled. "His best friend's son, you hear?"

As he hurled more insults and prepared to lunge again, Rhoddan grabbed his shoulder and swung him around. Shayth was past caring with whom he fought and threw a punch. But Rhoddan easily avoided the clumsy attempt and swung his right fist into Shayth's chin, sending him reeling to the floor. Shayth didn't get up. Then Rhoddan dragged him up onto his cot and turned to face Ilana.

"Nice shot," Maugwen cheered, though she withered when Rhoddan, who was opening and closing his fist in pain, glared at her.

"What do you think happened?" Ilana asked.

"No idea," Rhoddan replied. "But I've a sneaking suspicion that his discussion with the general didn't go too well."

The excitement over, they all retreated to their cots and went to sleep. When they were woken the next morning for breakfast and bucket duty, the guard glared at Shayth, who lay still on his cot, facing the wall. Prisoners were required to stand up when food was brought to them so the guards could easily see if someone was sick or dead. The guard hesitated but ultimately decided that he was not going to deal with Shayth.

"We'll be back soon," the guard announced. "You're to see where the celebrations will take place. You'll be shown what will happen tomorrow and where you should stand so you don't make complete fools of yourself. Very considerate of the general, if you ask me."

"What does that mean?" Ilana asked when he had left.

"It's a rehearsal. It needs to look good for the Emperor." Maugwen said.

"And if we don't cooperate?"

Maugwen shrugged. "I think you can do it the easy way or the hard way. But either way, you'll die."

Ilana stared at her. Maugwen was so young and innocent. She had no idea how insensitive she had just been.

Rhoddan was dozing when the guards finally came for them several hours after their evening meal. It had been a tense day. Shayth never spoke and refused to even acknowledge anyone. He lay curled up on his cot, not rising to eat or drink. Rhoddan eyed him with increasing apprehension.

The sixer stood in two groups of three, each trio holding a burning torch. A soldier unlocked Ilana's cell and signaled with his head for her to exit. He moved more cautiously to the other cell, opened the door and beckoned to Rhoddan.

"Walk to the she-elf very slowly. You try anything and we'll thrash you to within an inch of your life. Understand?"

Rhoddan nodded and obeyed. Shayth still had not moved.

"We can do this smoothly or shackle your legs and drag you," the guard said. "The general doesn't care either way." When he received no response, he stormed into the cell and cracked his baton against the wall by the head of Shayth's cot.

Shayth jumped to his feet and the guard almost fell over backwards. "A little jumpy tonight, aren't we?" Shayth hissed. "Why are we doing this in the dark?"

"Not our place to ask questions," the guard replied. "Let's move."

"Maybe it's because you're frightened of us and want us to be tired. Or maybe you're scared that we might outsmart you and run away."

The head guard sneered. "Maybe General Tarlach had more important things than you traitors to worry about during the day. I'd bet even his visits to the chamber pot were a higher priority."

Shayth took a wider berth than necessary on his way out of the cell, causing the guard to take another step back. The implication was clear to both of them, and Shayth grinned cynically.

Rhoddan glanced at Ilana. Was Shayth cracking? What had happened in Tarlach's office?

FIFTY-NINE

When Seanchai felt Sellia's hand shaking him awake, it was already well after sunrise. He had never covered any distance at such a fast pace and was surprised at the toll it took.

He chewed on some dried goat meat and recalled how Sellia had killed one for Rhoddan and himself when they had fled from Rhoddan's group towards Uncle's camp. It felt like an age had passed and he reflected on how much his perception of Sellia had changed these past few days. She had been so aloof and intimidating to him before, in Uncle's clan. Perhaps she had changed. Perhaps he had.

"You shouldn't have let me sleep so long," he grumbled.

"You needed it to restore your strength," Sellia argued. "You're going to be quite busy in the next few days. Anyway, I only woke you now because the road is packed and we should use the chaos to slip into the city."

He nodded. "Any ideas on how we can pass that checkpoint ahead?"

"Yes. With them." She gestured to an ostentatious caravan of brightly painted wagons, performers of all sizes and colors, and exotic, foreign animals.

"Who are they?" Seanchai asked in wonder.

"It's a circus troupe. They travel to different towns and perform tricks, acrobatics, and magic. Have you never seen one?"

Seanchai shook his head. "No, but I've heard about them. What's your plan?"

"We join them. If necessary we'll talk with the owner. But I can see a few elves in their party. Let's try them first."

They packed their bags and tied their horses to the trees. Sellia hid the saddles between rocks. Seanchai turned to Snowmane. "We'll be back soon, old friend," he said as he patted the horse.

Sellia thought to contradict him, but decided against it. She was worried about the young elf's feelings, not those of his horse. She noted that Seanchai took the bags with the book and the herbs with him.

They walked toward the road. Sellia still limped, but it was less noticeable. As they approached the circus caravan, she suggested that Seanchai hold back. She approached a group of elves gambling with cubes on the ground and crouched down by them.

"What do you want?" a stout elf asked , his eyes darting around. "We have no food to share."

"I don't seek food," Sellia answered. "My husband and I are traveling without papers. We want to join you and enter the city with your caravan."

The elves glanced at each other, back at Seanchai and then to Sellia.

"Why don't you have papers?"

"We're from Northshot. The baron there does not appreciate his tenants going anywhere that doesn't bring him a profit. He would rather we work his fields until we die." She drew back her hood and looked at the three elfes in the group. "The baron also has a taste for elfes. Those he takes usually don't return. If they do, they are broken. He…" she looks down at her feet, embarrassed. "He has taken an interest in me."

The elfes all tensed at Sellia's story, "We'll help you," one replied without hesitation, but the nervous elf slammed the cubes on the ground in frustration.

"They could put us all in danger," he said.

"And if this baron had set his eyes on me, Fredrich?" the same elfe replied, looking at him with what Sellia took to be a firm but loving expression.

He shook his head and sighed, defeated. Then he turned to Sellia. "What do you seek in Galbrieth?"

"We plan to find the baron," Sellia replied. "My husband will arrange for a little accident in the crowded streets. With all these people, and many of them drunk at that, there'll be chaos. We won't give up our little farm to him, and I won't let him abuse or torture me."

There was a nod of solidarity among the elves. Only Fredrich seemed troubled. "No one must see him." He nodded at Seanchai. "He'll hide in our wagon. You'll stay with the elfes. Can you dance? Sometimes the soldiers have their own price to relieve the boredom."

"I can," she replied, laying her hands on her slim hips and arching her waist.

"Good. If the soldiers find your husband, we can't help. We will act surprised, as though he smuggled himself in. Do you understand that?"

Sellia nodded.

"Take him to that wagon over there. I will meet him in a few minutes."

Sellia did not need to dance. The soldiers at the checkpoint were overworked and expecting the circus caravan. They paid no more attention to the women and elfes than what equipment was packed in the wagons. Seanchai lay under a sheet between two long boxes. He was concealed well enough to be overlooked by a cursory glance.

When the entourage reached their destination, the lead elf and Sellia uncovered Seanchai to let him out. As he struggled to get up, his hood fell back, and Fredrich gasped.

Sellia had a knife at his throat before he could react. "Don't do or say anything that we will all regret, do you understand?"

"Yes," Fredrich replied. "It was a shock, that's all. Are you—?"

Seanchai smiled and replaced his cowl, but didn't answer. The circus elf stared wondrously into his bright blue eyes until Seanchai grasped his hand. When released, Fredrich's hand held some coins.

"Not much, I'm afraid," Seanchai said, "but I want to thank you for taking a risk and, I hope, to encourage your discretion."

"Thank you," Fredrich said, nodding in awe. "This isn't necessary, but will be put to good use."

"Not in the ale house," Sellia warned. "Alcohol can loosen an elf's tongue, make him careless."

"The ale houses here don't welcome elves unless it's to lose their money gambling," Fredrich stiffened. Then he glanced again at Seanchai and smiled. "Go now. I've forgotten we ever met, but I'll always remember meeting you."

"We should have asked him where the inn is," Sellia remarked after they had wandered aimlessly for a time without locating it.

"No," Seanchai replied. "I don't want him to know where we are going. Mhari said the inn is in the rough quarter. It looks like we're getting near."

Thieves no doubt took in their ragged clothes and Seanchai's imposing size allowed them to make their way unbothered until a drunken elf grabbed at Sellia and attempted to plant a kiss on her lips. He found himself spun around and the knife she poked in his back kept him at a distance and prompted him to kindly offer to escort them to the Galbrieth Arms.

"Ain't no good of an inn, 'specially for us elves. I know a –"

"We aren't staying here," Sellia interrupted. "We just need to deliver something to someone. And you will forget we ever met. Understood?"

The pressure of the knife's blade ensured that his memory was already slipping. When they saw the sign for the Galbrieth Arms, they let the drunkard go. He melted quickly into the crowd.

They went inside, hoods up and hands on their knives. The main hall smelled of pipe smoke and stale alcohol and had a low ceiling with heavy beams crossing it. Several people were drinking in an anteroom where a band played.

Sellia asked a waitress for Jalkieth and was directed to a table in a shadowy corner. "The one in the yellow waistcoat. But he ain't hirin' right now, dear."

They approached the table and waited until Jalkieth's companion finished his business and left. Seanchai approached the table, leaned down and whispered, "I was sent by my master, Mhari." The man brushed him off, but Seanchai was prepared. "You will know me when I reveal myself."

Jalkieth stared at him and nodded slowly. Then he rose and led them out of the inn into a one-story courtyard. He turned to his left along a row of doors, stopping and unlocking one at the very end. He offered for Seanchai to enter.

Seanchai walked in and Jalkieth moved into the doorway to block him from view outside. Seanchai turned around to face him and removed his hood. The innkeeper gasped and involuntarily brought a hand to his mouth.

"I trust that this room is safe?" Seanchai confirmed. "We don't plan to stay long."

SIXTY

Ilana, Shayth and Rhoddan followed the staff sergeant and two soldiers out of the dungeon. Ilana realized she was actually glad to be leaving the stale air of the cells, even though it was to see where she would die. A thought occurred to her.

"What about the Tutans?" she asked.

"Didn't hear them request to join you," the officer said without turning round. The other soldiers laughed and it sounded particularly evil rebounding off the rock walls.

The stony path proved difficult to maneuver, and she tripped twice on the cobblestones. The second time Shayth caught her, she glanced up to thank him and saw his eyes dart from her to something above.

Ilana straightened and surreptitiously glanced up. Was that movement or wishful thinking? She locked her gaze on the stony path before her, wondering if Shayth, clearly blazing with fury and itching to vent his frustrations on someone's face, would stay disciplined. Not much, she thought, was preventing him from exploding?

They turned left into another corridor—this one with no windows or ceiling beams. Ilana sensed activity behind her, but kept walking so as not to draw attention. A grunt, a thud, and then a muffled yelp, which she tried to cough over. Not loudly enough—the sergeant swung round. There was only darkness behind the prisoners.

"Bolt? Grimwitch?" The sergeant strained to control his voice.

His remaining soldiers shoved the prisoners against the wall and rushed into the blackness, meeting a big, cloaked man with a long knife in one hand and a short one in the other. He killed both guards in one fluid movement, his short knife slicing one's throat and circling straight into the other's stomach.

The sergeant, instead of drawing his own sword, reached for a whistle around his neck. It never reached his mouth. Rhoddan's punch sent the officer crashing against the wall. Shayth was right behind him with fist raised, too. He glared at his friend.

"That was inconsiderate," he hissed. Ilana would have liked to see the comment accompanied by a smile.

"Next time," Rhoddan murmured.

Their rescuer was dressed all in black: boots, trousers, shirt and scarf that fully covered his head and face, leaving only his eyes revealed. He strode past Shayth and Rhoddan, put his boot on the fallen sergeant's throat, and stepped down. The sickening crack of bones echoed through the tunnel.

Then the figure turned, ran ten paces back down the corridor, stopped and nodded his head for them to follow. Shayth bent down and grabbed the sergeant's sword.

"Seanchai," Ilana whispered, a thrill coursing through her body.

They ran after him, down one corridor, up another, and through a door hidden in a wall. He was too agile, too fast, for them to catch up to, but they didn't care. They were escaping.

Still, Ilana couldn't help thinking: Why didn't Seanchai acknowledge them—her, especially? Doubt flooded her mind. This person was bigger than Seanchai. Though he used elven weapons, he was far more fluent than Seanchai. And he knew every inch of the garrison's underbelly—even that they would take this route at this particular time. Was there a resistance cell in Galbrieth?

When they next caught sight of the figure, he had dispensed with two more guards, and blood dripped from his blades. He threw a sword to Rhoddan, but didn't deliver the other to Ilana. Seanchai knew she could fight. Her heart sunk as she finally accepted that this wasn't Seanchai. It was ironic. She had spent her time in captivity praying he would stay away, and now she was desperately disappointed that he wasn't their rescuer.

"You're wounded," Shayth said to the figure. Blood leaked from a gash across his forehead, and he reached up briefly with a gloved hand before continuing up the tunnel.

Fresh air. Or, as fresh as it could be, given that it was in the middle of the city, but after underground incarceration, it felt rich. They entered the square teeming with people preparing for the celebration.

But they ran straight into a regiment of soldiers going through drills. An officer reacted quickly, drawing his broadsword and booming to his infantry: "The prisoners! Take positions. Light the beacon!" He pointed his sword to the group. "Don't move!"

Archers drew their bows as a fire roared up next to them. Shayth braced to fight, and Rhoddan and Ilana closed in. But their rescuer turned and fled back into the caverns.

A sixer went after him and disappeared into the dark tunnel.

"Follow him," Ilana cried to Rhoddan and Shayth, but, blinded by flames and smoke, they could not react faster than the two-dozen soldiers who surrounded them, soon joined by those who had run into the tunnel and returned empty-handed. The prisoners stood back to back, a ragged triangle, swords at the ready.

"We fight," Shayth roared. "We take as many down as we can."

"It's as good a day as any to die," Rhoddan answered his voice strangely serene. "It feels right with a sword in my hand."

But Ilana stepped forward, took Rhoddan's sword, and threw it on the ground, where it clanged on the stone. Then she turned to face her friends.

"No," she said, voice quavering. "It's not as good a day as any. It's just a waste. Save yourselves. Live another day. Who knows what could happen tomorrow?"

She was sure Rhoddan and Shayth could hear her disappointment that their rescuer was not Seanchai. But the possibility of seeing him again had filled her with a desire to stay alive as long as she could.

"Come on," she said and reached for Shayth's sword. "Please," she begged, and her voice broke. Shayth let go and Ilana turned back to Rhoddan and fell into his arms, sobbing quietly. "It wasn't him," her muffled voice whispered.

They were marched into the square and to the executioner's platform, where thick gallows with five rope nooses swung slightly in the breeze.

"We should string 'em up now," growled a soldier near Ilana. "Save a lot of trouble tomorrow."

"After what they just pulled," another added, "I'm sure the Emperor wouldn't care. Bolt and Grimwitch are dead."

Tension was high as Shayth glared at the soldier who had just spoken. The man, realizing he was referring to the prince, averted his eyes. But the tension remained.

"Actually, I believe the, um, Emperor would take great exception," a pleasant voice said from behind them. Bortand shuffled up the stairs. "He was most clear concerning when and how he wants the executions to take place. I read the orders myself. Does anyone wish to take issue with the, um, Emperor?"

No one spoke, and the soldiers shuffled awkwardly. Bortand turned to the commanding officer. "You reacted very quickly. I will make sure the general hears. Have you finished here? I suspect General Tarlach would appreciate a chat with the prisoners. I don't think we should keep him waiting, do you?"

"Sir," the officer saluted, "the rescuer escaped and might be around with allies. We need more soldiers to move the prisoners."

Bortand looked around, quickly counting the soldiers. "I should hope you can handle three scrawny prisoners, Sergeant, with your, um, twenty-six well-trained men. Don't you post them forward in stages or something?"

"Yes, sir. Strategic advancing, sir." The soldiers stood a bit straighter, smirking at Bortand's failure to know their terminology. He knew they assumed that a fat bureaucrat would not understand their tactics, but they were wrong. Bortand knew the exact terminology. He also knew his intentional blunder had both diffused their anger and boosted their confidence. He smiled back.

"Very well, Sergeant. Please strategically advance the prisoners to, um, General Tarlach's office."

"Yes, sir," the sergeant even saluted. "Men, surround the prisoners."

General Tarlach was not in his office when Bortand arrived. He was probably looking for those who had attempted to aid the prisoners. Bortand peered out of the window. The garrison was lit as soldiers ran with torches, many yelling orders. Hopefully the general would run a lot too, Bortand thought. Otherwise he'd be doing a lot of yelling when he returned.

Shayth was angry as it was, but having to wait outside Tarlach's office again was infuriating. He thought of their last conversation here and how it had affected him. That wouldn't happen this time.

It was two hours before the general appeared, breathless and sweating. He walked into his office and, pulling off his helmet, went to a bowl in the corner to splash water on his face.

Shayth, Rhoddan and Ilana stood waiting. With his back to them, General Tarlach growled, "Who helped you?"

Met with silence, he yelled: "I said, who helped you?" He threw his helmet across the room, and it bounced on the stone floor. He turned slowly.

"We didn't have time for introductions," Shayth replied, "and he was masked, before you bother to ask."

Determined to maintain his composure, Shayth glanced up into the general's eyes. There, he saw something he hadn't expected. There was dried blood crusting over a long cut across Tarlach's forehead. Shayth opened his mouth to speak, but Tarlach eyes went wide and he smashed his fist into Shayth's face, sending Shayth flying across the room.

The interrogation was over.

SIXTY-ONE

Seanchai fell fast asleep immediately. They had traveled hard these last few days, and he appreciated the luxury of sleeping within walls with no need to post guards or fear intrusion. Mhari had vouched for the innkeeper, and that was good enough for him.

Seanchai's growling stomach woke him this time. It was already dark, and he was hungry and anxious. He needed to begin scouting and formulate a plan before the emperor's birthday celebration and the execution the following afternoon.

Outside, he was shocked to see the throng of people on the streets at such a late hour—and even more surprised that he had managed to sleep through it. There was raucous shouting and laughter. Many reeked of ale and scented smoke, and were bumping into each other drunkenly. Given Seanchai's physical stature those who bumped into him promptly apologized, but he thought it weird how this was often followed by a fit of drunken giggling.

Sellia held his arm to ensure they didn't separate, and soon guided him into a packed eatery. They stood in a line of customers waiting to be served. When they reached the front, they were each handed a tray and charged two draktans. A full pewter was slammed onto each of their trays, sloshing up on their cloaks. It annoyed Seanchai even though his garment was torn and threadbare.

They weaved through the sprawl of tables and found a vacant one for two in a corner. As they sat, Seanchai noticed Sellia smiling to herself.

"What's so funny?" he asked.

"You," she laughed. "I don't need to see your face to know how uncomfortable you are. Try and relax a bit. Blend in."

"I'm not used to being around so many humans," he replied. "I miss my family, my village and being with elves."

Sellia took his hand in hers, sending a thrill through his body that was replaced immediately with guilt. She leaned closer. "I think you're going to have to get used to being around this many people. So for now, enjoy the anonymity and try to look as though you belong."

"Let's talk about what we need to do," Seanchai said.

"No," Sellia snapped. "There're too many people in here, with twice as many ears. I bet at least six are in the general's pay, bursting to hear something like this."

"So why not find somewhere quieter? Some places we passed were almost empty."

Sellia pretended to laugh as though he had just told the most hilarious joke. She dipped her bread in the stew and took a bite. "We would stick out to anyone passing. Here we're just another young couple in a hectic place. Now eat. It's going cold."

She washed her food down with ale. The dented pewter looked unruly in contrast to her distinguished cheekbones. Observing her made him think of Ilana. How was she holding up? Did she hope he would come? Did she expect it? More likely she would chide him for risking himself, but he had to find her. He needed to be with her.

Seanchai finished his food quickly and was contemplating going back for more when four soldiers entered. Instantly, the place went silent, and all eyes followed them as they ambled round the tables. When one moved in their general direction, Sellia leaned in and entwined her fingers in his.

"Take it easy, Seanchai," she whispered, having seen him subconsciously reach for his knives. "They just want to look like they're working. Soon they'll be given some food and sit down."

One of the soldiers came nearer, glancing their way.

"Say something," she whispered.

"What?"

She laughed and batted her eyes, an elfe totally in love. Seanchai was startled and then played along, reaching out to stroke her cheek. She sighed theatrically.

The soldier made a comment about patrons losing their appetites and went back to the serving counter. No one objected when the soldiers went straight to the front of the line.

Once the place had settled down and people began their conversations again, Seanchai and Sellia finished their food and left. They walked toward the square behind a couple. When the man put his arm around the woman's waist, Seanchai copied him with Sellia. The woman responded and put her arm around the man. Sellia smirked and followed her lead. But when the man stopped, bent down and planted a kiss on the woman, Seanchai leapt away from Sellia as if he had been burned. She laughed hysterically, almost falling over in the process.

"What's so funny?" he asked, already knowing the answer.

Sellia frowned. "What's so bad? We'll probably be dead tomorrow. Lighten up!"

Seanchai was sure the points of his ears were burning red, but Sellia's comment was sobering, and he had no response. They entered the great square and stopped for a moment to take in their surroundings before strolling toward the dignitaries' pavilion.

Seanchai bypassed the seating and approached the executioner's stage. When Sellia caught up to him, he was watching two men adjust the gallows. The trap door below the nooses was snapped open and shut several times.

Seanchai's stomach tightened and, clutching Sellia's hand, he followed the wooden structure as it wound back to a big archway in the rock face that led, if he remembered correctly, to the dungeons. They walked to the corner of the rock face and around the side of the garrison walls, but Seanchai couldn't see any way in. Suddenly, they came face-to-face with a patrol of soldiers.

"What are you doing here?" the officer in charge demanded.

"Just looking for a quiet spot," giggled Sellia, "if you know what I mean, sir. There are people everywhere." She pressed herself against Seanchai.

"Well, this ain't a good spot, so go find a room."

The patrol passed, and Seanchai and Sellia continued along the wall, but it was too dark to see higher than a hand or two. If there was a hidden ledge, they could not tell. Seanchai sighed.

As they rounded the corner, another patrol approached. Sellia pushed Seanchai against the wall and grabbed his face outside of his cowl. Then she kissed him full on the lips and lingered, waiting for the guards to continue their patrol.

"Bloody elves," one sneered. "Never could hold their drinks."

"Should be 'anging the rest of 'em tomorro'," another sneered.

Seanchai was glad for Sellia's strong grasp as he felt the rage rise.

SIXTY-TWO

They made their way back to the bustling square, and Seanchai stiffened as they passed the gallows again. A big, square circus tent had been erected next to the stage together with corrals of exotic animals. As they approached the tent entrance, two big guards stepped into their path.

"No entry until tomorrow," one said.

"Can I just peek?" Seanchai asked. "I've never seen inside a circus before."

"They're rehearsing. Them circus folk get real testy before a performance. Know what I mean?"

Seanchai nodded, but continued to stare at the tent. He smiled at the two guards. "I don't want any trouble. I'm just a little excited."

"See it all the time," the other guard smiled. "You get here early tomorrow and grab a really good seat."

"Oh, I will," said Seanchai. "What time will it start?"

"After the hangings. They'll warm up the crowd beforehand, too, I hear. Though since it's the Emperor's nephew, I doubt they'll need to, what with the terrible things I've heard he's done."

"The Emperor's *nephew*?" Sellia asked when Seanchai just looked shell-shocked.

"Yeah, you don't know?" the guard replied. "A violent murderer, from what I hear. Anyway, the circus'll start about two hours before sunset. That's why we were told to put the circus tent right next to the gallows."

Sellia thanked them and guided Seanchai away.

He stopped by one of the numerous declarations posted on poles. He had not read it closely before. He shook his head. "Prince," he said, his voice bleak. "When we met Shayth, he said half the empire was chasing him. He was correct - it was the same half."

He turned and looked into Sellia's rich eyes. He sighed and gently moved a strand of hair behind her ear. It was a tender moment, but he was thinking of Ilana, who often pulled an unruly strand back in that way. He winced and felt his stomach tighten.

"Let's see if Mhari has arrived. Maybe she'll have a good idea, or any idea for that matter.

Mhari was not at the inn and Jalkieth turned his back on Seanchai when he tried to ask the innkeeper. Back in their room, Sellia tried to sleep, but soon gave up. She could sense Seanchai was awake, but neither wanted to break the silence. Finally, Sellia rose and sat on the edge of Seanchai's bed. She cleared her throat.

"Seanchai? What would Mhari tell you to do if she was here?"

"She's *not* here," Seanchai growled.

"Yes, I have noticed, but what would she advise you to do if she was?"

Seanchai didn't answer for a while, and then quietly admitted, "She would tell me to walk away and not risk everything for my friends."

"And what would Rhoddan and Ilana tell you?"

"The same."

Sellia refrained from saying anything more. She rested her hand on his arm and sighed. They sat that way for a long time, each lost in their own thoughts. Then Seanchai abruptly rose.

"Let's go," he said.

"Where?"

"To the walls. To see if we can find something."

"Really, Seanchai? What might we find?"

He turned and snapped. "You don't have to come. Stay here if you want." He stalked out of the door and slammed it shut. Sellia was instantly after him.

It was the middle of the night and the streets were still crawling with people, but this crowd seemed harder and more desperate. Seanchai walked briskly and with such intense purpose that people quickly moved out of his way.

"Hey, wait up," she panted. "The garrison's in the other direction."

Seanchai didn't hesitate or change his course. Gradually the crowds thinned as they entered a rougher part of town. When Sellia finally caught up with him, she grabbed his arm and spun him around. When she saw his eyes, she gasped. His pupils seemed out of focus.

Seanchai wrenched away, and Sellia wondered if he was scrying. She recalled him telling her that he had tracked his friends into Galbrieth and saw how they had been caught. He led her into an alleyway.

"You should stay here," he murmured.

"I don't know what you're up to, but I'm not sure leaving me alone in this neighborhood is any less dangerous." Sellia said and glanced up and down the street. Seeing small clusters of shady characters, she made her own decision. "I'm coming in."

Seanchai knocked on the door with two quick raps, followed by a third after two further seconds. A slit opened and a bloodshot eye peered out through the peephole.

"Who goes there?"

"A simple traveler," replied Seanchai, making his voice sound hoarse.

"What will you have with us?"

"A meal. Some Grampton mead if you have it."

The slit on the door closed. A muffled conversation took place inside, but they couldn't hear what was said. Seanchai mumbled something about wondering how often these people changed their passwords. Suddenly, locks were scraped back and the door opened. Seanchai swept in, pushing the doorman aside so he couldn't prevent Sellia from entering.

They stood before a long table. The man sitting at the head looked completely unbothered by their entrance, though his eyes never left them. Seanchai's physical presence filled the small, dank room, sending several men slinking away into the shadows.

As the table cleared, a hand came to Sellia's shoulder from behind. She saw a knife glint, but before she could react, Seanchai thrust a fist into the man's face, smashing him into the wall, where he crumpled to the floor. Someone gasped. Seanchai had their attention.

"You do not know me," Seanchai stated. His voice was deep and commanding.

"So how do you know about us?" the man replied. "We guard our ... reputation."

Forced laughter drifted out of the shadows.

"I have been here in a way you can't imagine, but that is irrelevant. You will get me into the garrison."

"Your friends tried that," the man replied. "I assume you want to rescue the young prince. It didn't go as planned."

More laughter.

"You will get me in. Shayth's failure was because of treachery and is a black mark on your...reputation."

Muttering from the shadows. Sellia thought that these men obviously took their professional image quite seriously and did not appreciate the insinuation.

"We can never guarantee results in our line of work. Believe me, I'm sorry for Shayth. He was... *is* a character."

"I am not concerned with your sympathies. Can you get me inside?"

The man scratched his unkempt beard. "I really don't know. It's not even a question of money."

"I'm not paying. Can you get me inside?"

The man looked up, and a flicker of fear crossed his face. There were gasps from the shadows.

"Assuming we *can* get you in—and I'm not sure how we could right now, as they've blocked up both the entrances we use—what do you mean by 'not paying'?"

"Shayth paid you and was betrayed. There was an ambush waiting. Someone in your organization tipped off the general. You carry the shame for that failed transaction. Get me inside and I will spare your lives. That should be payment enough."

Blades scratched free of their scabbards.

"Don't bother," Seanchai warned, his voice slow and deliberate. "You are no match for me, especially in the dark." He looked slowly around the room, despite the darkness, locking eyes with each of them. "Which one of you is Rowan?"

No one moved.

"Which one?" His menace made them shuffle.

"I can't get you into the dungeons," the leader said, an edge of despair in his voice. "They have tripled, even quadrupled, the guard. We don't have a way. Does anyone here think they know a way in? *I* will pay for the service, in lieu of our good friend, Shayth."

The question was met with tense silence.

"Last time. Who ... Is ... Rowan?" Seanchai growled.

This time men moved away, leaving one standing alone.

"It's not my fault!" Rowan cried, his voice shrill. "They knew the risk. I got them in. That's all I was paid to do!"

Seanchai raised a finger toward Rowan, who immediately fell quiet. Then he turned his head and addressed the man at the table. "What is the price for betrayal in this business?"

The leader didn't hesitate. "Death."

While Seanchai's eyes bored into the leader, his palm turned toward Rowan. The Wycaan pulled his hand back and pushed with his entire body, driving his feet into the ground. Rowan flew into the wall behind him, the sickening crack of bones shattering brought gasps from even these hardened criminals.

"No one," threatened Seanchai, "will ever recall I was here. No one will follow us out. If I find either of these demands were disobeyed, I will find all of you, and you will suffer the same fate."

He backed towards the door, keeping Sellia behind him. She opened the door and they left. No one followed. No one so much as moved a muscle.

SIXTY-THREE

Sellia had to scurry to keep up with Seanchai as they left the alley and headed into the main street. She kept looking over her shoulder.

"They won't follow," Seanchai snapped.

"Remind me never to do business with you," Sellia said. "Some customers have such high demands."

Seanchai continued without answering, but a moment later he stopped abruptly in his tracks and stared down a dark alley. They heard a scuffle, and his eyes lost focus again. He ran down the alley, his unsheathed knives glinting in the light of a bonfire nearby.

Sellia followed him into the alley, but by the time her eyes adjusted to the dark, three men lay dead on the ground. A small, familiar elf stood glued to the wall, staring in terror at Seanchai. The Wycaan's white hair was free and wild. His blades dripped with blood.

"Hey. You're from the circus caravan. Fredrich, no?" Sellia exclaimed. "How did you get stuck in this?"

Fredrich glanced at her but his eyes zoomed back to Seanchai.

"Answer her," Seanchai hissed.

Fredrich just pushed himself tighter against the wall.

"Seanchai," Sellia forced a smile. "Put your knives away and cover your head." Seanchai did as she said while she turned to Fredrich. "What happened? You said the bars don't welcome elves."

"Gambling," he muttered, finally able to speak. "And they were cheating me. I shouldn't have called them out. I shouldn't even have been there." He stared down at the ground, now embarrassed. "I could have passed the money you gave me to Esrelda."

Seanchai kicked one of the bodies. "Do they still have your money?"

Fredrich stooped and retrieved his bag of coins from one of the men. "Thank you," he said. "I guess now I owe you. Someday, I hope—"

Seanchai grabbed Fredrich's collar as he was mid-sentence and pushed him up against the wall. "Tomorrow, you will repay the debt. We will walk you back to your caravan to make sure you don't get into any more trouble. On the way, we will show you where you will meet us in the morning. Understood?"

The rigid circus elf nodded vigorously and squealed his acquiescence.

They walked without event. When they arrived at the restaurant near the square where they had eaten earlier, Seanchai turned to Fredrich. "We will be here two hours after sunrise, tomorrow. Bring us each a clown costume. Make sure one is big enough for me. Understood?"

"I-I will come," Fredrich trembled. "And I-I will bring you the costumes."

After Fredrich scampered away toward the square, Seanchai led them back toward the Galbrieth Arms. Back in the room, he flung off his shirt and poured water over his head and face.

"You've got a plan," Sellia said excitedly.

Seanchai turned to face her water dripping from his hair. His broad chest was taut, and his deep blue eyes sparkled.

"Oh yes," he said. "And it's a good one." He wiped the water away and shook his head. "I just wish we had even the remotest chance of succeeding."

"Rhoddan? You awake?"

"Yeah, Ilana."

"You're not doing your exercises? You always exercise at night."

"No. I'm not."

"Why?"

"Not sure it's worth it anymore."

There was a pause before Ilana spoke again. "Rhoddan?"

"Yes?"

"You afraid?"

"No, I don't think so. It's as good a time as any to die."

"Really? You're not just saying that?"

Silence. Then resigned, he answered, "I would rather die fighting."

"Me, too."

"You gonna miss him?"

"Yes. I'm going to die tomorrow wondering what might have been between us. That's what's really making me sad."

"I'm sorry, Ilana. I would have liked to see you grow together. I would have liked to love someone and be loved like you love each other."

"Have you ever been in love, Rhoddan?"

"No."

Ilana sighed. "Then it's not the right time to die." A moment's silence then, "I'm sorry. What I meant to say—"

"I understand what you mean, Ilana. We're just too young to die."

"Yeah."

"I'm too young to die, too," said Maugwen out of nowhere.

"You aren't going to die tomorrow. Stay out of it," Shayth snapped in reply.

"I am," she said, quivering and they all looked at her. "My parents have run away. The guards told me when I emptied our bucket earlier."

"That's terrible," said Ilana reaching out to hug her.

"No it's not," Maugwen said, her voice muffled in Ilana's embrace. "My mother is sick and needs medicine. I have two younger brothers and a sister. I understand my father's decision. I just wish I'd had the opportunity to tell him so he won't feel so bad.

"Also, the guards had told me that I could go free if I found out where your special one is hiding. I didn't, and at some point I kind of stopped trying."

Both Rhoddan and Shayth came to the bars of their cell and looked over at her.

"Hey kid," Shayth said, his tone soft. "I'm sorry, really I am."

"Thank you," Maugwen replied. "That's the first nice thing you've said to me."

"Yeah," he replied. "I thought you were a spy or something."

"Me, a spy?" she laughed. "Well, actually, I guess I was. Not a very good one, though."

"Maybe you still can be," Rhoddan suggested, excited at the thought. "Tell them you have some information on us or something. It can't hurt us now."

"What can she tell them?" Ilana asked.

They all went silent,. They were out of ideas, out of energy.

"Dumb suggestion," Rhoddan admitted.

Shayth patted him on the shoulder. "Yeah, pretty dumb."

Suddenly they were all laughing uncontrollably. It surely echoed up to the guards, who didn't bother coming to silence them. Their laughter rebounded off the ancient rock walls. It woke other prisoners and the ghosts of the condemned, those who had died in the prison before them.

"I'm glad I met you all," said Maugwen when they finally were able to take a breath. "Maybe I'm a better person for knowing that elves are good people. Maybe it'll count."

"It'll count," Shayth confirmed, and there was a rare softness in his tone.

Ilana stared across the alcove at him. "I think you've been racking up some points, too, Shayth."

"I doubt it." His voice went cold again. "You never got the whole story."

"Wanna tell us now?" Ilana asked.

"No," Shayth replied looking at her. "I think I should quit while I'm ahead."

"Tell him," Rhoddan suddenly said to Ilana.

"Tell me what?" Shayth demanded.

Ilana looked from one to the other. "Before you were born, did your parents ever have any contact with elves?"

Shayth bristled. "My father did. He spent time with your people, officially negotiating treaties and overseeing policy implementation. The Emperor got very angry with him for advocating for their rights. Why do you ask?"

"Have you always worn black and been drawn to the color?" Ilana asked.

"Yes, ever since I could choose for myself. Why?"

"Because in the elven tongue, Shayth is a rare black rock. It's very valuable, very precious, and is sought after for its incredible resilience and beauty. What's interesting is that the reason it's hard to find is that it's often encased inside more common-looking stones, where you wouldn't think to look.

"We think that you are your name, Shayth. Elves believe that names have power. You have had to endure so much with such resilience that you have encased yourself in common stone. You're a rare human and, for your friends, you have been so valuable. I think that inside of you, there is great beauty. Like the rock you are named for, Shayth."

He turned away from the cell bars, rubbing a hand through his spiky, black hair. He bowed his head and sunk down onto his cot. "Thank you," he said, his voice cracking.

SIXTY-FOUR

Breakfast was brought to the prisoners later than usual, but all four had been awake for hours as thousands of feet pounded in the square above.

Three priests served the breakfast with the guards standing back. The food was not the usual congealed gruel, but steaming fried eggs and thick slices of fresh bread straight from the ovens. Their smell wafted through the cells. The priests were wary of the prisoners, cautiously sliding the trays under the bars. Only the oldest priest stood, regarding them.

"Would either of you like to talk with me, children, before you are taken?"

This was directed to Shayth and Maugwen as he didn't even acknowledge the elves. Shayth turned his back on the man, but Maugwen hesitated. The priest turned to her.

"I would be happy to listen to you, child. Unburden your sins to me before you face the judgment of the gods."

Maugwen bit her bottom lip. When she spoke, it was measured. "What about my cellmate, and him?" She nodded over to Rhoddan.

The priest played with the thick golden chain around his neck. "They are not children of our gods," he said, his tone still pleasant.

"Then neither am I," Maugwen replied, standing as straight as she could.

The priest sighed and began to turn.

"And for your information, I haven't committed any crime. Your patron is putting the sins of the fathers on his innocent children. And you and your gods are turning a blind eye because it suits you to do so."

The priest turned to face the small girl. "I will pray for you, child. In your fear, you know not what you say."

As he left, Maugwen withered. Her family had believed in the gods, and she feared their wrath. Ilana gave her a hug, but found nothing to say.

Rhoddan, however, was proudly defiant. "You told him, kid. Well done." Then he picked up his tray of food.

"Don't eat it," Shayth warned.

"Why not?"

"They've drugged it so you'll be submissive when they take us out."

"Doesn't sound too bad to me," Rhoddan responded, but he didn't touch the food. At the same moment, he and Ilana both stared at Shayth. "You still think…"

"Who knows?" Shayth shrugged. "No, I don't. But if someone tries, you'll endanger their lives if you can't run and fight."

Ilana looked across from her cell, her hands clutching the bars above her head. "I want to believe it, too, Shayth. Right up until the instant that trap door opens, I'm going to believe someone will come."

They emptied their food into the buckets and slid the trays out of their cells.

Four sixers of soldiers came for them in the afternoon. Ilana held Maugwen's hand and could feel her clammy sweat.

"We don't want any trouble," the officer said to Shayth.

Shayth laughed bitterly. "Really? What can you do to us now? Beat us after we've been hanged?"

More guards joined them, leading the Tutans. Neither of them acknowledged the others, preferring to keep their eyes on the ground in front of them. The company climbed the steps and walked along the stone corridors. Shayth, Ilana and Rhoddan all glanced up, hoping to see the man in black again, but this time there were soldiers posted. General Tarlach was taking no chances. The noise from outside became louder and nearer. A wave of laughter erupted, and a soldier grumbled about missing the circus.

"Yeah," Shayth jeered. "You all could have played the clowns."

The guard raised his hand, but his commander quickly intervened. "The general wants them untouched."

Shayth noted the guards were carrying swords instead of their usual wooden batons. Once out in the sunlight they stopped as their eyes adjusted to the bright light and they took in the square. It looked splendid. Huge banners bearing the Emperor's coat of arms, a tower's dark silhouette with the sun peering out from behind, hung from every wall and building. Hundreds of flags in all sizes and colors, flapped in the wind that swirled above the crowds.

Every seat in the dignitaries' stand was taken, and the square was packed with people. The crowd cheered and howled with laughter at the circus clowns' and acrobats' finale. Shayth saw that a sixth noose had been attached to the gallows and glanced at Maugwen. Her eyes were staring at the ground. He gently rubbed her arm and smiled at her when she looked up.

Then a slow, heavy drumbeat commenced, and the crowd quieted. A man walked onto the stage, carrying a horn to amplify his voice. The drumming stopped, and the crowd craned their heads to see.

"My lords and ladies. Good people of Galbrieth. Let's give a rousing thank you to the amazing circus!"

The crowd cheered and whooped. As soon as they had quieted, he riled them up again. "Happy birthday to the Emperor!" Thousands cheered hysterically, their fervor amplified by their sheer number and the large amount of ale they had consumed. When their cheers receded, he cried out again: "Long live the Emperor!" The crowd chanted: "Long live the Emperor! Long live the Emperor!"

It took a while for them to settle down enough and when they did, the man raised his horn and spoke. "My lords and ladies. Good people of Galbrieth. The Emperor is wise and kind. He defends his subjects from the wicked hordes who try to invade our borders. He dispenses justice to protect the weak and vulnerable. But not everyone appreciates his generosity and compassion. A few misguided and wretched individuals plot to overthrow him, to cast this great nation into poverty, hunger, and crime. Such people must be brought to justice and pay the price for treason."

The drums began a slow, mournful beat, and the circus troupe retreated to the side of the stage. The announcer moved closer to the gallows, where a hooded man stood by the lever. His presence sobered the crowd, A few moments before, tens of thousands of people had laughed, chanted and sung. Now an eerie silence descended over the square.

The prisoners were marched forward and onto the stage by the armed troops. Those behind had to push the prisoners into step. They solemnly marched out to the middle of the stage. Then the guards moved aside as each was positioned in front of a noose.

From somewhere in the crowd, a woman's voice cried out: "She's just a little girl!" Ilana glanced at Maugwen. The young human stood with her head bowed.

"You okay?" Ilana asked quietly.

With effort, Maugwen raised her head to stare defiantly out into the crowd. "We are *all* prisoners," she cried out, and her voice was firm.

A guard stepped forward to quiet her, but hesitated when a murmur rolled through the crowd. Maugwen didn't have anything else to say, anyway, and everyone settled. The announcer read out their names and alleged crimes. The Tutans were just referred to as rebels. No one knew their names. No one cared. Maugwen's name had been added to the others, and she was declared a traitor, as well. Shayth's name was called last and followed by a long list of people that he had purportedly murdered.

When the announcer finished, the executioner stepped forward. In a hoarse voice, he offered each a hood. Shayth just glared at him, Rhoddan shook his head defiantly, and Ilana quietly said no. The Tutans also shook their heads. Then he stood before Maugwen, who shook her head, too, though her chin was again resting on her chest.

"Are you sure, little one?" he offered kindly.

"Yes," she said loudly, though her voice quivered. With a great effort, she picked up her head and looked into his eyes. "The last thing I want to see before I die is my city and my friends."

Maugwen reached out her hands, taking one of the Tutan's and offering her other to Ilana. Ilana grasped it and offered her other to Rhoddan, who in turn held his out to Shayth. When it was ignored, Rhoddan said, "We're in this together, Shayth. Friends till the end."

Shayth turned his head. No smile was forthcoming, but he nodded. "Yeah. Friends to the very end."

And he reached out and took Rhoddan's hand tightly in his own.

SIXTY-FIVE

Laughter erupted from the crowd. The executioner and prisoners all looked toward the circus tent as a lanky clown lurched onto the stage. He wore a bright white wig and a mock executioner's mask. He staggered under a humpback and two sticks protruded under his cloak, suggesting he was a puppet with strings cut.

A second clown ran after him, calling out in a female's voice for him to stop. They ducked and wove as they made their way to the gallows. The crowd roared with laughter, relieved from the intensity of the moment.

The clowns pretended to fight the soldiers, who laughed along with the crowd. While they were distracted, the female clown threw smoke bombs and fireworks into the crowd. The thick, green smoke caused panic, and people ran in all directions. The bigger clown waved his arms in a wide circle and the rows of soldiers on the stage flew back into the crowd as if yanked by invisible ropes.

The tall clown dove for the prisoners. One blow sent the executioner reeling. Rope cords were slashed, and all six were released from their bonds.

"To the crowds," cried the tall clown. "Stay close."

The soldiers reformed their lines and the order to charge was shouted above the melee. But instead, they let out a collective scream as a cloud of arrows descended upon them. They were in dress uniform, not armor, and had only swords with which to protect themselves. No shields, no helmets.

Another volley of arrows yielded more screams. Ilana saw the clowns' surprise despite their makeup. This had evidently not been part of their plan, but they recovered quickly and ran through the crowd, which parted before them without resistance.

Horns blew from all directions. Soldiers took up positions on the mighty battlements, gates were hastily closed and a drawbridge raised. Other soldiers ran to assemble at the main arteries out of the square. As the prisoners and rescuers banded together and confronted one such group, the big clown ripped off his mask. He drew a long knife, which he threw to Rhoddan, and a short, which he passed to Ilana. As she grabbed it, she looked up into his blue eyes and gasped.

But there was no time for anything further. Sellia had an extra sword for Shayth, and they turned to face the lines of grim-faced soldiers. Ilana watched Seanchai draw two long, thin swords from a sheath on his back and charge forward.

The soldiers were mesmerized by his huge presence and weren't prepared for the Tutans' attack. A mass of hairy, gray-clad men and women descended upon them from the side with a ferocity that offered the soldiers no chance to defend themselves.

The Wycaan charged on, as well, dropping soldiers in their tracks as he passed. No one moved as fast as him, his double swords a deadly blur. Alongside him was Mhari, her narrow eyes sparkling. Despite her age, the old woman moved with graceful speed, and it was she who led them through the streets.

Ilana looked up at the great battlements. Soldiers were falling before them, shot by arrows from the ground. The mighty walls of Galbrieth offered excellent cover from enemies trying to get into the city, but not from those who were already inside.

Mhari had planned her route out of Galbrieth carefully. They entered a part of town where the streets narrowed, and the soldiers found it difficult to run more than two abreast. Their superior numbers now offered no advantage.

They headed toward what was known as The Farmer's Gate—a smaller entrance used by traders and the poor. But the Tutans that had tried to secure the gate had encountered stiff opposition from the guards and failed to take control of the levers that opened and closed the portcullis. A soldier sacrificed his life to release the catch that held the chains locked. The iron gate crashed down, and their exit was closed.

They stood for a moment, staring at the portcullis. Battalions of troops would soon be upon them from two directions. A decision had to be made. Mhari turned to a frowning Targs. "Cover us," she yelled. "I won't let you down this time."

Then she grabbed Seanchai and dragged him into an alley. Between narrow walls, she shoved her student up against the bricks and grasped his shirt strongly with both hands.

"I told you before we parted that friends, however close, might one day have to sacrifice their friendship for the greater good. Do you remember?" When Seanchai nodded, she continued. "You have a great destiny, Seanchai. You must gather the elves from the Markwin forest and the islands of the west. You must bring the dwarves out of their mines to honor the ancient alliance. Find the Azuri if you can. Only you can possibly unite them all. You wield the magic of the Wycaans, but your greatest gift is the loyalty and friendship you inspire. Swear to me that you will do this."

Seanchai hesitated.

"I am your master," Mhari roared and she grabbed her apprentice even tighter. "Swear to me, Seanchai. Swear you will reforge the alliance."

Seanchai's body shook. "But I came all this way to rescue my friends, and we are so close. You helped me achieve–"

"Not them," Mhari yelled and Seanchai felt a massive wave of power growing inside his teacher. Then he knew. Mhari was not referring to Ilana, Rhoddan, and Shayth.

"Not you," the young elf pleaded. "Please."

"Yes," Mhari's eyes were wide, her skin glowing red. "I failed the Tutans once before and, still, they answered my call. I have dedicated my life to this moment. You accepted me as your master. Swear to me. Let me fulfill my destiny, and swear that you will fulfill yours."

They stared at each other. Seanchai shook his head, but couldn't avoid Mhari's iron gaze. He felt the intense heat emanating from his teacher's body and knew then what was about to unfold.

"I swear," said Seanchai, tears welling in his eyes. "*Ashbar,*" he whispered the binding oath in the ancient language.

Mhari released him and strode out to the others. "To Seanchai!" she boomed. "To Seanchai!"

And as the desert men and the elves gathered around Seanchai, Mhari cried out to them. "THE ALLIANCE! REFORGE THE ALLIANCE!"

Then she turned and strode toward the great walls of Galbrieth. Arrows rained down on her. Some missed, others seemed somehow to be repelled, but too many reached their marks. With arms out-stretched and palms facing the wall, she continued forward, summoning the elements of earth and wind.

The ground let out a mighty shriek as a crack appeared near Mhari. Rock plates, dormant for millions of years, yielded, and the power of the land of Odessiya herself flowed up from the bowels of the earth and through the Wycaan Master. Her body was bathed in yellow and gold as the power released through her palms smashed into the great stone walls. The wind howled above them and people clasped their hands over their ears in terror.

Mhari walked on.

Most soldiers fled, but a few remained frozen in terror on the battlements. The old woman reached the wall and the huge stones dissolved at her touch. A flash of golden light left her fingertips, followed by a second, and a third. A mighty groan came forth from the rocks in the wall, where stones at the top, battered by the wind and the hewn blocks at the bottom crumbled as the earth beneath it buckled and gave way.

And the mighty walls of Galbrieth collapsed in a colossal explosion. Soldiers screamed and fell, and the huge rocks crashed down on Mhari, Wycaan Master of Odessiya.

SIXTY-SIX

Seanchai felt his teacher's life energy dissipate. He screamed and whirled, looking for someone to fight. Rhoddan grabbed him and shouted into his ear. "Now. We must leave now." Seanchai threw him off and the elf flew back. Seanchai saw only white, hot, pure fury fueled by the image of Mhari crushed under the wall, as she died to save them all.

He wheeled around, both swords held high. He needed an enemy to kill. Those surrounding him shrank back in fear. Only Ilana stood her ground, tears streaming down her cheeks and her arms held out wide.

"For Mhari," she said, her voice shaking. "Don't let her sacrifice be in vain. Fulfill your oath for your teacher, your people, and for us, Seanchai."

The white-haired elf glared at her, his chest heaving as he struggled to contain the boiling rage. Time froze. Then Seanchai turned and stepped over the rubble that was once the great walls of Galbrieth. Soldiers caught outside the wall fell swiftly under his swords and his grief.

They fled into the Vale, turning toward the mountains and running through a plantation of trees planted by General Tarlach as a gift to the city after he had conquered it. When they came out the other side, Seanchai saw the gorge that would take them up into the mountains. But as they ran into the open, a horn blew and a line of cavalry charged down on them from the north. General Tarlach's reinforcements had arrived.

The Wycaan looked around for a path to take, or even a defensible area. There was nothing. As the warhorses thundered toward them in unison, Seanchai ordered everyone to form a wedge behind him at the point.

"Together," he cried. "Elves, humans, and Tutans. An alliance. We stand as one. Be brave. Hold strong."

Just then, another horn blew, this one he recognized was hewn of elven craft. More horsemen poured out from the gorge itself. "Elves!" someone cried, and as the two cavalries clashed, Seanchai raised his swords above his head and roared.

They charged forward and attacked Tarlach's cavalry from behind. Seanchai tore through his enemy, sorrow fueling him like a flame as he cut down countless soldiers.

A bearded officer jumped from his wounded horse and charged Ilana. She backed up and braced herself, but tripped over a body lying on the ground behind her. The soldier laughed and raised his sword. But as it came down to deliver the final blow, a huge body crashed into him.

"Get up, girl," a voice roared. "I tasked you to look after Seanchai."

"Father!" she cried.

But there was no time to talk. Uncle turned and killed the officer he had sent sprawling, then disappeared into the melee.

The battle did not last long and when it was over, Uncle led them deep into the mountains. As the sun set, it bathed the valley in blood red light. Seanchai stood on a rock and stared down at the dust cloud that still hung above Galbrieth. He could think only of Mhari, crushed beneath the huge stones. Shayth and Rhoddan came to stand on either side of him. They were cut and bruised, but victorious, and together. A huge elf strode toward them, one muscular arm circling Sellia's shoulders and the other around Ilana.

Seanchai stared at him in disbelief, using all his energy and discipline to focus. When the Wycaan spoke, his voice was soft, his physical and mental fatigue washing over him. "I didn't think you'd arrive on time or even heed my call. Thank you, Uncle. Your help was critical."

Uncle beamed at Seanchai and then bowed his head. "How could I not come to rescue my daughter? Or refuse the call of a Wycaan warrior?"

"Your daughter?"

"Seanchai," Ilana smiled for the first time in ages, "meet my father."

Seanchai stared at the huge elf, who laughed and then pulled Seanchai into a tight hug.

"I'm sorry for the death of your master," Uncle said once they had disengaged. "But now is not the time to mourn. You must decide your next move."

Seanchai nodded, and his gaze went back to the city where his teacher lay. In a commanding voice he called to the elves, men, and Tutans around him. "Bear witness. Many brave friends died today so that we might be free. Under the stones of Galbrieth lies Mhari, Wycaan Master and Teacher. She died fulfilling her destiny. May we all have the honor to die as she did."

There was respectful murmuring and nodding of bowed heads. Then Uncle asked again. "What now, Seanchai. Where will you go?"

Seanchai addressed Uncle, but his voice carried to all. "I will fulfill the wishes of my master. I will head into the west and, with the free elves, rebuild an alliance that will stand for ten thousand years. With their aid I will return and liberate the people of Odessiya."

Rhoddan stepped forward and drew his sword into the air. As the blade left its scabbard a rasp filled the dusk air. He thrust it into the air. "And I offer you my life to fulfill your task."

Shayth joined them, raising a nicked and bloodstained broadsword. "And you have my sword, Wycaan."

Ilana glanced up at her father. He sighed deeply and nodded.

"And my heart," she said, leaving her father's side to stand beside Seanchai.

The Wycaan drew his swords and held them up with the others, a many-pointed arrow reaching into the sky. The setting sun cast one final bright beam and, as it bathed the swords in a rich, red glow, Seanchai cried: "The Alliance!"

As one, all present answered his cry.

EPILOGUE

General Tarlach stood on the dusty rubble that had once been his fortifications. Bortand approached with a scroll and quill. No one else dared come close.

"My general," he said, his voice soft but steady. "We must, um, send a message to the Emperor."

"Yes," Tarlach replied without looking.

"Sire. What should it say?"

Tarlach stared out to a distant hill, where a flash of sunlight on metal momentarily blinded him. He sighed. "Tell him the Wycaan elf is real. Tell him that I believe he will try and reforge the alliance. Tell him," the general hesitated, "that his nephew rides with the Wycaan."

Bortand scribbled and then asked. "Anything else, my lord?"

"Yes. Tell him that his worst fears have been realized. Tell him... it has begun."

WYCAAN MASTER: AT THE WALLS OF GALBRIETH
END OF BOOK ONE

AUTHOR'S NOTE:

Dear Friend,

If you are reading these words, you have probably arrived with Seanchai, Rhoddan, Ilana, Sellia and myself to Galbrieth. I hope you didn't get wounded in the battle. These characters have become firm friends and I will continue the journey with them into *The First Decree*.

I know your time is valuable and am honored you decided to share some of it reading *At The Walls Of Galbrieth*. Please consider leaving a brief review if you purchased this book online. Feel free to contact me at anelfwriter@gmail.com or sign up for my weekly blog post at http://www.elfwriter.com. I also tweet at @elfwriter.

Thank you, again,

Alon

NON-FANTASY NOVELS BY ALON SHALEV:

A Gardener's Tale (Three Clover Press, 2011)
The Accidental Activist (Three Clover Press, 2010).

The Story Continues:

WYCAAN MASTER, BOOK 2: THE FIRST DECREE

by Alon Shalev

ISBN: 978-0-9884428-4-9 (paperback)

Tourmaline Books, Berkeley, California

Coming out in 2013

When history inscribes its impassive judgment on what transpired after the fall of the Great Alliance, let it include a chapter about the dwarves. For though men and elves will dominate its pages, the story of those who dwell underground should be known.

It was I, King Hothen the Elder, who led his warriors from the battlefield, at least those who survived. Our numbers were small and the prospects harrowing. We left our dead to the vultures and the crows, including my own father, King Goldenore. For all I knew was that I must keep our people alive.

Dwarves are brave warriors and when the armies clashed, our battalions fought in the fiercest encounters. So it was that when the piles of bodies grew, many, too many, were of noble dwarves.

With our armies decimated, I took our people to a deep cave far away and there we built mighty Hothengold. When completed, and with our numbers beginning to recover, I sent out the leaders of the six clans, ordering them to secure other such underground fortresses and seek mining opportunities as only we understand.

But also I instructed our leaders to hold faith, for as he lay on the battlefield, his soul precariously balanced between life and the great halls of our ancestors, the Wycaan Master Perridor, shared with me a vision. The Wycaans, he revealed, was massacred but not obliterated.

"Hold fast to our ways," he whispered. "Bide your time underground in the shadows where the greedy eyes of men cannot see. Rebuild our nation and wait. For with this promise I leave you. A Wycaan will come to lead us. And he will find friendship among the dwarves, and return us to our rightful place."

And so I took my people underground. The first law we passed was one of survival and became known as the First Decree. Following the great treachery, no man, elf or any save dwarves were allowed under the mountains. Those who wandered our way fell to our axes, and the great dwarf nation drifted out of sight and mind of ambitious Emperors.

But hearken to my words. The land of Odessiya will never heal itself until the dwarves, elves and humans are reunited. Whether with promises or blades, the alliance will one day rise and the dwarf nation will take its rightful place alongside the other great races.

Until then, my people, I counsel patience, never a strong trait among dwarves. Let us grow our clans and our wealth away from the sight of the empire, but let us never forget. Be vigilant, be patient, and wait the coming of the Wycaan.

These are the last words of Hothen the Elder, High King of the Dwarves.
From the Chronicles of King Hothen the Elder